MILL'S FOLLY -
A Journey with Evil

P. A. Sirko

ISBN: 0-6155-7038-0
ISBN-13: 9780615570389

Library of Congress Control Number: 2011963359
P. A. Sirko, Woodland Park, CO

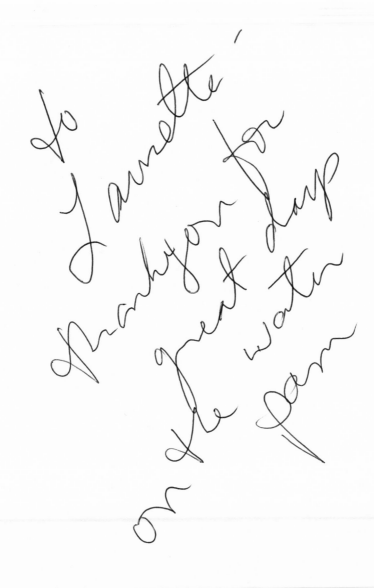

to Janette'
thankyou for
great day
on the water
Pam

DEDICATION

Dedicated to Randy, Zachary and Matthew.
People to thank, Karen Betlejewski, Coordinator Del Norte County Historical Society in Crescent City, California and cool historian.

Mike Stull, a dedicated volunteer of the Campbell County Historical & Genealogical Society.

Norman & Jack Anderson who helped with the area and lent me a shovel! Thank you.

John E. Springer, Sales/Service Manager, Dukane Seacom, Inc., for valuable deep-sea diving facts.

Breeders Cup Races throughout the United States and Canada that I have been fortunate enough to attend and the kind people on the Backside of Churchill Downs.

The Maritime Heritage Project. Legends of America. Portland State University. Oregon Encyclopedia Project-Kelsey @ Wordpress.com. Ben Campbell, Chief Deputy PVA Administration, New Port, Ky., who's advice lead me to Millwheel Farm. Florence Jesberg for her generosity and creativity.

Rene Peters, Barbra Simpson, and Bernice Beams for their hospitality.
And to my muse, Addie Sublett.

CHAPTERS

SEPTEMBER 1996   1

1- JULY 30, 1865   21

2- SINKING of the BROTHER JONATHAN   45

3- The GRIM REAPER   53

4- ST. LOUIS and CINCINNATI   59

5- The MAGNOLIA, a PACKET BOAT   69

6- PROSTITUTES and EXPLOSIONS   81

7- LEW MILLS buys a HORSE   93

8- The LAND and the NEIGHBORS   101

9- FREED SLAVES   113

10- The KENTUCKY FARM 1868   127

11- The REAPER BREEDS   139

12- MILLWHEEL PLANTATION PROSPERS   145

13- The MURDERS 1875   151

14- Part 2—OCTOBER, 1998   161

15- LAWYERS, GHOSTS and DEEDS   171

16- ADVICE and LOST JEWELRY   179

17- INDIA INVESTIGATES   187

18- A DEATH at the BREEDERS CUP   199

19- NEW YORK, GOLD COINS and CAMELS   209

20- MILL'S FOLLY   221

21- STEAMBOAT HISTORY—JEFFERSON'S
RETURN   229

22- A GRAVE MENACE   239

23- NIC'S EPIPHANY   249

24- SEX and REAPERS REVENGE   261

25- DEATH and DIARIES   273

26- ROAMING GHOSTS   279

27- INDIA'S EPIPHANY and the STEAMBOAT
CREW   287

28- OBOL'S for the JOURNEY   295

SEPTEMBER 1996

This was the last night of Nathan Curran's life. Doing what he loved, he was thinking that past diving adventures into the abyss were now passé.

"This is the night." he whispered, shaking the sand from his goggles.

Pulling air tanks from the rack Nathan looked down to examine his equipment. He couldn't wait to slip into his familiar swim fins, fondly named "Thelma and Louise" by his best friend and partner, Jeremy Kolomyjec. With the waves pushing their chartered boat dangerously close to the rocks that rose up from below, each man used one hand to adjust their goggles and the other hand to stay secured to the vessel. Falling overboard unprepared was a concern. Until the regulators, cameras, bags, then weights and other paraphernalia were in place it would not be wise.

The Pacific Ocean was lonely and dark that evening. The sky above was painted with a thin veil of clouds seeking a port to rest. Below, the ocean's surface was brutal, pushing up from the depths then crashing down upon it, an open mouth to consume each wave. This was a familiar condition of the northern California coast in any season, but the squall tonight would also accommodate a pair of divers who planned to tackle their exploit as quickly as possible. They would need to finish this job, avoiding discovery by the Coast Guard or the returning salvage crew along the shore of Crescent City. Both young men were counting on the twilight to cloak this voyage.

Turning, Nathan glanced back at the newly hired crew made up of three local guides that had proficiency in fishing, drinking and Spanish. Mostly Spanish. So the business relationship between Nathan, Jeremy and the crew was restricted to cash, which worked in any language. The guides left the loading and lugging of the gear entirely in the hands of the two divers but that was a small problem compared to what lay ahead on this September night.

Diving since 1981 during their high school years off the Florida Coast the two young men had gained experience in every tropical ocean and inlet. Dodging sharks and alligators, chasing friendly manatees and even having arm wrestled an octopus made them 'Hero's of the Sea' or so they told the six foot beauties at the bars along the beaches. Sometimes it even worked. But their quest for fame was becoming more expensive than profitable, their reputations preceding them with tour groups, local shipyards and other harbors along the coast. Dubbed 'reckless, troublesome and unpredictable' they still remained sincere in their pursuit of an "income with flexible hours." Their profession also required charming the local ladies who, in most cases, held sway over their boat owning husbands. The boys would carefully flirt with any lady over '50 feet', eventually producing job offers of diving, mastering a sailboat or fishing instruction.

"And Margarita's after 5pm." They crowed.

Originally from Cocoa Beach, Florida and still in their thirties, they were finding it more difficult to satisfy their needs and desires. Both boys dreamt of succeeding beyond entertaining the snowbirds from November to Easter break. Forever together, Nathan Curran and Jeremy Kolomyjec were 'partners in crime.' They shared everything including financial distress. Right now they were broke.

Nathan's twin brother Nicolas Curran just called them crazy. Identical by appearance, their personalities collided head-on. Nicholas was a history teacher in upstate New York, having what Nathan considered a settled life that revolved around correcting homework, PTA meetings, and an occasional trip to Saratoga Race Track. Nathan believed those soirees were the extent of his brother Nicholas' reckless life style. Unfortunately, now kismet had steered Nathan away from contacting his twin brother for quite some time. Unexpected events while diving in the spring of 1992 off the coast of Bodega Bay just north of San Francisco would push both Jeremy and Nathan to take chances to dive deeper and put both their lives at risk more often than not.

It began as a routine dive. A shiny object was discovered under an old coral ledge where eels would typically pop out to greet swimmers as they passed. At 30 feet below the surface they did not anticipate finding anything beyond a wristwatch, cancelled credit card or earring at best. But there it was. A bracelet of some kind, corrosively green from a life underwater, and as they plucked it from the sand it appeared that this discovery was not of a recent design.

Swimming to the surface they climbed anxiously into their old rubber raft and headed into Santa Rosa with their find. In their eagerness they walked directly to the east end of town where they knew of a local antique store that also carried assorted jewelry. While having no indication of what this bracelet might be worth, and so naive in rarities such as this, they handed the piece to an older gentleman that had introduced himself as Matthew, proprietor of the store. Matthew examined the piece, and passing it back to them said, "Return in the morning and we'll talk more."

As arranged, Jeremy and Nathan arrived at sunup only to discover that the store didn't even open until 10am. They bought some coffee and sat on the sidewalk until the proprietor returned.

The jeweler was pleased to see them and again appraised the piece, silently turning it in his hands. Unclean, gritty and slightly bent it still had shine in places that indicated a woven rope design with open ends suggesting a tassel or flower shape.

Matthew determined, "Yes, it is silver, but with the economy it will only bring a small amount." Interrogating them once more, he wanted to be clear, "Where did you find this again?"

Jeremy and Nathan repeated, "Bodega Bay."

The jeweler cleared his throat. " Six hundred dollars would be my best offer in this matter. You might shop it around, but I doubt you'd get a higher price anywhere else."

Their excitement was too much. Celebrating into the night, yelling at each other over dinner, they both declared their shared epiphany. The boys knew that more fortune lay below the surface of the ocean than what they had been delving into before now. Over the years they had stumbled upon exploration and recovery ships that made no secret of finding treasure along the Pacific coast. Newspaper articles and nightly newscasts touted the discoveries, which by now most residents along the west coast considered commonplace. The boys had learned that the seaboard was littered with over 1,600 reported shipwrecks from Mexico to Canada. Experience was another matter.

Two years earlier in 1990 they had saved up a considerable amount of cash and traveled to Dahab, Egypt and the 'Blue Hole,' a cave located on the coast of the Red Sea. Commonly referred to as the 'Divers Cemetery' it had already claimed the lives of over 40 swimmers. Nathan and Jeremy felt prepared to tackle this new adventure after diving in such places as Milford Sound, the Toucari Caves in Dominica, and Half Moon Wall near the city of Belize. With those experiences under their belts what could go wrong?

Besides finding the bracelet, Nathan had high hopes of additional bounty along the coast. To convince Jeremy he reminisced, "We researched the Blue Hole before taking the plunge. We studied the diving time beneath the surface and found that we had maybe twenty minutes to go down 130 feet. Hey, we did it! Passed through the cave, remember? We got below that underwater bridge, the 'Arch,' then swam against current into the Red Sea. I dared you to do it, buddy, and you made it!"

"I still had a two day headache from the bends," groaned Jeremy.

The boys had learned a great deal in Egypt, staying for several weeks watching and listening to the other divers.

"We got this down," Nathan bragged, "Nitrogen narcosis messed with other divers heads. They had passed below the arch at that depth with not enough air and changed direction, got lost, unable to correctly become buoyant after rapidly descending 300 feet back to the surface. You and I pulled it off. We had sufficient oxygen and lived to dive again!"

With experiences gained in Egypt they had returned to the United States, earning money so easily in Santa Rosa from the silver bracelet that Jeremy Kolomyjec and Nathan Curran were now consumed with the idea of diving for treasure.

Nathan summed it up, "Some ocean vessels have sunk for no other reason than a loose plumbing fixture. With so many derelict ships reported along the west coast, everything from schooners to fishing trawlers to steamboats, there should be plenty of treasure for everyone!"

❧✺❧

For 133 years the Brother Jonathan has slept quietly 260 feet below the surface of the Pacific Ocean. Sailors, fisherman and scavengers who knew of the gravesite tried to approach her since the day she melted into the angry depths off the coast of Crescent City, California. Searching, regardless of the dangers, there remained a chance to find gold. On July 30, 1865 the 'Jonathan' had left San Francisco traveling north along the Pacific coast bound for Portland, Oregon. After hitting a rock the ship was doomed. Of the 200 who had boarded the ship that summer day only 19 passengers survived. The one thing on everyone's mind since that fateful day was the question of the safe. It held $200,000 in military pay for U.S. Army troops and gold for payments to the Indians in the Northwest Region. Then there were the crates of Double Eagle gold coins to be delivered to federal banks along the west coast. New technology during the 1960's opened the door to explore previously undiscovered shipwrecks in seas around the globe. These opportunities proved to be a weakness for any experienced diver.

In late September 1993, Nathan Curran first heard the news of the discovery early one morning in a marine supply store north of San Francisco.

"Yup, finally found her! Never saw such frenzy. And the gold's not just what those scientists found! Trouble too." The proprietor behind the counter of the store kept pointing to the TV on the wall and stuffing a rope Nathan had just bought into a bag too small, "The state will take it all anyway. California claims that it's within their boundaries, sunk too close to Crescent City's coast. Guys diving believe its far enough out, four and one half miles. Hell, it's spread all over anyway, both on the international side and inside the coast line. Guess they'll just have to pick up only those gold coins that are farthest from shore!" With that the storeowner laughed hysterically.

Nathan remained silent and he was not laughing. "When did you hear this?"

"All day yesterday and last night too! The research vessel says it covers about 9 miles of ocean floor. Could be quite a catch for those salvage people if the state doesn't step in and try to stop em."

Nathan carried his bundled ropes outside and sat down on the tailgate of his aging Toyota pickup. "What a windfall! And just a few hundred miles north!"

He needed to find Jeremy.

Last seen drinking beers on a beach the night before, Jeremy had been cooing a girl with cropped blond hair and the body of a surfer. Hard to resist. Thinking that she probably lived in town Nathan began driving around, anxiously searching apartment parking lots within a couple of blocks of the beach for Jeremy's Chevy Bascayne. In about 25 minutes he spotted the car next to a small patio apartment. Noticing a screen door slightly ajar, Nathan tore inside and frantically announced the news, "Underwater, north up the coast! A ship! They're finding gold, stuff, historical stuff! On the news, discovered yesterday!"

Jeremy lay quietly under a thin sheet with his eyes tightly closed, his young friend trying desperately to cover her nude body with pillows and towels from the floor.

"This is great news! We can go there. We can head up this weekend, check it out, ask around!"

"You're drinking to much coffee." Jeremy whispered.

"And with the crappy raft we bought we can cruise around after dark and see what's up!" Nathan exclaimed.

Jeremy's girlfriend was not as enthusiastic. "Who is this person and why is he standing in my room yelling at us?"

"Nathan, may I introduce Kim…Kim, Nathan."

"Please ask him to leave," she hissed with her teeth clenched.

Nathan leaned over and scooping her up threw her naked body over his shoulder. She began kicking her skinny legs but he walked across the small flat, luckily choosing the correct door and set her down on the tiled bathroom floor, quickly slamming the door between them.

He turned to his buddy, "So, you'll get home now, right?"

Jeremy, eyes still closed, rubbed his shaggy head with both hands, "Ya, can't wait."

At the same time in Crescent City, California, meetings with parties interested in the Brother Jonathan were underway. The media had arrived to report on the discovery. With careful preparation Nathan and Jeremy could become a part of it as well, but after inspecting their pitiful collection of diving equipment it was obvious that it would be unsuitable for depths below 150 feet.

Then there was a matter of breaking the law.

Newspaper articles where already reporting that the sheriff and local authorities were watching the five-mile perimeter of the ocean around the wreck site for scavenger divers. This increased security came after an innocent trawler unknowingly traveled within the research vessel's position near Jonathan Rock. Named for the tragedy, it resembled a tall chimney invisibly standing just below the waters surface four and one half miles off shore.

Since the boys had limited funds, they started doing research at the local historical society. Soon it became a second home until one of the librarians began asking them questions, not about the books they wanted, but instead inquiring as to what they wanted the books for. The boys remained vague, "We're helping with our family's genealogy research. We think some of them may have died aboard the Brother Jonathan when it went down in 1865."

She rolled her eyes, and said, "Fine. It's true there is a great deal of excitement surrounding this new discovery of the paddle steamer, but remember, collecting undocumented treasure is still against the law!" She advised, loud enough for other library patrons to hear.

They smiled and left, making no further plans to return.

"She's wise to us." They both agreed.

With a small amount of research and little cash, Jeremy and Nathan packed up their belongings, kissed their landlady goodbye and set out for their destination north: Crescent City. Immediately applying for work, they both found jobs at a local bait shop. After that they hit on Jeremy Kolomjyec's parents begging for cash, "We found a nice deal on a larger raft. It has an 80-horse power engine!" The boys knew that it would only get them out to the dive site on calm nights, but it was a step up from the dingy they had been using.

With the new northern California environment they also sought additional experience, never assuming that they could jump overboard into the ocean, swim 240 feet down and just pick up gold doubloons. They spent evenings cruising north along the Oregon coast. Nathan stayed on board the raft while Jeremy took the plunge. Later the young diver reported, "Lost my knife, other gear. I slammed into the rocks, ripped my wetsuit. Fish swam past the size of Moby Dick! It was all very unexpected."

"I suppose we should be grateful," Nathan surmised, "We'll list our mistakes so with the next dive we'll be better prepared."

"I'm still pissed about all the lost gear," Jeremy grumbled, "But this can't happen when we reach the Brother Jonathan. We'd be in a real pickle 250 feet down with torn wetsuits and sharks."

During this same time the Coast Guard and local police were stopping rogue divers so the boys needed to construct a plan to avoid arrest in restricted waters. At the bait shop they met girls in town who owned boats.

Nathan said smoothly, "We'll build a campfire, serve champagne. Bring your girlfriends and sleeping bags.

Travel northwest for ten minutes until you see the jetty. We'll meet you there."

After given directions to this rendezvous, their lovely victims were purposely sent across the research vessel area to meet with the boys later, unaware of the restriction. If the girls made it past the police boundaries then the coast was clear and the boys would follow seeking marker buoy's left by the salvage team. If the girls were caught then the boys would turn around and go home. Each time they sacrificed girlfriends, but they figured in the long run it was worth the price.

More investigation about the Brother Jonathan's whereabouts were needed. Now the boys found an older tourist named Burt who loved to fish.

"Burt, you'll catch a ton of fish! We'll be in our raft at sundown out about four miles northwest. Look for us. We'll be fishing, too."

They sealed the deal with a picture of Nathan's father standing next to a very large Pacific Mackerel that had been caught years before. Showing this to Burt, the plan went better than expected. That night Burt tried to outrun the Coast Guard crew on duty, which allowed Nathan and Jeremy to get their closest look at the research vessel. Floating silently about 1000 yards away they tried to record signals or messages, but it proved impossible, the research boat having been cloaked carefully. Throughout history scavengers were notorious for ransacking valuables from sunken vessels while destroying other significant finds in the process. Illegal without a permit, their dive would be considered a crime.

Nathan studied the dark water as Jeremy drove slowly back to shore, "We need to find the 'sweet spot,' the wire leading down to the treasure. The research vessel would have dropped it earlier from the beginning of the discovery making it convenient to return with less effort each day. It simply follows the beacon that leads out to the dive spot marker. It's here somewhere."

With the season growing short, the boys threw caution to the wind and rented a larger boat from a family of vacationers, the Woodruff's. Consisting of the Captain, Ken Woodruff, his wife, Irene, and their 9-year-old son Benny, the family agreed to provide a 55-foot SeaRay Cruiser for one evening. The boys had concocted a tale about their $20,000 catamaran blowing off it's mooring and drifting up the coast. Although the night was windy, the Woodruff family was in need of funds so the boys offered Ken $300 to help them 'search'. Pointing northwest from the Crescent City harbor the group left shore hunting for the 'lost sailboat.' Just as Nathan and Jeremy predicted, with such rough weather the research vessel's usual spot was empty, the captain having the good sense to stay in port.

Waves nearly 6 feet high and a wind of 10-12 knots pushed the SeaRay boat towards the coast but the boys were determined to point Captain Ken in a westerly direction farther from the town. For the last 14 months Nathan and Jeremy knew which area to search for the reference marker. By selling Jeremy's Biscayne they had even found enough cash to purchase a Dukane Seacom

Underwater pinger and locator kit. Tonight they planned to drop the pinger below the ocean surface. Set at 37 kHz, it was adjusted to their unique frequency, which would avoid detection by the salvage vessel when it returned to gather up the rest of its own markers, perhaps as soon as tomorrow.

Because the month of September found the weather no longer compatible for salvage operations the research vessel in town was already packing up to leave. The boys knew that if they did not achieve setting their marker tonight that soon the vessels marker buoy would be pulled up, and the sweet spot would be forever lost.

Just a small blinking red light, the boys finally spotted the beacon raising up and submerging with each wave. Thrilled, they grabbed their pinger and activated it, asking Ken to move closer as they dropped their own marker 240 feet, hoping that it would rest near the original marker still below.

Now the SeaRay had been out too long and Captain Ken was beginning to get wise. His wife, Irene had thought the boys were so sincere and polite, feeling sorry for their bad luck with their catamaran, but Ken announced that if they did not return to port that they would surely run out of gas and be lost at sea. Making their way back to the docks of Crescent City by 5am, they returned just as the engine died. Ken was livid, but his wife was totally understanding and very sympathetic with the loss of the boys boat. They happily accepted another $100 from Jeremy as they secured the yacht and bid each other farewell.

On September 6, 1996 the salvage team left Crescent City for the season. The sea had turned wild. From the waves above, to the shifting tides below, the water pushed and pulled around the rock mountains that rose up from the abyss. On the bottom hundreds of feet below, a quiet layer of sand and sediment slept, remaining in its ancient form, ignoring the chaos and havoc overhead. For centuries this ocean bed cradled the remnants of vessels that had passed above, met their fate, and died. Soft silt swirled across the floor like a veil covering goblets, Queensware and small coins, floating like a butterfly to rest silently upon the treasures.

That morning the crew of the research vessel packed up their gear, loading trucks with necessary salvage equipment, documents and computers that had served them throughout the summer months. The departure was big news. Crescent City residents had enjoyed the added population of reporters from newspapers, magazines and TV stations. Curious sailors from faraway ports came to gawk, while historians visited hoping to stumble upon any new stories concerning the Brother Jonathan and its history. This batch of "rubberneckers" even included a young lady writing a paranormal mystery. Motels, car repair shops, restaurants, marinas, grocery stores had all profited from that fatal day on July 30, 1865.

As the next evening arrived Nathan and Jeremy were prepared. By 11pm they successfully located their pinger using the large diving boat owned by the Spanish crew. They hoped the low tide would pull the sea's surface far enough out to expose any additional rock pinnacles that rose above the surf. They had finished their study of the salvage vessels departures and arrival times and noted any changes in the weather and waves. Their observations over the last two years were crucial, focusing on tonight. Renting additional equipment, hiring crew and a strong enough boat, even the newer technology, it all had to come together this evening.

The Spaniards were instructed to tie off the vessel on to the calmer side of a rock. The two boys, already suited with tanks, and with the confidence of two seasoned professionals, fell over the side and into the abyss.

The nighttime coast from San Francisco to Vancouver is always angry. Sound travels faster, gravity and heat disappear, optics in the water change their vision and the world around them becomes denser with water weighing 800 times more than air. The divers felt that they had done their homework for this situation.

Jeremy touched his belt, taking inventory, "Connecting bags, safety rope to the boat. Knife, check, check, check." He reached one last time for his cave flashlight and watch containing lume pigments which helped in low light conditions. Agonizing, he was still ill at ease, *"We should have done this next spring."*

Making their plunge off the side of the boat it immediately became difficult to swim down. The strength of the tides were pushing them up and then sucking them under again, spinning their bodies. Numerous times Jeremy corrected himself, not wishing in the darkness to confuse the bottom with the surface. Nathan was having less trouble climbing downward by clinging to the rock with one glove, holding his torch with his other. The lower he swam the more seadust that rose around him blackening the area. Octopus made their homes at this depth and the murky water camouflaged their whereabouts. Neither boy wanted to have a wrestling match during this important dive so they knew to remain vigilant of strange stirrings.

There was an additional fear that with all of the wrecks spread across these coastal waters they could be searching the wrong remnants. "In 1883 another ship, a two-masted schooner named the J.M. Wall had sunk in this same location." They had earlier remembered, "Who's to say we'd find out too late that we've pilfered booty off the wrong ruins?"

Nathan's body had to keep fighting to remain heading south. Kelp dipped and swayed consistently with each current. The lack of natural light limited his vision to judge the width and distance of objects appearing every few feet. He knew the bottom would eventually draw closer. Pushing against the tide to reach the sand, the bottom became visible. He needed to reconnect with Jeremy. Both of them had functions to perform such as bagging many of the items that people warned them not to take. His endorphin high was screaming now, as it was his responsibility to get them safely to the surface and de-compress.

"Where the hell is Jeremy?" With no time left to search, Nathan began to panic, "I hope he's still connected to the boat to find the way up!"

Turning, Nathan noticed a tiny flicker of light off the floor, then another. Excitement swelled up quickly. It was the moment where all of their planning would pay off. As he pushed his body closer he reached into the sand, dragging his fingers through it, searching, feeling every shape as the silt swirled around his hands.

The water was colder here, denser at this depth than from 100 feet above. He needed to pick up speed with the search, but groping around was the only chance of finding anything. The glitter noticed a few moments ago had now disappeared. Crawling across the bottom he still stopped to feel and identify objects.

Then it was in his hand. Round, flat, somewhat rough, a shiny gold coin. First one, then another, Nathan dropped them both into the small bag attached to his waist. Holding the light at a downward angle he began shifting faster and faster across the ocean floor grabbing at any loose object within his grasp.

Jeremy, are you near? Nathan hoped as he continued gathering the prize. Could Jeremy's rope have slipped off? The water around Nathan's body was now growing colder and the sensitivity to that change had taught him to recognize other changes around him as well. *There's definitely a presence nearby, a large fish perhaps or an octopus? They're common in these waters.*

The change in temperature caused him to look up from his work. He was no longer alone. In the distance a dark object approached, hidden by patterns of the currents and movements of the kelp, making it difficult to guess how close it was. The image was very large and too distorted to judge but it was still possible that Jeremy had finally found him.

Floating closer the image was now clear, a man walking.

Nathan was terrified that the nitrogen narcosis was driving his mind to madness, a consequence that until now he had always been able to avoid.

The intruder moved closer, the body large in stature, a beard waving with the current on his dark face, old clothes from another era snaking around his huge frame. A black hat covered his eyes, yet with no tank or goggles the man simply looked ahead and smiled at Nathan. Reaching out he extended his hand, opening his fingers to expose a palm covered with double eagle gold coins. There was no time for Nathan to think about the coins, or his best friend, or even his twin brother Nicolas.

There was only now, and now it was over.

Chapter 1
July 30, 1865

Looking down Lew Mills spit in the water and pondered a thought, *For such a huge phenomenon as smallpox it was a poorly conceived name. Epidemics come and go. One time it's measles, then yellow fever. Why, I wonder, had been called small?* Leaning against the bulkhead he quietly contemplated this, only to conclude that even something as minute as hiccups could slow down a huge ship.

All morning he had waited impatiently as 190 people boarded the paddle steamer, not counting the crew of 54, and it seemed to have taken weeks. Slogging on and off, kissing goodbyes, more people than needed for this trip.

Frustrated, he remembered, "I'll need something to eat and a place to sleep. A cot in the crew's quarters perhaps? Something down below near the berths?" The idea made him wince knowing that dirty Indians and brats with runny noses may have slept there before him. "On the other hand, there's the fact that after so many days in San Francisco, and the ship now underway for Portland, I'll find warm, dry beds where young tarts are waiting for men like me to arrive."

His hidden corner at the aft provided privacy since the cook would soon be searching him out to set the tables in the dining salon. The pounding of his head matched the pounding of the surf, a token of last night's

21

antics. Last evening, wearing his ratty tweed coat and his pantry shirt from the ship he had found no luck with the maids at the town pub. To cap the climax, Mills drank up more than enough ale and was thrown out. "Fine. It was a dump anyway." Now he was very glad that Captain De-Wolf was setting sail and would eventually move inland to enter at the Columbia River, away from the strong Pacific winds that made him miserable.

"Mills!" shouted the cook, Charles Rice, from the top of the main stair, "Get your ars to the kitchen and watch your breads. They are falling from the cold!"

Lew Mills had a talent for his job as a baker and the cook never asked questions concerning a man's reputation. Mills was good with biscuits and breads and that was enough.

Spitting again from a plug of tobacco he got up and made his way up the main stair, then through a companionway into the galley which had temporarily been adjusted from berths into a kitchen for meals. Grabbing his apron he pulled the raw bread from its rack to examine it. "Yes it has fallen some. Best move it closer to the heat."

The captain above could be heard from the pilothouse barking out orders to be heard from starboard to port side, the same directions he used on every departure. Dressed in his stiff uniform, he created a charming image. White gloved ladies swooned hearing the commands, feeling safer. Children, frightened by the water, would find him a colorful chap by the end of the journey. Now leaving Crescent City, California, they all felt the tide pushing and pulling against the boat from the waves that would stay with them into the Pacific as they traveled north, passing Gold Beach, then Coos Bay finally turning inland to enter the Columbia River which would transport them east to Portland.

The ship was named the Brother Jonathan. The name had been taken from a primary symbol in the United States before the Civil War and known as the original name for the states. Later, the name "Uncle Sam" would be known on a federal level, replacing the term 'Brother Jonathan' after the Civil War.

Built in 1851 in New York she was a steamship of the highest caliber, measuring 220 foot keel, 36 foot beam, a wheel on each side 33 feet in diameter, the engine having an impressive 21 inch cylinder. Made of wood, iron and copper she was of the finest design. Because of the passengers, sometimes as many as 365, the steamer was outfitted with such luxuries as salons with white enamel, touched with gold, and ventilation for hot weather.

During the years 1851 and 1852 she sailed between New York and Chagres, near Panama. She was then sold to Cornelius Vanderbilt who had her rebuilt to accommodate 750. Business was brisk, but with greed involving government, stockholders, investors, and even the crew, it appeared everyone wanted to control the profits. In 1856 the Nicaraguan government discontinued any transit across that country, stopping the transport of goods and passengers crossing the isthmus, so the Brother Jonathan was sold again.

Under the guidance of the new captain, John T. Wright, the ship was re-named the "Commodore". She would now sail along the Pacific coast with stops in Seattle,

Portland and Vancouver. On this voyage some of the passengers on board were looking to join the "Western Gold Rush" now significant news in the east. Black families, some legally free and some not, were willing to travel far looking for a better life even in the wilds of Canada.

The Brother Jonathan's fame peaked when she was asked to deliver the most important dispatch in the ships history. Congress had decided to admit Oregon to the Union on February 14th, 1859 and President James Buchanan wanted to send the notice immediately. But this was a new land, yet untamed by any technology beyond smoke signals. The news could only be wired as far as St. Louis. Arriving there it would be transferred by stagecoach to San Francisco. The official announcement was to be carried on to the only large steamship traveling north, the 'Jonathan.' Entering the Portland wharf, she arrived with the bill granting Statehood to Oregon.

But the ship's fame was not to last.

Early in April 1862, Indian tribes camping from Victoria to Vancouver Island to southern Alaska were dying of smallpox. The epidemic was being blamed on the arrival of an Indian booking transport on the infamous ship.

That fateful voyage had begun from San Francisco bound for Puget Sound. Carrying as many as 125 passengers, the cargo consisted of hats, books, glassware, butter, vegetables, shoes and many other necessities, including 20 mules and 75 sheep. The smallpox virus had been carried on board as well. By April 25, even with the vaccine being available, over 500 natives became afflicted. During the month of May thousands of Indians would be vaccinated, yet death would follow them from the docks, across the western territories and into their camps. It spread among them from San Francisco to camps in Alaska, then moved east to where tribes that had, until now, successfully avoided epidemics for generations. Hundreds of families were lost. The plague would take Indians, blacks, and whites to the grave. The Tsimshian, Haida, and Tlingit tribes, which lived along the pacific coast would be infected causing 14,000 deaths between 1862-1863.

❦

Strong winds that morning of July 30, 1865 kept the passengers tucked inside their staterooms and off the decks. Steerage was mostly empty as tickets for this trip were purchased mainly for cabins. The decks were abandoned except for the helmsmen near the bridge wearing ropes tied to their waists to keep from washing overboard. There were few women. Groups of miners, foreign laborers and several government officials were passing through this part of the country, but not necessarily to stay. Rogues, gamblers and scamps made up the rest of the 190 occupants. Tucked away, the travelers drank, exchanged information in the ships salon or gathered in the pilot's cabin to play cards.

Mills moved about the kitchen now with urgency, spilling the soups as he pushed them away from the counter.

Raising a knife at a pantry boy he yelled, "Get out of my way or I'll stuff you in the oven!"

The passengers began filling the dining salon with conversation and laughter. Talk of illness would not be welcomed today. Now leaving port, after having been deemed clean by authorities, Captain DeWolf wanted to avoid his ship associated with the terms like "scourge" or "disease". This was 1865. With bad news behind him, the captain made plans to travel the coast quietly while still keeping his commitment to a record time of sixty-nine hours between San Francisco and Portland. Rather than sail the inland rivers it pleased the captain to take this ship out onto the open water of the Pacific. Unfortunately, as the captain would soon discover, the Brother Jonathan had not originally been built as an ocean going vessel.

After the dinner fare had been cleaned away, the galley swept and temporary staterooms replaced, Lew Mills moved into the wardroom. Several passengers had already arrived. Some seated, others standing, they gathered together around a card table in the company of the steerage steward and the second mate. The quarters were tight but even with the limited space they still found enough room to play a game of euchre.

As he entered the tiny room the players took no notice of him, which was fine. Lacking extra chairs he made his way to a corner wall, slid down to the floor, crossed his legs and closed his eyes.

A man in his fifties, looking to have more money than most, began to rant, "Damn fools in Panama tried to accuse me of everything! Kept me for weeks sitting pretty while they dug into the mud—swam around for days. Finally found it."

Cards were shuffled as the man continued, "I hired a man, good diver, not one of the local idiots they had out there, and he finally recovered the strong box. And what do you think? Nothing in it! Payroll funds gone. I learned more everyday. Captain of the Golden Rule took it! Figures. Just looking at him I knew he was a crook."

The man speaking wore a wool frock coat, tailored with wide lapels and covered buttons. Another man to the right was wearing similar attire but didn't seem to be listening, instead studying his own cards.

Into the center of the table a tiger card was thrown. Everyone groaned.

" Why didn't you take him to court?" The second mate asked the storyteller.

"No proof, no money, no time. My family had been eating bananas for two weeks already, you heard, near Roncado Reef. I wanted to get back with them. Later, when rescued they made it back to Panama, jumped a train to San Francisco. Glad to meet up with them again. But my wife, she sours on me. Would like to see me gone. Says it would be nice to settle in someday with a store, garden, a dairy, all in one stick."

Everyone grumbled in agreement at the man's description of events as the steerage steward shuffled the cards once more.

Lew Mills was enjoying the moment. Any conversation about gold or money was a favorite topic and so he stayed invisible, slumping further into the corner and hoping to hear more. He had already caught some of this gentleman's adventure before setting sail a few days earlier from their port in San Francisco;

The Golden Rule had been a steamer out of New York leaving for San Juan (in those years also referred to as Greytown). During the end of May, 1865, with over 500 passengers and a crew of 100, the rain, wind, and darkness caused her to stall onto a reef known as Roncado, about 250 miles northeast of Aspinwall, a town later to be known as Colon. Amazingly, there were enough lifeboats available to lower the passengers into the Atlantic Ocean, which at that time was stormy but shallow. Over a period of two days everyone was moved onto the small flat island just northwest of where the floundering ship lay. On about 12 acres of beach the fates were on their side. Small fresh water springs were found and with a condenser salvaged off the ship additional drinking water would be available.

A community came together consisting of the men, women, children and members of the crew. A village was created complete with amenities such as bedding from the ship used for shade and tents.

Eventually the Golden Rule began breaking up, disappearing into the abyss. Surrounded by sea and waves they had no way to predict when they might be rescued, but they felt that they would have enough food for 20 days. On June 9th an officer and the ships purser set off for Aspinwall and successfully returned with help. In less than two weeks all passengers and crew had been rescued and delivered to the Panamanian Isthmus.

Scandal remained. A strongbox, containing one million dollars in government notes and gold had been the responsibility of the agent for the Treasury Department, Victor Smith. His mission was to deliver the payroll to San Francisco, yet the strongbox was missing. Divers eventually rescued a similar box from the bottom of the sea, only to find it empty. The blame fell on Smith, but he in turn blamed the Golden Rule's Captain Dennis who was greatly in debt at the time. Nothing was proven and Victor Smith was reunited with his family in San Francisco a few weeks later. A steamer docked in the same location, the Brother Jonathan, was traveling north to reach Portland, Oregon and once again Smith was assigned the task of delivering $200,000 to the Forts in Fort Vancouver.

Lew Mills glanced up and with a wicked stirring in his soul quietly proclaimed, "So this is the great Victor Smith?"

The Captain spoke while keeping his eyes on his cards. "Yet now your carrying payroll again so I guess your word was good?" Captain DeWolf's eyes rose to meet the storytellers expression. "How's that come to be, Mr. Smith?"

"Like I told you," Smith responded, "After they questioned the diver who had first opened the box, me and the Captain Dennis, well, the authorities figured the money went down into the Atlantic with the Golden Rule. But still consider that everyone got off in a good way! Happy they were too, to move on to better designs before they were eaten by natives!"

Chuckles and a laugh were heard among the men.

As the group relaxed back into the card game Smith slowly rose out of his chair and was quickly supported by his companion, Rufus Lieghton, who took Smith's arm tightly, guiding him toward the door.

"Deal me out. It's getting late".

Smith collected no coins as he turned to leave, apparently finding the game less than profitable. Leaving the wardroom the two men closed the door and with small steps toddled down the darkened portside. Two other passengers quickly grabbed the empty chairs.

Waiting until the footsteps could no longer be heard one of the ships officers spoke up, "Hell, his wife didn't jump any train to Panama, that's crazy! His wife had six weeks traveling alone while Smith played dumb on Roncado beach with the police! She collected the chest of gold coins after being rescued no doubt, dragged it onto the next ship, the America. Probably has it tucked under her bed now. Soon as they get off this boat I'll bet they head straight east back to his place in Cincinnati. Why he needed this trip I'll never know."

A different player from across the table spoke, "Maybe he likes his job. Just think. Any man or crook, handles money all day for a living, fox in the henhouse for sure. And he brings along government protection, having that Mr. Lieghton to feed and coddle him."

With greed in his heart Mills decided, "Think I'll take a walk and make some new friends." Pulling himself off the floor he straightened and stretched his 6'2" body to remove the pain received from the hard redwood planking.

His ass was still sore as he left to pursue the two departing scoundrels, Smith and his bodyguard.

Violent seas had been the rule for most of the voyage since leaving San Francisco early that July morning. The harbor was now three hours behind and the trip slow with waves 20 to 30 feet high over the bulwark and cargo exceeding a safe measure. Since leaving port it had been a fools voyage. A crew of 54 and a passenger list of 190 was a small order for this trip, yet the problems did not stem from human cargo.

A month before on the Columbia River the Jonathan suffered hull damage after colliding with a barkentine sailing ship, the Jane Falkenberg. Cargo intended for the Jonathan had been piling up. Not to be shorted on this voyage a company agent ordered all cargo loaded on board, nearly 500 tons. Captain Samuel DeWolf objected, but some items were necessary in Vancouver and the town of Victoria, such as books, hats, cigars, furniture and even equipment for a woolen mill. Some questionable. Several prostitutes caught a ride, perhaps following the 346 barrels of whiskey loaded below. To finish this menagerie a three-stamp ore-crusher weighing several tons was brought on joining a horse and two camels being delivered to a circus in Oregon.

Mills had not joined up on this voyage for entertainment." My justification is for sport." He thought to himself as he strode down the deck, "Moneys the passion for all men and often their downfall. Not love, nor health but money obtains power with no concern for others of the human race. I'll remain aboard long enough to enjoy this game. Strength, domination, that's the drug for these men and this affair of the ship must be executed if not by me than by different demons who would gladly step up to take my place."

The ship careened as Captain DeWolf now back at his wheelhouse turned weatherly into the gale. The boatswain tightened lanyard ropes, holding down loosened yardarms and a torn sail.

Mills followed the pretentious passengers as they made their way back to their staterooms. He noticed the two men as they stepped aside long enough to allow a young cabin boy, known as Moran, to pass. Mills was far enough down the walkway to squeeze next to one of the four lifeboats and turning his body, pretended to light a Lucifer. The small boy Moran stepped quickly around Mills not wanting to find out if the large man would swing around and propel him overboard. Suddenly Mill's had an idea. Galloping after the boy as they approached midship he pulled the small sailor around to face him. Mills spoke loudly into Moran's seawater soaked face, "Boy, glad I caught you! Seems a family has got the sickness with all the backing and filling. They found themselves peaked. Left their room to walk above. Can I have the key to clean?"

The cabin boy had no problem passing the key. The thought of mopping up puke from the floor caused him to feel sick as well.

"Thanks, I'll get it back to you" And with that Mills turned, grabbing handles along the wall planks trotting quickly back to a room located directly next to Smith's, letting himself inside.

The Brother Jonathan had been refitted several times since 1857. The reasoning was that extra weight had to be reduced above to compensate for additional cargo below and in doing so, the berth walls were as thin as paper. Closing the door behind him Mills locked it to keep out any visitors or high waves.

A woman's voice could be heard from the next room.

"Loved seeing our little ones again, but mind you the trip back to Cincinnati was no picnic, Indians and all. Once we reached Newport I felt safer. The babies are fine. Our Cincinnati house is in a grand way and the chest is aside for now, carefully hidden."

As she spoke of her family, Caroline Smith fingered her new bracelet. It had been a gift from Victor when they had been united once more in San Francisco. After their harrowing journey on the Golden Rule he had purchased this to show his gratitude. Carefully designed it was created of silver. The links were woven or meshed to resemble lace. Two flat leaves made the lock and on those Victor had engraved her initials CVS.

Mills then recognized Smith's voice, "We need to get off this ship and back on land. We'll then be able to find conveyance to Kansas- get us closer to Ohio anyway."

Caroline agreed, "Once we come into Portland and drop off this payment to the Treasury, we'll be free to leave. Maybe get another commission east!"

With that the swindlers laughed harder.

"Caroline, how did you survive on Roncado reef? You don't look any worse for wear."

"Your a gent, yes you are Rufus Leighton. Wish you could have been there. Warm days, plenty of nothing to do. Sun, sand to lay about. Shells the size of my hand, every color, and fish too! They'd come up to the shore for crackers. Every shape. Such creatures."

Leighton interrupted, "Then where were the notes, the gold coins?"

Caroline Smith went on, "Some of the yanks got their plunder off the ship before it sank. I made sweet with a widower and pleaded for his travel chest just before we left ship. He obliged and with that I was able to pitch his trousers overboard. Rolled the notes and coins in a dress. We needed to bustle between coasts. Dispatching the chest to Cincinnati there was little time at home to kiss the boys and hide the treasure. Still we arrived to meet Victor in San Francisco a day early!"

Mills quickly found this attitude between Victor Smith and the woman, his wife, deceiving. "Earlier tonight Smith's story described a downhearted bride ready to fly away. What a lie! A yarn to promote another plot." Grinning he decided, "These thieves will soon leave this world once I'm finished, and become the wandering dead. I should be the one to enjoy the bounty they left in Cincinnati!" An evil inside of him awoke like a hunger but it was a power to be suppressed for now. "How long?"

Mills felt out of control.

The storm outside embraced the ship, causing a thrusting and twisting of seawater to fly across the vessel. Tales of money and crime were causing him to feel a bit left out. "I've played the game of greed many times before and always enjoyed it. Think I'll join in."

A pounding in his head drove him to act then but the voice of Rufus Leighton stopped him momentarily.

"We will need to unload at the next docking. This sea is unpredictable much like your last voyage. At this rate you two may once again be the victims of a shipwreck!"

Chortling was again heard through the wall.

Alone in the empty stateroom Lew Mills waited still as death, feeling the boat bucking about as he listened to the villains close by. He thought to himself, "This is such fun. Fools out on a lark, codfish aristocracy." Convinced this was not the first or last crime for these Yankees he had an afterthought, "Good, no souls worth saving."

With the consistent bang of the waves hitting the door he looked over and noticed water crawling underneath the frame toward him. As the wetness approached he considered an obstacle, "Victor Smith", a common name. That chest of gold in Ohio? How many Victor Smith's living in that city will I have to hunt down and murder to obtain it?"

Sounds of the sea enveloped the floundering ship. Ropes flew against masts, canvas folded and snapped, bells mysteriously rang without being asked. A stranger walking below shouted a warning ahead to the steerage compartment, "Stop, man overboard!"

Movement could be heard below, people running toward the starboard bow.

Moving off the wall Mills opened the door placing his hand on the grip as the cabin door next to his opened at the same time. Thinking momentarily of his good fortune, he yanked his door clear and moved quickly out towards the sea. Victor Smith and Rufus Leighton leaned over the rail looking ahead to the bow interested in seeing the excitement, never noticing the large man looming over them to the right.

Assuming that Smith's wife had no interest in this fatality or was too fearful to step out, luck had placed both scoundrels alone where Mills needed them to be. Seeing no traces of weapons he reached out with his immense hands grabbing the closest man first, pulling the front of his jacket up high and threw him like a rag over the side. Without turning towards the ocean to acknowledge the event he stepped instantly forward grabbing the back collar and trousers of the next man, Victor Smith and thrust him into the Pacific like a bail of hay.

Now Mills was free to take a moment and scrutinize the murders.

"The waves took both men leaving nothing to view, yet I feel someone may have been aware of my actions." Looking about, he could see no one to the starboard aft and back toward the stern. He thought everyone had rushed forward earlier after the warning but suddenly below the deck he spotted the hem of a skirt. A dark green velvet, it swished away out of sight before he could see more.

"Have my actions been noticed?"

Leaning further over the rail another huge wave slapped the ship causing Mills to step back and cling tighter with his hands. "No time to investigate for witnesses."

Grinning now, he turned and entered Victor Smith's stateroom.

Caroline Smith had her back to the door as she looked through a porthole into the distance. Solace must have seemed miles away. He marched up behind her, while at the same time she turned, and not recognizing him gasped.

Mills asked in a quiet voice, "Nice to meet you too. Now tell me, where do you live?"

The tiny woman whispered something about their home in Port Angeles.

"Wrong answer." Mills said.

She seemed faint and the demon became concerned that she might scream and attract others. He placed his right hand over her mouth and his left hand around her slim neck.

"Now I'm going to let you tell me where you live in Ohio. Cincinnati, isn't it? Just nod your head."

She nodded yes.

"Your husband and his friend have left for awhile so it's only you and me. Victor asked that I visit your domicile next time I travel east. Lets agree that you would want to see me again. Sound nice? Nod your pretty head."

All he could see were two wide eyes staring over his hand that covered half her face. She began to gag from the odor of the tobacco on his breath but managed to nod a yes..

"Good! I can't wait to see you again either. What was that address again, in Cincinnati?"

She whispered from under his hand, "Water Street, the river."

"Then off you go, to a new place you've never been. I'll join you there soon, but for now lets just say 'Keep your chin up!'"

She stared at him never blinking or moving her eyes away. Not to be trusted and to avoid any additional conflicts he moved her head a little to far around until he heard a snap. Her body slumped toward the floor. Weighing less than a leaf he dropped her into a water closet and closed the door. Looking outside he paused to glance left then right. "I have only a few more chores to accomplish before Captain DeWolf seeks anchorage from this horrendous storm. Portland was our destination but in the four hours since leaving Crescent City this boat has only traveled about 13 miles. If we get closer to the coastline I could jump and swim to shore or hide somewhere inside the ship until dark. That sounds like a plan except questions of the missing passengers may arise, not to mention the death of Miss Smith. How can I remain on board and pretend nothing has happened?"

Waves sloshed high enough against the Brother Jonathan's side to reach over the companionway.

"A clever move now would be to find a place to be noticed, an alibi, removing me from any accusations that could arise later. An appearance amongst the crew would be valuable."

Mills stumbled back to the aft where he knew men were inside the engine room throwing coal. Stepping inside the black chamber he lingered quietly until one of the men noticed him. "Mills, Mills, give us a hand! This boat needs a great deal of power to stay pushing across the top of this squall. Step in here and help us!"

Three men were franticly throwing fuel into the flames of the furnace in a battle to beat Mother Nature's wrath. The floor beneath them moved up and down making it difficult for them to remain erect as each full shovel heaved both coal and man toward the glowing hatch.

"How long have you been resting there?" A crewman named Drake asked Mills.

"Long enough to dry out some. I'm soaked through, relieved with the heat."

"If you want to get warm, move over here and grab a shovel!" Drake's muscles were black with dust and sweat, black lines snaking down his face, arms, and neck.

Mills shuffled over to the furnace pretending to loose his balance as the floor pitched beneath everyone's feet.

"I know you need more help as this ship might fail today but I'm weak from the sea and soon I'll be called back to the galley to fill my place there."

Filling their shovels they ignored Mills, too busy to challenge the baker in an argument.

As the men shoveled coal below Captain DeWolf at the helm above had given up. Passengers were pleading for him to turn around and head back to the safe port of Crescent City only a few miles east. Waves now reached above the pilothouse. Captain DeWolf had found no rocks marked on the charts to show any danger in their location. The only apparent reef was behind them toward the coastline, so to satisfy the frightened passengers requests the captain began the turn, to guide the ship portside south/southwest returning them slowly to the cove at Crescent City. It was now 12:30 PM. The wind pushed the ship backwards causing the paddles on either side to become independent of each other, one side lifting the paddle above the surface causing it to spin uncontrollably, while the other side sank and the paddlewheel disappeared below.

As Mills made his way along the main gangway a first officer shot past heading toward the engine room to check for any leaks of saltwater. Changing direction the men above spotted foam heaving up from the pillars of rock just below the surface. A man handling an anchor on the bow yelled the warning to the wheelhouse, but the fate of the Brother Jonathan was sealed. As she fell with the last swell, it brought the front hull directly down onto a rock that had for centuries crested up from 250 below the ocean floor. Slapping down, the bow was impaled and the destruction of the ship traveled as far up as the bridge.

As people screamed and cargo washed overboard hundreds of barrels of whiskey floated away, perhaps toward the lucky tribes of Klamath or Yurok Indians along the shore. A dog, a horse, and two camels swam as several men fought to secure themselves to debris or rocks that popped into view only to recede again in the blink of a wave.

Suddenly slapped from behind Mills turned to discover the purser's door had come ajar. While commonly locked, it was swinging wildly, opening and closing with the gales. Entering the tiny room Mills discovered the purser, John Benton out cold, apparently knocked unconscious from flying objects following the impact against the rock. Having no scruples to slow his decision Mills stepped across the body and rolling it over, groped the pockets of the young officer until a key was located. The officer also wore a money belt hidden beneath his coat but unbuckling it Mills spat out his disappointment, "No good out west, these flimsy greenbacks. And what's this?" He fingered a tintype picture of a woman wearing a veil and lace blouse. "This is of no value to me!" and he pitched it into a corner.

His interest was the two safes bolted securely to the floor ahead. Relocking the swinging cabin door and using Benton's key Mills unlocked the smaller of the two strongboxes. Only certificates and an old coat lie inside. The larger of the safes was a Doblier, impossible to open without a combination.

As the boat twisted into its fatal position he could hear screams and sobs, feet running and the last pushing of the giant paddles. Someone outside the purser's cabin was struggling with the door latch yelling, " Benton, let me enter or you'll suffer a court marshal on the mainland!"

Ignoring the demand Mills began pulling open drawers and checking under receipt books. He was surprised to easily discover a sequence of numbers written on the drawer bottom. He spun the dial to find the numbers needed and in a flash heaved open the heavy lead door discovering a clutch of coins laid out nicely in a wooden box. In lines for a count, hundreds of them, a gift of gold for the Klamath Indians that the government assumed would for a short time keep peace. Mills was not concerned with treaties on shore, "Shoot them all" would remedy the problem.

Pulling the soiled green backs from the coin belt the baker now grabbed handfuls of gold, dropping it into the money belt pockets. Filling each small cavity to the top he buttoned the flaps. Someone was again yelling outside the door, pulling at the handle hoping to retrieve his fortune from inside the office. Mills grinned to himself, "Sorry, your money has been reclaimed to provide for my retirement."

Looking back at Benton he noticed a movement of the small man's body. The waves crashed through the window and entered the room like an uninvited guest filling the floor with foam from the sea. Water mixed with books and the paper money washed next to where the officer lay. Mills, satisfied with his take, crossed over to the man and slid him nearer to the pool of briny sludge that had collected in the corner. Grabbing the purser's hair Mills turned the man's head and held it down firmly under the surface until any movement from his body stopped.

The sound of the yelling passenger disappeared from beyond the door as another wave hit, sweeping the man and his dreams from the ships walkway. Screams and wails of hopelessness from below seemed to surround Mills as he now moved to leave the purser's room. Stepping outside he paused for a moment looking for a way to escape the damaged vessel. Knowing life vests were stored below, he began his descent toward the bulwark side of the ship where a few vests stayed nestled away for the crew. The ocean was now filled with a population of travelers, whiskey barrels and floating cargo. Women in whalebone skirts swam past hoping to reach objects to stay afloat. The irony of their bad luck eventually found them descending below the cold black surface of the ocean to return to the giant mammals what had been stolen long ago for their frocks.

On the hurricane deck Captain DeWolf asked his third officer Patterson to help the women and children into the lifeboats. Additional assistance was offered by first officer Hallen, and George Wright, a Brigadier General on route to Vancouver. Several men had already begun boarding the lifeboats only to be pulled aside by the crew and made to wait as protocol dictated families of ladies with their charges had first honors. Carrying four iron lifeboats and two wooden surfboats the Jonathan was badly unprepared for this situation. The first attempt to lower a group to the water's surface failed as the small vessel swung back, crushing it against the hull. The occupants were swept under the stern of the damaged ship, losing all. A second boat was lowered with more ladies but again they were slammed into the waves near the paddlewheels, twisting the surfboat and crashing it back into the side of the ship. Mr. Allen, a first officer, was able to lift most of the ladies back on board the Jonathan before the lifeboat was smashed beyond use.

Mills watched the show from above clutching a wood stanchion. Several minutes had gone by and the steamer was breaking up, much of it already below the surface or floating away into the distance.

Making one more attempt, third mate Mr. Patterson gathered a small group of ladies and some children. A few strong crewmembers also climbed into the small vessel to assist with the ropes as they slowly descended toward the waves. Mills was feeling confident now, *"Harm or danger is only a mortal problem. I'm a Reaper and as an angel of the dead the tides are agreeable wherever I travel. Lives on board connect only for the wink of an eye. Soon I'll separate myself again, find other catastrophes elsewhere to engage in."* Moving quickly down the iron steps from above he ran toward the lifeboat and jumped in.

Chapter 2
SINKING of the BROTHER JONATHAN

Jumping over the rail and landing hard into the lifeboat Mills heard curses from sailors above. Even the Captain raised his voice in disgust over the fact that Mills showed no respect for the women and children still left on board, perhaps to drown today in this godless storm.

Mills fell directly upon an Oriental woman and her small son. They had placed themselves on the seat at the bow of the wooden craft, taking up only a small space. Landing, his body had crushed her shoulder and as he crawled off her tiny body others on board mocked him for his cruel tenacity.

"She's my wife!" he spit at them, in his gruff voice, "So leave me be!" Barking out additional obscenities he placed himself at the bow. Glancing over to the cowering boy on the seat he offered, "Here son, sit upon my lap for security."

The other men near the back of the boat grumbled curses while shoveling water over the side with a fire bucket. Others on board cupped their iced hands to throw the unwelcomed water away, hoping to make a small contribution. Having been with the Brother Jonathan crew for some time Mills recognized some of the group. The survivors consisted of a coal passer, a fireman, one of the chief engineers, a pantry man from the galley where Mills had worked and a watchman. Others he did not know directly. It didn't matter in the least who rode along. He had made the play and now had gained a free ride to shore.

Two of the crewmen in the middle, one a large black man, struggled with the oars as they pushed the boat through the surf away from the derelict ship as quickly as possible.

Jacob Yates, a quartermaster directly in front of Mills and his newly appointed family said with a frown, "Didn't know you had a wife Mills. Congratulations on your acquisition!"

Mills growled something in response and turned to watch the end of the Brother Jonathan as it moved further from view. In his opinion it was a lucky rock that found the bow, selfishly reaching up to grab at a life above the sea. And such a pathetic crowd of humanity. They had sailed ignorantly into their futures, becoming victims penalized for having chosen a ship that would steal them from their homes and families. They rolled the dice, winning a trip into darkness.

This flock of lifeboat survivors counted only nineteen: four sailors, two black men, and Mr. Sevener, a hired entertainer who would not be amusing the crowd today. There were Portuguese seaman, a fireman named Lynn, and a few sobbing women with their frightened children. Edward Shields, a waiter and William Lowery, a fireman were taming the oars. The third officer James Patterson was out cold having hit his head while sliding off the ship too close under the rail. Worthless.

46

In a bustled skirt and lace collar a woman named Mary Tweedale shouted above the storm to ask the oriental woman squeezed against Mills, "Miss Lee, are you all right?"

The tiny women smiled in response while pulling her soaked shawl above her head. It promised no sanctuary from the ocean yet under the cover the dainty women could almost disappear. Waves still flew and fell upon the small boat as it slowly pushed its way back toward the quiet cove of Crescent City. Half a day earlier they had left that cove to reach Portland and the Columbia River entrance but after a terrifying four hours at sea the steamer had only traveled approximately ten miles west.

Officer Patterson now began moving, regaining consciousness. The other travelers noticed but had problems of their own. Although they kept bailing, it seemed hopeless. The ocean continuously washed inside deep enough to meet the gunnels. The women were using their skirts as shovels, looking all the while back to the floundering steamship for help. Their prayer was that another small craft might follow them to shore. Eventually, with short views from the top of the waves, they saw that the large ship had faded. Now they were trapped alone in the storm.

Still afloat after two hours of rowing a new threat tested them, the breakers. Their boat was being sucked closer to the shore with the tide as the men heaved the oars around the rocks. One of the men pointed ahead and shouted, "The rocks are not our only jeopardy. Indians!"

Yates, the quartermaster, had noticed as well and in a whisper said to Mills, "They've been camped along these shores for thousands of years, staying vigilant. They watch the vessels that sail this coast. Hazards of the Pacific provide them bonuses on many occasions. Any bounty in this wilderness territory is valuable, being both new and rare to them. From the ship even our scalps make for valuable trading. Looks like their crawling down from Bird Rock now, eager to have the tide wash us ashore and make their hunting day complete."

With this new fear the crew pushed the lifeboat south loosing sight of the natives while avoiding the shallows. Moving around Battery Point they were spotted from a distance by men and boys from the town waving their arms as they raced to the water's edge. Some men waded out into the surf grabbing the bow to pull it closer in and save the ladies from having to swim. It was a silly gesture, finding that all aboard were drenched worse than the rescuers. Helped to the shore, some of the ladies fainted simply from being totally fatigued and overwhelmed by the catastrophe. Questions and inquiries of the sinking made for loud conversation as the townspeople shouted for answers of the whereabouts of the Brother Jonathan.

Lew Mills jumped over the side, wading to shore. As he watched the chaos leaving the small boat he had an idea. Spotting a villager who, from the purple on his fingers appeared to have been picking berries, he asked," The sheriff, is he about?"

"Well yes, most likely at the end of that first street. Brown door, chairs out front. Might be there. Why?"

Mills puffed out his chest and spoke with a false sincerity, "Indians watched the boat go down. Likely to attack any survivors that wash up. I'll find him while you help get these ladies to the inn."

Most of the men from the village were already walking the victims up the beach, some embracing the survivors, others carrying the limp children draped across their arms toward the motel.

Pretending to take the berry picker's advice the Reaper walked quickly across the wrack scattered along the sand and over a tall berm that would forever separate him from the sea and Crescent City.

Now that he had a small amount of wealth and a tattered reputation Mills began his quest to reach Cincinnati. Stolen gold waited there and he fantasized about plans for a retirement. Distancing himself from the Brother Jonathan had been easy but his future was dicey. It had only been a few hours since the lifeboat had washed up on shore and decisions must be made quickly and carefully lest he be associated with the disaster.

"My days of employment on the ship had been filled with stories of gold and mining camps that followed the Salmon River, Elk Camp, Thompson's Ferry. I need prospector's trails heading east that would eventually land me in Ohio. There's additional treasure to claim. The town of Yreka may be a good place to start, hooking on to the Siskiyou Trail. The ship's gossip had people sharing stories about the hundreds of gold camps throughout the mountains. But how would I travel? Jumping on a horse was one way to consider for my quest, but I hate horses. They bite in the front and kick in the back. When ignored they usually go back to the place they started.

Why have one? Better to eat them than feed them. Still, buying one is an option."

He walked through the woods to distance himself further from the Pacific town, "I could travel down the coast and canoe the Klamath River. Then south on that until it joined the Trinity River. But local boatmen might just be talking about the Brother Jonathan catastrophe, so perhaps it'd be best to look elsewhere. A bath and some food would be nice." His clothes were salty and his stomach was beginning to hurt. Still damp from the night on the lifeboat he wanted to avoid being noticed by any passing wagons until sunup but surprisingly the road was crowded with activity. Stagecoaches' flew past, miners shuffled by with mules, ex-slaves dragged along behind buckboards and Mills observed one badly worn carriage carrying harlots on route to they're rendezvous with John's.

With the dawn he felt confident enough to flag down a group of five young men with a wagon half full of provisions and ponies full of juice. They slowed down just enough as Mills called out.

"If you'll oblige me I'll pay the fare to ride!"

Thinking opportunity they pulled up their horse and stared at him. A boy behind the driver asked in a thick accent unfamiliar to Mills, "Which route do you travel?"

Mills needed to think one moment, "To find a stage stop east"

"We go to Happy Camp, no more" the boy replied with a friendly grin.

"How much further is it into Yreka?"

The boys had a verbal exchange suggesting foreign lands unknown.

'How can they understand each other?' Thought Mills.

"We go east to Happy Camp, no more." All five smiled, more to share an understanding rather than to offend this stranger.

"Fine," he mumbled, "Any place from Crescent City will do. In the future these lads won't mention this accidental meeting to anyone but each other."

Chapter 3
The GRIM REAPER

Love, guilt and empathy were all foreign to Lew Mills. He obtained personal satisfaction by observing man's perils. He did not relish emotions although rage came into play occasionally. From time to time he had dealt with the frustration of dealing with mortal men, having been beaten over the years by good Samaritans that wanted him jailed, hanged, or shot.

Insufficient penalties at best.

Their anger had been memorable and well deserved. Communities condemned him with "moral insanity," hunting him down, seeking revenge for the victims that had died while Mills stood and smirked. Some considered him a scourge, pursuing him to rid the earth of his pestilence. Mills had learned something from these attacks having been imprisoned when his plans had not gone properly and nearly beaten to death. After those violent events he had simply picked up his soul, moved on to another place staying evasive as well as anonymous.

Traveling through time it was demanded of him to forever be engaged in *the game*. There were others like him, 'Participants in Death' holding their black souls close, only reacquainting relations with each other as they passed through history. Reapers of every archetype, they stopped only long enough to brag or boast of their own ghoulish games and profitable adventures. Strength

was gained through notoriety of numbers. Large tragedies such as fires, floods, lightning strikes or even earthquakes in heavily populated areas would count in their
favor. That was the game. Points were awarded for attending extreme events that sliced off bits of mankind,

When it came to death 'the more the merrier' Reapers shouted!

The players felt exhilarated when attending 'something for the history books.' Their evil glee even extended to annihilations of each other. No, there was no love
lost between any of these spirits. If danger lay ahead for a
player, warnings were never uttered.

Did Lew Mills know all of the players? No. Reapers
would emerge from other places and eras to partake in
the consequential nightmares that historians would record over time with great pain and sorrow. Mills juggled
cultures, changed some, even removing a few. Populations of gentle, naïve individuals that had no experience
with evil were the pawns. Problem seemed to be that
there were still too many players in this game.

After leaving the Brother Jonathan Lew Mills did not
feel a lost but instead refreshed. He delighted in watching the terrified eyes of the passengers, their shocked ex-
pressions revealing a loss of hope as they sank beneath
the waves to be ground up below the surface. It made the
game simple when the pawns were so vulnerable.

This trip east across the new territories during winter
would give him several opportunities to observe death at
its best. Born victims such as Indians were crossing paths
for the first time with settlers and miners. There were
new laws that the white man was prepared to enforce.

If Lew Mills chose to stay and sample the hatred festering within the tribes it could prove to be jolly entertainment.

And the soldiers. Frustrated from hunger, cold and lonely, they too would soon be entering winter. Like bears starving from a sparse summer the temptation to sleep comes too soon and the fear of dying in a winter's abyss will test a man's morals.

Then there were the miners. Their mountain hell shared little hope and no guidance. The Klamath Mountain range takes more than it gives and even the strongest man can crumble under the fever and cold. Mines collapsed beneath the earth, falling onto the innocent. It would be a last testament for them, yet Mills would be pleased to join them below, wait until each breathed his last. Contentment would not come from their demise but more so in the circumstances. Attending episodes of disease, starvation, accidents, that was the fun. To participate in tragedy was to the Reapers like enjoying a fine meal. Savoring each selection, hot or cold, bitter or sweet.

The many flavors of death.

❧

Indians seemed preoccupied elsewhere and few people roamed the land going in an easterly direction. Unfortunately for the dark traveler any sickness or violence was far away. Nights on the prairie brought a cold that chilled Mills to his center. Surrounded by tumbleweeds and screaming dust his wagon had traveled less than 40 miles that day and the sun that earlier had warmed his back had been gone for hours. Between Colorado and

St. Louis Lew Mills acquired a buckboard. His revulsion for horses made even this convenience agonizing, yet compared to the hardship of walking it was tolerated. Food had been the only gratification since Salina, Kansas, but a few feet ahead his luck changed.

In the dark the buckboard thumped over something other than a rock. Looking down at the black sand below Mills gazed upon the body of a man quietly at rest. Mills was still hours from his next town, Jefferson City, Missouri, and was glad for this unexpected surprise. Jumping off the seat he tied the horse to a boulder nearby and began investigating.

"Just a corpse now, but the body's still intact. In only a short time the smell will carry and coyotes will be moving in closer to gnaw on it."

Mills pulled the wagon back closer adding to the distress of his spooky horse. Feeling the body, no, the miner wasn't warm. Rolling the body over helped to detect a bounty of clothing along with the man's Hackensack. Picking it up it seemed quite heavy. Checking the contents he counted several picks, a book, matches, some jerky and a hemp rope. "A lot of rope."

Grinning, Mills thought, *"Perhaps this man pictured himself siding down into a cave, the walls lined with solid gold and a lake at the bottom filled with whiskey where he could swim all day and whore all night. Hah! This man's dreams had come true quicker dying than living."*

Pulling the valuable coat off first, Mills than tucked the rope under the dead man's back. Digging in the man's bag once more he found a match. Needing to light it he stepped over to the downwind side of the cadaver so the stick would hold a flame. Dryer than Grandpa's jokes, the rope proved combustible and soon the body was roasting nicely, heating the night and sending the cremated remains to disintegrate into the smoky sky.

The next morning Mills had awoke from his first decent sleep in some time having been comfortably swaddled between the buckboard and the campfire. With his knife he again began cutting the last crispy parts away but found that he no longer had an appetite. "Three helpings were enough for any man. I'll leave the rest for that scraggly pack of coyotes in the distance, howling with hunger. If they choke on it and die the worms will be the winners. Someone always profits."

Chapter 4
ST. LOUIS &
CINCINNATI

Reaching St. Louis, Lew Mills found himself fitting comfortably into the river city lifestyle. Riverboats were stacked like cordwood along the Missouri shore. The wooden giants passed along the muddy waterway while others slept in their slips as crewmen loaded and unloaded cargo. Lowly mud clerks moved in every direction finishing one job, then quickly beginning another. Pursers in their cabins counted while cooks in the galley stowed foodstuffs away for the next trip out.

As he moved through town he would leave a gold coin here or there to purchase a meal, a room or a girl, careful not to distribute too many. A twenty-dollar coin could bring questions. He wanted to avoid explanations of the rare currency with nosey proprietors. News of the Brother Jonathan may have already reached this part of the territory. Word traveled fast among river rats.

Needing a drink Lew Mills limped into a corner bar and moved up to the front of the room while searching his pockets for small coins. The ragged soles of the boots he had worn since leaving Crescent City slapped open with each step exposing calloused heels. "New boots would be in order."

The bar was busy. Workers looking for lunch stood in line ranting on about recent river misfortunes, but the bartender had the floor, "Wrecks far and wide, steamboats, exploding in this town, sinking in that town. Snags hiding in the river like alligators ready to jump right out and bite 'em through the hull." He wanted to be heard above the twenty or so crewmen drinking and conversing around the room. "It's the leagues of loggers, don't ya know! No love for the ships, just the pay. Selling fuel from the shore, banks are weak from Hannibal to Cairo. Nothing left to hold the mud back. My wife says the trees find a way to slip into the river at night, lay on the bottom waiting for a boat."

The bartender found Mills staring from the end of the bar, wearing a scowl to accent his already course face. Walking down he asked, "Whiskey?"

"About time," Answered Mills.

Another big man at the back of the room kept the conversation going, "Captain McKinney's Twilight was taken not long ago, the steamer Tempest, too!"

As Mills sipped his shot of rotgut the barkeep answered, "It's the boilers more often than not. Thin from the heat. Hot, cold, then hot again. After a couple of years they are happy to explode. Puts them out of their misery."

Mills ordered a second shot. Hearing that the public was so often close to death brought him a great deal of satisfaction and he wondered if St. Louis might be a place to stay and forget about Victor Smith's gold trunk waiting in Cincinnati.

Glancing down to examine the holes in his boots Mills perked up as the discussion changed to a topic familiar to him. Three men opening a second bottle at their table were saying, "In Crescent City they're still picking the bodies up along the coast. Sixteen washed up between Gold Bluffs and Trinidad. North of that there was even a camel on the beach, dead of course. And a horse from the Brother Jonathan, stiff as a stick."

A man next to them piped up, "Indians wanted to take the bodies but soldiers from Camp Lincoln ran 'em off. Before they got there the injuns took shoes, even scalps, any valuables. Boats still going out to search with so much gold left to find."

The barkeep added, "An' I heard some hands walked away from the sinking. Nineteen came ashore that day in a skiff. Eighteen stuck around. I heard one man up and left. Had enough and didn't stay around to tell the tale. The law in California is curious about what that man was doing, why he left. There might be money in it for someone if they find him and can get him back to the coast."

An older well-dressed man spoke next, "Last month I read in an article stating that the authorities know the man. Seems he worked on the ship. Rode back to shore with the ladies, children, other crewmembers. It should be easy to catch him if he's still in the area."

"Well, is there a reward?" The barkeep asked.

"I believe there is. But so many questions left to ask, terrible tragedy. Families lost. People simply vanished into the sea. Heartbreaking."

An older woman came down the bar and offered another drink to Mills. "Later" was his answer. He glanced down at his hands that had been tightly squeezing the small glass nearly crushing it. "They must know my name of course, somewhere between Crescent City and here." He looked around the room at the men's faces, "The crew, they knew me. And Peterson, that moron, making light of my fraudulent family. At the time they had served a purpose."

The man spoke once more, "An Oriental woman and her son, seems they reported the man carried contraband. The boy told of a money belt beneath the man's coat. Reward of $250 if the man can be caught and held to answer questions."

Smells of leather coats and cigars filled the room as the whiskey on the Reaper's tongue began to sour. He mumbled to himself, "Plans have changed. Time to leave St. Louis."

Walking out of the saloon he headed for the stage-coach ticket office. Once he had established the hour of departure there might still be time enough left to hunt down a different pair of boots.

cVo

He grabbed a stagecoach out of St. Louis with a swing station in Vincennes. From there it went on to Louisville. The entire trip cost $15.50.

Approaching the station keeper Lew Mills growled, "The rate's too damn high. The Queen travels cheaper!"

A stage driver, referred to as a "Charlie" was notified as well, "The fare's a robbery! Its no wonder you bandits are shot and killed so often!"

In Louisville he grabbed some johnnycakes from a stand and walked across town to the Ohio River catching an empty keelboat going against the grain upriver to Cincinnati. Giving the boys onboard a dollar he barked, "Here, keep the change." They proceeded to push up the waterway. It was already late afternoon so the trip would not land them into the city until some time after midnight two days later.

The water barge was about 60 feet long, and 15 feet wide with a cabin in the center of the boat. Lew Mills was their only freight and because of the cold he took the opportunity to make himself at home inside the small hut. Finding some moldy pork jerky to eat he eventually fell asleep.

As he stepped off the boat at the Cincinnati shore it was quiet and dark.

"Hungry as I am, it's more important to find Victor Smith's gold cache and be done with it. Food will have to wait. The bounty off the Golden Rule has been haunting me since leaving Crescent City nearly three years ago!"

Milk wagons were already moving through the town so he asked a boy driving one, "Would you know the house on Water Street owned by a rich man, Victor Smith?"

The boy answered, "Yes, there was a house, but it's been empty. Very dark now. Used to deliver there with my Papa until I got my own route but with no one inside it was crossed off the list."

"Do you still go past the house?"

"No, a different boy drives that street."

Mills pushed his face hard into the young man's face and whispered, "Take me there."

After about ten minutes the boy stopped the horses in front of a tall two story home. A mirrored image of itself on both sides, it was trimmed with a short lacey iron fence in front of a stone porch. In the middle of the structure was the large front door. Above that door on the second floor was a trio of windows, each with a gargoyle perched in front to watch for intruders. Giving them a dirty look of his own Mills dropped from the wagon onto the cobbled street and moved up to the home's entrance. Behind him he heard the wheels of the cart quickly move off, the horse at a gallop.

Rattling the knob it seemed obvious at this hour of the night that it was locked. He stepped to the side window and looking inside saw only dark shadows displaying a few items of furniture. Making his way around to the back he passed under the carriage entrance and found a second door. It was locked as well, but loosely. Mills applied his shoulder and with little effort had it open. This seemed the kitchen. Its shelves were bare and dusty. No kettles to warm some tea, no sticks to heat the stove. Moving towards the middle of the house he passed through the butlers pantry, the dining area absent a table, and into the vestibule.

Open and at one time airy it now held the dilapidated steps leading up to the second story. Mills stopped to listen. Small sounds, some mice, a bat. If there had been anyone on the first floor he would have detected him or her. The home seemed deserted. A candle or oil lamp would come in handy now. Mills searched the entry room around him and found no help. Walking to the tall vestibule walls there was the loveliest French wallpaper hung with great care from floor to ceiling. With his fingernails he felt for an edge. Finding one he ripped a long slice of it away. Rolling it tight, he then lite the end with one of the matches that he had saved from the dead man's Hackensack. He started up the long stairs. At a halfway landing was a decision, left or right.

"The dust on the right is gone in the middle of the step as well as on the handrail. The left direction was dustier from little traffic." Turning right he moved slowly holding his wallpaper torch to see both the hall and any obstacles waiting to cripple him. Moving about 15 strides he discovered a platter in front of a door holding two tea-cups, the tea leaves dry.

Mills waited, wanting to catch a creak or whisper from the other side of the door before someone shot him first, making him even more agitated about this trip than he was now. He could knock, but that to him seemed pointless.

Kicking the door open he jumped into the room and yelled, "Who's in here?"

He detected a tiny whimper from beneath a tattered coverlet. It appeared two bodies were hiding in a small bed, both half his size. They were children or maybe women. Throwing the covers off he looked down onto two old maids huddled together. One seemed to be protecting the other who was, from all appearances, sound asleep even after the scare.

"Are you Victor's Smith's mother?" Mills shouted at the helpless woman, hoping to scare the bejesus out of her.

The tiny voice replied, "No. It's just me. The Smith's left long ago."

"When did they leave? What for?"

"There was no one here to care for the children. The parents died in California. Drown on a ship. Others came, took the children, the clothes, most of the furnishings."

"So what the hell are you doing here? Is there food? Bread?"

"No. Only my friend and I." Pushing her nose into the hair of the woman beside her. She began to cry.

"Wake her up! Lets see if you can get a fire going, find something to eat!"

The woman cried harder, "She's dead. My friend. Left this world yesterday, maybe the day before. My companion's gone."

Looking about the abandoned room Mills rolled his eyes and thought, "Geez, now I'm stuck here in this dump with two old spinsters, one dead, no food and perhaps the money's gone as well."

Still clutching his torch he left the room feeling quite secure that the only resident would not jump him. Walking across the rest of the house he searched closets in the breezeway, drawing room and great hall. Going down to the coal room he looked inside the furnace. "Nothing. The wine cellar's barren. No reserves of cheese or potatoes left. My goal was to find the trunk of coins but there seems little reason to hunt. January in this cave holds only spiders and rats who've already enjoyed the last of any crumbs."

Lew Mills shuffled back upstairs to the woman's resting place. Crossing the room he discovered that the lady had pulled the covers back across herself and gratefully stopped crying.

"You're still warm, just enough to thaw my feet. You move over and we'll get cozy."

She studied him for a moment, her face changing to a wrinkle.

"And no crying! You start to blubber and I'll throw you outside!"

Removing his boots he marched back across the room and pulled down the only drapes he'd seen in the house. Covering only the two of them, he was unconcerned about the cadaver. As he pushed up close to the quivering old maid Mills soon fell into sleep.

The morning dawned cold. Mills rolled over to see his breath leave his lips. His hands and feet were hard to move and as he wiggled them he noticed the lady next to him felt even colder. She was dead.

"A good decision on her part. This was no picnic with January, no food and a dead friend. Would they be walking together on the other side?" He surprised himself with this inquiry of their salvation. "What do I care? Since leaving Louisville I've felt emptier than a whore's purse. Time to spend some of this gold around my waist and investigate this fresh port town."

With only the disappointment of Victor Smith's missing trunk from the Golden Rule to swallow, Mills felt ready for something new. A warm feeling enveloped him. "I'd like a nice explosion, a fire, maybe a torrential flood in the future. That would cheer me up. Or something capable of wiping out a slice of the Ohio population. Hell, with the commonwealth of Kentucky on the other side I could envision some hangings and perhaps a bad batch of killer bourbon to boot." Smiling for the first time in days he left Victor Smith's mansion contemplating this new waterway and experiences of yet another type of foul amusement.

Chapter 5
The MAGNOLIA, a PACKET BOAT

After a night in bed with two dead women and no food Mills was feeling peevish. Victor Smith's house briefly crossed his mind as he made his way down to the docks along the shore, "No money found. What a joke. And it seemed the joke was on me. The trip across the territory was useless. Two and a half years of forging rivers, nights on the ground, my ass killing me from long hours in a trapper's canoe. What a life. And now I'm starving. Would the other Reapers know of my bad luck? Not a good situation to be considered weak among my competition. California, that was better. Less to do. It's time to change my luck. Whatever gold coins left can be used to became a man of leisure once more. This never-ending life between two eternities brings retirement to mind more often than a warm whore on a soft bed."

Frustrated, Mills growled to himself sliding down a mud trail toward the steamboat docks that edged the Cincinnati shore. In the distance was the cry of a faraway boat as it pushed up river. Calling ahead from it's stacks the boat would be looking to join the rest of the herd, tied safely to wooden moorings wanting to rest. The water going past smelled dirty. Early morning traffic from flatboats, ships, barges and even canoes had stirred up the worst of the bottom. Far away Mills noticed pieces of wood floating along the surface, painted planks drifting downstream. These were the last remnants of the sunken vessel, most likely the victim of a deadhead. Following behind was a boat and crew of snagpullers, each relentlessly doing their job to keep the river free of such flotsam. Paddling franticly to catch the debris Mills laughed at them. "Glad to watch them labor. I'd want no part in that."

Standing on the dock, several workers passed near, all busy and all much shorter. Some turned to notice the big man with seemingly no responsibilities but quickly rushed off to safer surroundings. Mills was beginning to feel whole again. He loved the water. A sudden surge of contentment washed over him, a feeling he had not felt since leaving the Pacific coast. As he watched the river flowing beneath the dock he heard soft laps become voices calling to him.

"Could this be the retreat to support my slothful lifestyle? I'm more than ready for such a holiday."

Around him activities of sailors on the ships reminded him of the Brother Jonathan and its crew. Now it was January 1868. Cold and clear there was plenty of winter ahead. This realization forced him to obtain a goal: a bed to call his own and a meal, morning, noon and night.

Walking as royalty Mills took to the shore traveling east. Along the icy boardwalk were stacked cotton bails, boxes of whiskey, fuel oil, gunpowder and other cargo to be loaded. Each pier held a different opportunity. Some steamboats were older, not seaworthy any longer in Mills opinion. That was not his problem but he wanted something a bit more luxurious. Mills was shopping for a place to rest. A vessel of little notoriety, average in size with no reputation and a warm bed.

Still walking the wharf he savored the thought of any tragedies along here in the future and hoped this busy port would supply them. "A boat sinking, a few fires, some untimely collisions. For myself, I picture sitting on the forward bow of a craft, smoking a cigar, sipping whiskey and watching."

Nearly at the end of the Cincinnati port he saw from a distance across the river much of the same floating clutter skirting the New Port docks of Kentucky. It was time to make a decision. Passing perhaps twenty of the small steamers he saw a ship just pulling away from the last dock named the Magnolia. A packet steamer that ran between Cincinnati and Maysville, this would be its first turnaround of the day. Feeling spry he ran ahead and jumped on board just as the crewman pulled the gangplank away.

"Say, you're a bit late! Wake up earlier next time, mate!" the cross sailor spat out at Mills.

Ignoring him, Mills marched inside the salon to check out the crowd. A few men in good suits and a spattering of women wearing their nicest dresses to travel in as they herded a passel of rowdy children. The kids were eager to run across the boat, bend over the bow to watch the water moving past or ring the bell. Tight with their grips, mothers would keep them from escaping until the boat docked later in Maysville.

Mills grinned. "Another mess of humanity. What was the point of their journey up and down the river? On, off,

71

back and forth, fools along for the ride. Like the pacific, just one faulty ship is all it takes. Floating coffins, the lot."

He did like it here. Now he wanted to stay.

Jumping up the stairs to the pilothouse he swung open the door. Although he knew the Captain was busy at the wheel, Mills stepped up, "I'm here to bake."

The Captain, James Prather, did not turn his head. He seemed deep in thought but Mills sensed differently. From the odor he recognized that the Captain was drunk. Three sheets to the wind to be exact. The man's condition made no difference to Mills, "Wanted to stop up and apply to you for a job. I'm a seasoned baker, sometime cook. Had plenty of years to show for it on the Pacific coast. San Francisco, Fort Bragg. Circled the horn, too."

"Oh, shut up, for the Christ sake."

Prather coughed, spewing a white foamy puddle on to the floor, "I don't give shit where you been. First trip today up this river. Will do the trip twice more before dark. What the hell do I care if you're the King of Siam?" He giggled, "I know, lets do this trip blindfolded!" His evil laughter sounded across the top of the ship.

Hearing a burst of laughter across the deck two men stopped their chores, said something to each other in German and then went back about their task.

"Fine, cook something. Bake yourself to death if you like. We could use a man with fortitude." Prather coughed up something else, pulled down the window and spit it away, "So many come to me cowering, needing work since the war. They won't get rich here, nor will you. Keep the crew and travelers fed for me, agreed?"

72

"Fine. And do you have an extra berth?"

"Somewhere. Go find Fradford. He's the cook or chief mate, or whatever he wants to be today. Tell him you'll need some yeast!"

Mills left the pilothouse listening to great gales of laughter from the Captain as he closed the door. Going down just one flight of stairs he swung around the corner looking for the galley and hoping desperately to find food.

His size parted the crowd as he walked behind the partition to the cooking area. Just as he remembered it from the Jonathan, pots, knives, a stove and sink. The cockroaches and silverfish were new, but the room was well lighted, helping to keep the crawling life forms away during the daytime. The cook, Benjamin Fradford, was slamming a strip of pork against the counter in the company of flies.

"I'm the new baker." Mills announced. "Ready to begin if there's space."

Fradford rolled his eyes as he swished a bug off his forehead, "You may need to wait. No provisions for you on board. No yeast, flour, lard. That'd be back at the city we just left. The go round takes about four hours. You can cool your heels in the cargo hold or the slops 'til we return."

Grabbing a bread roll off the cutting board Mills went out to the bow. "This was perfect," he thought. "An irresponsible captain and cook with a crew of Germans…. Accidents waiting to happen."

Folding his body onto an old wooden deck chair, Lew Mills stretched out his legs, pulled down his hat and enjoyed the ride.

◦✲◦

Since 1787 steamboats traveled throughout the United States on inland rivers. Considered cheap, dependable and the safest way to travel before railroads became common in the new territories this link between cities was only $5 per person for a cabin and $1 for a seat on the deck. Deck seating included any weather, from sunshine to tornados. Cargo was a mix of whiskey, foodstuffs, cotton, wool, animals and ammunition. Called a packet boat, the Magnolia also ran correspondence to Maysville and on occasion, to Vanceburg three times a day.

Before her stint taking day-trippers up and down what the Indians called the "Good River," the Magnolia had a history all her own.

Built 1857, she was a wooden side-wheeler constructed to sail both the oceans and inland waters. A cargo ship in the British Isles during 1861, Civil War Union vessels had been tracking her down hoping to capture the Magnolia for a large bounty. With the war effort she was carrying cotton and secret confederate letters containing plans to import arms. Pursued, the crew of the Magnolia chose to destroy her cargo, burning the boat rather than hand it over. Confederate sailors exploded a boiler as Union vessels quickly caught up, boarded, and put out the fires.

Flying a new flag, she switched allegiance to capture Confederate ships as a blockade-runner. Additional wartime history on the Magnolia would include a period spent as a hospital ship and as a temporary office for Ulysses S. Grant. Now as a packet boat on the Ohio River, the Magnolia remained valuable. Often carrying a full consignment of between 150 and 170 passengers and assorted cargo with each trip, she was old but fast and profitable. In New York her owners had her insured to her full value, guaranteeing revenue whether floating or sinking.

❦

Mills had found contentment on the Magnolia. As soon as an area for baking was cleared in the galley he crossed the river on a flatboat to New Port, Kentucky and hired two boys to be his indentured slaves. Not hard to find, Winston and Noah were orphans. Neither of their fathers had returned after the war. Noah's mother had died of pneumonia a year earlier and Winston's mother had died delivering her next child. Both boys relished the thought of employment. Mills just wanted to sleep. During the year of 1868 both boys had been homeless. With the experience of living on the lamb they had gained a street sense and their talents made them easy for Mills to teach.

"I will only show you once how to test for the correct temperature of the yeast by dipping a finger in the warm bowl of water. Learn to test the warmth of the water. Not too hot or cold. If done wrong I will cuff you across the head. Now watch me roll and knead this dough. Again, any mistakes and I'll knock your skull again in the same fashion!"

Noah seemed to take the abuse best. After correcting his mistakes for Mills he would then go down to the water barrel on the lower deck and soak his head. Winston just solved the problem of receiving any punishment by having a good memory. Within a week both boys were producing 30 loaves of bread a day and cornmeal biscuits each morning.

February came with a cold that drove customers away from the docks. Only one trip a day was necessary between Cincinnati and Maysville. Most of the steerage compartments below were beds taken by the German crew. Long days were spent writing letters to family abroad or playing skat. Mills, Captain Prather and the cook, Fradford stayed in the empty dining room playing cards or darts. Poker was the game of choice but boredom invited whist, cribbage and euchre.

Kentucky winters consisted of freezing rain more often than snow. The river had sheets of ice reaching out from the banks almost 10 feet so leaving port might serve to damage the hull. Even with the use of axes or rocks Winston, Noah and the crew proved useless against the frigid water.

Evenings the men would move the table down into the boiler room. There was enough wood to heat the small space, but little beyond that. Like a room in Hades they joked that the blackness invoked a card game in hell. Officers from nearby steamers, the Panther or Falcon would also visit to wager. Meager bets were placed. Captain Prather seemed to be the worst card player Mills had ever seen. Into a stupor from alcohol, Prather would throw down bets that would make a blind man sit up and notice.

"What the hell are you betting a pair of 6's if you don't know what anyone else has got?" Yelled the Captain of the Falcon at Prather.

Prather burped, making another attempt at upping the kitty while eyeing the crowd.

"Jeez, man, everyone here's got you beat. All the low cards were played in the last hand! Best you rethink your wager."

Embarrassed, the two Captains decided not to play longer. Bidding the others adieu they made their way to warmer cabins on their own boats.

Prather, Mills, Williams Edwards, a barkeep and the cook Fradford remained at the table. "Shuffle the cards, you bunch of lily-livered bastards. I still have money to lose so get your cards and make your bets." Prather spat out just before he had another taste of rum.

"I'm cold and need to find dry clothes to sleep in," Edwards said to the captain as he sheepishly retreated from the room.

"Same here." Fradford said, rising from his chair.

"Oh, sit down." Prather begged, "You don't have to play. Just watch. I still have one mark up my sleeve. Lets me and Mills go for high card than call it a night. What do you say?"

Edwards and Fradford sat back down again, curious to see the outcome.

Mills lied, "I'm tired and need to wake those two rag-amuffins or we'll have no bread at dawn."

Lifting a bottle to pour another dose, Prather cried, "Nonsense! There's no need for bread tomorrow. There's no ship that sails. I'll fetch my bet and we'll have one game!"

Prather rose up and stumbled to the top of the fly-bridge alone. The other three men waited below to see what he had planned. Mills fantasized Prather's feet slipping off the gangway, grabbing for his bottle rather than the rail and kissing his life good-bye.

A few minutes later the silhouette of the Captain stood in the metal doorframe. "I've got my bet! It's all I can gamble on such a cold night but if Mills wins this it may warm him up!"

Prather fell back into his chair and threw a paper document onto the table.

"Whats this, your last will and testament?" the cook cried, and both he and Edwards laughed out loud. Mills was not amused.

"High card gets the boat, the Magnolia and all of her treasures!" Prather commanded. Then he cackled to himself, readjusting his seat to shuffle the cards.

All three men looked at the paper on the table, then the two men looked at Mills.

"What do you bet?"

The black lifeless eyes of the Reaper flashed at the trio, "My soul."

Prather mixed the deck in his hands, "Worthless. But I am a spiritual man and will grant that you keep your good-for-nothing soul. Instead pay me with your labors for one year if you lose."

"Done. But keep in mind the fates are on my side. Are you sure you're choosing the right bet, the boat or your eternity?"

Prather smiled, "No, just the boat tonight. That bet you suggest would only disappoint you since my soul has no value either."

He dropped the cards on the table, "You cut first."

Mills picked up the stack near the middle. Finding a three of clubs he laid it in the table. Fradford dimly shook his head.

Prather picked the deck just above the surface of the table. A two of diamonds.

Edwards and Fradford both shrieked with delight, screaming about the three and the odds of the draw. Mills looked at Prather but saw no anxiety. The man had just lost his ship so it would seem that there would be some show of remorse.

"There you go, old chap. The boats yours and you can be captain now."

"All well and good," Mills agreed, "But as captain I choose only to command. If you wish to stay aboard than you still must drive. I will find my own duties and have the crew keep the galley filled with bread and pork."

Prather rubbed his face while Edwards asked, "And who of you will keep the manifest, load the mail, count the stacks?"

"The boat is Mills. Let him hire more hands to help if need be. I'll drive for a time. It keeps me off the streets and out of bordellos. Perhaps Mills will find a simple-minded operator with no soul, and then I can move on."

Mills stood up, towering over the other men, "I already have."

Chapter 6
PROSTITUTES and EXPLOSIONS

"A dying boat, beat to hell since the war," Prather thought, satisfied for the loss of responsibility, "Now its Mills problem. With the owner, David Gibson forever in New York it could be anyone's boat. And Mills never read the deed. Didn't even glance to see if I owned it. Both of us happy with the results. He can yell all day at the help. I'll be the one now getting sleep and drink, visiting the girls and doing cards in town."

Walking up the steps of an old hotel Prather did feel uneasy about the fact that Mills was not whooping it up after winning the card game, "It's a wait and see with that spook. He may have control on the ship but I've started my holiday today."

A girl Prather pays for favors, Martha, was waiting in her corner of a room shared by three other ladies. Prather handed her his coat, settling in for their weekly tryst. His grinning was a surprise catching her off guard.

"You're looking tonight like the cat that ate the bird." She purred.

"Right you are, sweetie! Lost my boat in a card game and got the better end of the deal to boot."

"But you were Captain!"

"Now I have just to drive a bit. No more hiring, firing, Germans to yell at, Indians to kick off the boat. And the bloke that won the boat is the cook! He says he'll feed me, get the mail. I said 'have at it'. He doesn't seem concerned with me or the boat. And what a rat's nest. It'd be lucky to make the trip even one more time down the river."

"Is it dangerous for the trips, down and up each day?" Martha asked, remembering that in the time she had lived along the Cincinnati shore many boats on the Ohio lasted less than ten years, most sinking with passengers on board.

"Damn thing leaks, needs a new everything. The real owner in New York, David Gibson, he has no interest. Insurance will pay more than the boat is worth when it goes."

"He'll find out your playin' around."

"Never stops to check. We get a collector once a week to take the ledgers and moneys from the safe. That's it.

Loosening his shoes Martha complimented him, "You do have the best. You lost a boat you don't own and get to eat and sleep on board, plus the fool cooks for you. Your life is a lark!"

"Lets celebrate now while the fires hot!"

They both laughed as he slipped his hand up her skirt.

On the other side of the river in New Port, Lew Mills was told of a girl living in a closet that entertained men for the evening. He was more interested in her warm bed than her favors but for human company away from the ship anyone would be an improvement.

Pulling his skivvies down the harlot named Willa noticed the improvement in clientele instantly, "My, you're big all over!"

"Glad your pleased." He mumbled, sitting down on the bed to untie his shoes.

As promised the room was tiny with three walls tightly surrounding the bed, the fourth side only a door.

"Been in town long?"

"I suppose you could say I've been passing through this world forever."

"How long?" She asked while helping Mills remove his shirt.

"Since the beginning of time."

"It sounds biblical. Are you religious?"

"I've been to hell, if that counts. Preachers are always shouting about that place in one way or another. It's actually not so bad, but no, I have no religion."

"So what kind of people are you?" Willa whispered to him, trying to stir up an erection with her hands.

More interested in his own history than her professional expertise, he exclaimed, "I'm a observer of catastrophe. It all started with a group of dead...very early... about the time of Cain and Abel. The first was Odin and his buddy Valkyries. Occasionally they roamed with Charon to lead souls to Hades." He put his hands behind his head for comfort, "I don't follow that line of thinking. The souls can wander from hither to yon, for all I care."

"Oh, that's silly. It's the work of the devil."

"Well, the devil might have caused it but we get to watch. Voyeurs, so to speak."

Playing with his hair she prattled on, "I can't stand funerals, stay away from anything sad."

"But that's a part of your culture, a religious ritual so it would be your duty to attend. Personally, I've decided that funerals are usually an excuse for old women to catch up on gossip."

Finally getting stiffer results she felt her remarks stimulating, a sort of erotica, so she encouraged him with another question, "Don't you feel remorse for the injured, the dying?"

"No. It's what keeps mankind going. We need the room. You need the room. Consider this. If everyone stays and no one goes the population would be a lot worse, terribly crowded."

"But people die. Important people who are full of ideas, talent, imagination and knowledge."

"And there it is. Makes room for others to take their place. Sort of gives everyone that didn't die a better chance to succeed, don't you think?"

In a manner of a speech Mills went on, "Death? Why this fuss about death. Use your imagination; try to visualize a world without it!…'an essential condition of life, not an evil.' Someone I once knew named Charlotte said that. Poor soul will be committing suicide eventually, but isn't she right?"

The conversation was growing darker and Willa was now uncomfortable with this morbid discussion. She tried once more to make her point, "I understand dying. Both my parents' are dead. I could never take their place.

They fought in wars, raised a family. Others remaining can't always fill those important positions after a loved one goes."

He lay next to her quietly, contemplating that soon she would be joining the deceased. As much as he was enjoying this debate the intercourse he was sharing with her tonight would carry with it 'bad blood', later causing her to die. He did not consider himself cruel, only an escort through time.

Breaking the silence Mills articulated, "My place is simply in the numbers, multitudes and populations. We go where tragedy occurs and witness what causes life to be altered."

"Like scarlet fever in a town?"

"It's a good start. Lets multiply that, say, a hundred times. Forest fires, earthquakes. A few of my favorites have been the potato famine in Ireland and that small pox malady covering the Pacific coast just recently. How about the Revolutionary War? About 10,000 soldiers bit the dust then."

"Oh gracious, your not that old, you scoundrel." She pushed her breasts closer to his chest and sighed, "If you're not the devil are you an angel?"

He pushed himself closer to cover her, "Yes. Of death"

❧

Hangover or a new intoxication, Captain Prather seemed to keep the Magnolia coming safely along side the piers in either Cincinnati or the small town of Maysville. Now with below freezing temperatures only one trip a day was necessary for the old steamer.

85

A cold wind blew down the river on that morning of March 17th, 1868, as the driver stumbled up to his seat in the pilothouse. The packet ship would launch at it's usual hour, noon, and head for one stop near Higginsport for additional mail before heading further upriver.

Mills stopped as he heard loud gibberish coming from overhead. Chief mate and cook, Fradford, was just coming down the stairs from the wheelhouse, "Into his cups, he is. Never slept last night or so I've heard. Got a new girl in town and played the fool until the sun came up."

Puffing a cigar and clutching a bag of correspondence, Lew Mills bent around Fradford to observe the Captain at the wheel. The driver seemed to tip and sway with the wake of the river.

"He'll be fine," Mills assured, "It's a grand day for a big adventure. Lets say we leave him be and check on the passengers instead."

Fradford thought this attitude a bit reckless considering that over 80 people had already bought tickets in town and more beyond that were boarding. The chief mate shook his head in worry.

The two men followed the rusted metal steps down to the gangway that would take them to the galley. Checking the kitchen Mills found Noah and Winston to have the breads and pudding already out. Mills raised his arm as if to attack. The boys ducked and Mills response was to laugh at his sadistic trick.

Ignoring them, Fradford said, "I'll stay and get the pig out. Too many riders now for just the boys bread today, they'll run short quick!"

Mills noticed that the steamboat had already passed New Richmond and was up to 9 knots against the current and leeward into the wind. "What's Prather's hurry? Must have another girl waiting to be poked in Maysville before he turns for home."

Before the locks and dams where installed downriver the Ohio was only 10 to 30 feet deep in the center, 40 feet at the most. Meeting another vessel going downstream was tricky having so little room to pass. Mud shoals falling from the banks could snag their boat and ground it. For a moment Mills considered taking the wheel himself. *No,* he thought, *It would not be sporting for me to interfere with fate.*

The crowds of riders that day were from different walks of life. Farmers, loggers and a few businessmen checking on investments were making the voyage to other port towns. Fishermen, a few ex-slaves and two Indians happened on to the boat that day. Mothers and kids made up the bulk. Racing past the older passengers the children were noticed by Mills with a scolding received by their mothers for not saying, "Excuse me or I'm sorry," as they tripped and ran around the open deck.

Edging along the outside gangway Lew Mills came upon a short bearded man wearing a long gray coat that seemed to hang loose from his small frame like a blanket. Fussing and pulling at the garment the man suddenly noticed Mills as well, "Sorry sir, no room to move around here. Its such a narrow ledge as one can see."

Mills, never a man for pleasantries, rudely grunted a reply, squeezed past, then after a few steps he stopped to ponder, "What would cause a man to reorganize his clothing on the outside of a ship?" Mills turned around and staying silent observed the backside of the bearded man once more pulling at his sleeves, coat and waist, obviously seeking some sort of comfort.

"He could be carrying a pistol or a bag of gold dust. Important papers?"

The long gray coat now moved away toward the bow turning left to disappear into the main deck. Curious, Mills retraced his path just enough to peak inside an opening on the wall. Sitting down on a bench the odd passenger looked very much alone. He spoke to no one, nor did he look around for a missing companion or wife to appear. Again he began to wiggle inside his oversized coat, using his hands to realign a bulge over his chest just to the left of his shoulder.

"Not a gun," Mills speculated, "Maybe a purse of greenbacks. But so much trouble for such worthless paper. Won't buy much around here." Imagination caused Mills to smirk, "Perhaps its an alligator he caught for a pet!" Smiling, the Magnolia's new captain walked off to find a perch for the ride.

When the boiler exploded everyone on board entered a different time and space. Happening so quickly the noise first stopped the conversations, then as bodies flew past falling into the water, screams ensued. Some men already aware of the danger jumped from the boat and started swimming toward shore. Confused at first, ears ringing, passengers ran to the rails hopelessly looking for a place to step off the vessel to safety. Flames from the back of the boat grew to life enveloping the sides and top, crawling forward toward the bow.

A second explosion, most likely from the gunpowder below decks propelled chairs, food and glass into the river. The wheel had ceased to turn and now the flaming ship was moving downstream with the current. A child ran past Lew Mills, clothes on fire, through the galley and off the side into the water. Mothers screamed in search of children, calling names, turning to scream again and having no place to run. The back of the boat had disappeared with only the bow still intact. Mills ran up to the pilothouse, not to save Captain Prather but rather to check the safe. It was far enough into the week that there would be cash inside to retrieve before the Magnolia was sucked under for eternity.

Marching up the steps he found the door jammed. Lifting his foot he kicked it open and stepped in. Oblivious to the chaos below Mills stalked across the small room stepping over the Captain. "Passed out most likely and missing all the fun." Moments slipping past and crew members now franticly calling for Prather, Mills ignored their cries and casually reached under the control panel to find the concealed safe. Having the key Mills opened a hidden panel and scooped items into his pockets, some gold coins, papers and a woman's handbag. Smoke had followed him up the stairs and it was becoming difficult to see. Squinting out the window he could see people coming from shore in skiffs as well as a tug, the Falcon, traveling in their direction to rescue swimmers.

"Best to jump off now," Mills murmured, "Rather than be the subject of talk tonight at the police station."

At the bow he readied himself for the plunge. Around him people were floating downstream, some dead, others nearly there. A woman gripped a large piece of railing as another swimmer paddled toward her, pushed her head below the surface and seized the wooden float for himself.

No hero, Mills turned his back to the crime and jumped in. The rivers narrow width made it possible to kick across the stream in less than a minute depositing him onto the Kentucky shore. Standing in mud to his knees his first goal was a trail out. Behind him the sounds of fear and dying could still be heard. Passengers splashing, calling, screaming. Upriver a group of farmers were launching yet another rescue boat. Ashes from the fire blew past and smells of cremated bodies lingered above the waters surface. As Mills watched the destruction his eye caught sight of his acquaintance from the boat, the small man with the long gray coat. He had made it to shore but his coat was now smoking and his hair had mostly burned away. The man coughed up sludge as he gasped for air.

"I'll introduce myself," Mills said as he walked over and without hesitation he flipped the man over, pushing his face into the mud. Arms and legs moved in panic but only for an instant. Sure that the man was dead Mills rolled him over and began rifling through pockets and waistband. Pulling a packet from under the dead man's vest he examined it to find a name, Thomas Curran, printed inside. Searching for locations to hide the stolen items in his own clothes he came up short but found a solution, "This gray coat looks inviting. Obviously it was too large for you. With my build I believe it would almost fit!"

Satisfied with his bounty, Mills lifted the man's carcass and tossed it back into the Ohio River. "We'll meet again, I'm sure," Mills crowed as he made his exit up the muddy bank of the Kentucky shoreline and away forever from the Ohio River.

Chapter 7
LEW MILLS buys a HORSE

Mills pushed along the trail edging the field, his jacket soaking wet and hair full of sludge. River water caused his boots to slip on his feet. Clearing a field for planting, several dark women paused to see the large man as he dragged past. They quickly turned back to their chores remembering that curiosity would only slow their task.

Mills mind traveled back to the Magnolia. By now, it would have sunk into the slit below the surface. Survivors would have been pulled from the current, resting and exhausted on the banks. The dead, now food for catfish, would drag downstream along the bottom until someone found them later caught in a loop of the flow.

He didn't think on that very long. The packet containing the document in his coat was still a mystery needing to be pulled away from dampness before the ink inside bled making it impossible to read. The coins in his sleeve felt good giving him confidence. Other men had worked their entire lives to have such a reserve, never acquiring such a prize.

After having walked about two miles he approached a wooded area undisturbed by man or cattle. Gentle shadows shared the floor of the forest with ferns and bamboo. Hardwood trees reached high overhead to stay safe from spring floods. Low recesses held pockets of icy water, typical for a gloomy March such as this. Stepping across the mud he pushed aside bramble to clear his way to a fallen tree. Dropping down, he sat for the first time since leaving the Magnolia. A huge sigh left his body as he dropped his head into his massive hands. Time to take inventory.

Digging out the coins only took seconds. Over the winter the old money belt stolen from the purser off the Brother Jonathan had broken up crossing the prairie. A new leather purse having a tie at both ends held them now. Loosening one end he peered inside to check the double eagle coins still intact. Retying the purse he reached into his coat flap to the hole under the lining for the packet. Damp from the river swim it had been wrapped in oilcloth and the pages were rolled rather than folded. Undoing the sheets there appeared to be no damage or tearing. The thin parchment was weak from the moisture so he proceeded to lay the pieces out to dry on the log. Evening would be here soon and the hope was that the sheets would dry and stiffen by morning. He would study the documents then.

With the dawn noisy jays in the canopy above caused Mills to open his eyes and glance around at the glade that served as a bedroom. Wiping his hands across his face reminded him how long he had been without a razor. "Lying among salamanders and grubs I doubt that they would be good judges of cleanliness."

Lew Mills rolled over to examine Thomas Curran's documents. They consisted of two large handwritten sheets showing the 'Metes and Bounds' of a property. At the top of the first page was a large ink drawing of the land listing dimensions using poles of five and one half feet to measure. Other features had been roughly added to represent trees, streams, rocks, corners and ponds. Neighbor's bordering properties were listed as well. Curran's name on the map was followed with the term 'heir.' Below on the bottom of the second sheet was Curran's name again, a woman Elizabeth and two children, Winston and Isabella.

On the second sheet was a written explanation of the property.

" Names of the seller, the Governor's signature, the date of the survey and the surveyor's name." Mills grinned, "This deed states the number of acres totaling 1904!"

There were tiny x's on the map and he could only guess as to what that may represent. "A sinkhole? Perhaps. I've passed several between trees and hillsides. I've heard that if one were to crawl down inside there might be a chance of finding crystals. If the passage was extremely tight a slave child could be lowered." Mills snickered, thinking of the rope slipping off and the child falling away into the dark abyss.

Lying there in the moss Lew Mills was very much alone. He thought back to working on the sternwheeler Magnolia. Like a floating town, each boat had made up a different tribe in river society, each with their own set of rules. That was then. It was now becoming obvious that no one would lord over him again except the weather.

Raising his head he noticed the noise above was almost deafening. Every bird in the forest had discovered him and needed to discuss it with any other bird that would listen. As Mills began collecting the papers he saw tiny ramps pushing up through the peat. In a few weeks the muddy glade would burst forth for summer with blankets of violets, ivies and wild ginger. Watercress was the only source of food now for it would be months before the blackberries and nuts were ready. Birches, cherries, maples and hawthorns would soon finalize the isolation of this hidden hollow. Mills was certain that any additional traffic to this place would only be whitetail deer. Fine by him.

"For the future I aim to lose the law, stay clear of other Reapers, avoid starvation and reign as nobility in my 'brotherhood of one'".

⚘

After two days walking Lew Mills passed a muddy field scattered with last summer's corn stocks and a different group of ex-slave women clearing the ground. Walking further for a time he stopped, turned around and retraced his path back. Returning to the field he saw that the women had gone, but there was a clear direction to follow showing their small footprints. He followed it away from the meadow and up a steep embankment to a ridge. At the top there were three cabins built of stone and log, one in good repair, others crumbling with age.

A group of perhaps twelve Negroes saw him approach, a dingy assortment ranging from very young children to old men who seemed to look as worn out as the cabins. Tall elm trees surrounded the yard. Goats grazed, momentarily raising their heads to notice the intruder as dogs' barked warnings. Mills smiled, waving his hand as he drew closer to the small settlement. The freemen that were able picked up the children and ran. Others carried the elderly away and the women shrieked as they pulled up their torn skirts to rush off. One man stood his ground as Mills approached.

"Sir, are you needin' to speak to the master?"

Mills thought that all blacks after the war had been freed. These may have been able to stay on their farm becoming indentured servants to their ex-owner. For starving blacks running north this farm may have been a heaven.

"Yes. I need to buy a horse."

"Follow me sir."

The man turned and led Mills to the last cabin. Walking fast Mills could hardly keep up having already traveled for two days and covering at the most ten miles a day, his feet were painfully blistered, his pants tight and scratchy. He considered, "I may even be lost miles from the Curran property, all of my walking now pointless."

At the end of the ridge this cabin was newer, a stone place well kept with bluebells and daffodils blooming along the foundation. Redbud trees had popped lavender and the white blooms of dogwoods were not far behind. In this environment separated from the river he felt out of place.

The Negro knocked on the cabin door and for no reasons that Mills could see took several steps back. They waited together patiently until the door swung free to find a man standing in front of them that caught Mills by surprise. He was perhaps thirty years old. Average in every way except for his beard. His hair started from under his nose and fell in torrents all the way to his belt. Mills had a difficult time keeping his eyes off the man's beard and hoped an introduction would keep him from laughing, "My name is….." and Mills stopped talking.

No one spoke, all three men floundering in an uncomfortable silence.

Mills had a decision to make. "Should I remain Lew Mills or change my name? And why not? My river reputation has gone to hell and with this new land ownership opportunity I could use a new identity to accompany any cleaver finagling."

"Thomas Curran." Mills said, extending a hand.

The shaggy farmer extended his hand and bellowed, "And I am Maliki Balut, sir, welcome to my farm."

They walked together across the yard toward a corral built from birch rails. Up so high Balut's hill preserve served as a lookout for the entire valley below. In the distance Mills was able to see spring floodplains and short segments of the Ohio River.

"Beautiful isn't it?" Thumbs in his belt loops, Balut's acreage had made him a proud man.

"Its notable." Mills agreed, but having no interest in relations for the future he lied, "Hope to come back this way once I get established."

"Where you headed?"

Mills remembered the names written on either side of the Curran property from the deed pages. "My land is between the Craft place and the Yobel's. Are you familiar with either family?"

Balut thought for a moment as he kicked a stone into the pen, "Think I met Craft in town once. Went to Alexandria long time back to get nails. A man introduced himself. May have been Craft. Looking for wire in implements I believe."

"Alexandria is where exactly?"

"Boy, you are lost! Head south from here about another half day off. Don't go too far west or you'll fall in to the Licking River. Don't go east or you'll fall into the Ohio."

"I could use a horse."

Balut looked Mills over. There was nothing to insinuate that the visitor was a horseman. Wrong boots, coat and pants, not correct attire for a Kentucky rider. He thought that this man would look much better on a boat. But money was always welcome so he offered, "Your pretty big. I have an ornery mare. She won't respect anyone here. Needs some intimidation and when she sees your size that will do the trick."

"I'll need a rope, maybe a saddle?" Mills quickly added, "And some biscuits. Not for the horse. It's been some time since I ate."

"Lets get you some biscuits first. You do look a bit wasted."

After eating both men returned to the corral to find the mare saddled and bridled. Taking one of his twenty-dollar gold coins from his coat Mills asked if the man had change. This amount was extreme for just a horse and saddle. Balut said no, but that he would add blankets and more food to the deal. Mills, being a bit desperate thought a moment and asked, "Would you have some socks, maybe a different pair of trousers?"

Balut went into his cabin. After a few minutes he returned with more clothes. "These belonged to a trapper that stopped here, then died. He didn't have a sickness. We thought he might have been hit over the head. Had these in his pack."

Placing the worn clothing and blankets behind the cantle they sealed the deal by shaking hands, and on foot Lew Mills lead the horse away.

Chapter 8
The LAND and the
NEIGHBORS

Pulling on the mare for over four hours through rivers and swamps, Mills stopped to rest on a rock. Barefoot now, he had thrown his boots away in Alexandria after finding a cobbler that supplied him with a newer pair, but they fit a bit snug. With pain either way he had voted for the soles of his feet rather that the pinch of a boot. He was happy to just plod along like this but his horse was becoming lazier by the mile.

She was a cinnamon color, maybe a light sorrel. Mills didn't care. Her head hung low, shoulders winged out and she had withers that could cut meat. Gall sores spotted her sides and her tail was mostly bone. When Mills looked into her eyes he saw clouds, with occasional lightning.

In the last hour they had been following a lane, the lucky result of advice from the same shoemaker who told Mills that a logging road would skirt the Craft place, turning at Yobel's and eventually leading him to Thomas Curran's land. Unrolling the document he established this distance far enough from Alexandria to be the correct property. Now at the highest point on the road he could examine the land around him. Yes, there were properly placed cricks, swamps and a large sycamore tree on the map coinciding with the other drawings on the paper. Cedar hills softly rising and falling grew with brush, grasses and marshes filled with cattails. His map emphasized this fact with lines to show elevation. Rimed now with small trees this area may have been victimized years before from a fire that had opened up avenues in the hollows. This may have been a relief to any other man, 1900 acres of promise, but not to Mills.

"A tangle of hawthorn, maple and birch with one scrawny pear tree in a distance. And it looks old. Branches bare from years of standing alone, attracting few bees having no one but deer to share its fruit. I'll ride down later and see if there's any food left."

Around him bushes and scrub of every kind rose entwined to such a web that even the sun could not find the ground. There were hundreds of acres of this, some having never changed for centuries. Sitting back down he rested his head in his hands and looked around his feet. Wildflowers had been pushing up braving an appearance knowing that April was just a few days away. Bloodroot, Dutchman's britches, crocus, and grape hyacinths were already revealing spring blooms.

From this perch he could see that there was still much beyond so with a stick he slapped the mare on the ass and pulled her down into the hollow. She unwillingly followed, lowering her haunches to slide down the muddy slope to an even wetter area below but Mills needed a drink and there was water in the ravine. When they finished with that he jerked her head up and dragged her back up the hill.

A main road followed the front of the property. The map was clear showing a well-defined line. Hiking further they passed a deer trail that entered the land, but thirsty once more his horse spotted a small creek and crossing the road she pulled to get to it. Once satisfied with another large drink he lead the mare back to the little used path thinking, 'Glad to know waters established throughout this location. Better that than a parcel of land plagued by drought.'

Now they were off the main road. The tiny path that entered the Curran property proved difficult with the tree trunks in the forest so close that branches scraped the sides of his jacket. The mare shuffled behind, nose down, tripping over every root. Walking five or six minutes the trail turned again to cross the same creek. Deer had traveled here often providing the dry narrow path that followed the waterway. Proceeding ahead they walked until they met a bog. Dead-ended, Mills stood looking over this weed-covered, bug infested home of copperheads and porcupines. A thousand years ago it had looked exactly the same save for a few more cattails. Glancing behind he noticed the horse, 'She's growing weary of moving and needs a field, any flat place to be hobbled for rest. That might perk her up but I'll think about it later. This damn land goes on forever.'

Now breaking trail they edged the bog, sometimes jumping over a sandy shoals only deep enough for birds to get their feet wet. Later the crick would appear once more, flow a few feet and fall into blackness, spinning under shady roots of oaks where frogs and minnows could hide. Never needing rest the water would rise up again to jump some flat stones, bump around some fallen branches and, satisfied with its performance, meander on its way to someplace more important.

Pushing their way Mills and the mare traveled another 20 minutes to find a second bog larger than the last. In the distance open water could be seen if Mills stood on his toes. Wanting to get a better look he tied one of the mares reins to a birch tree where there was a little dry grass for her to nibble around the base. Pushing the cattails aside he plunged into the thicket. The swampy footing was not stable and with each step the ground would collapse from his weight and cold puddles would instantly appear around his feet. It seemed impossible to find steady footing. His fear was that if he stopped walking he might sink into the bog and be consumed forever.

Pushing faster now to stay afloat he glanced to his right and noticed a beaver lodge in the distance rising up about 5 feet above the surface of the swamp. Relief at this discovery changed his steps to become more of a polka. Dancing to reach the beaver mound he grabbed onto the sticks covering it and pulled himself to the top. The view he found was of open water perhaps an acre across and with the sun shining down it appeared to be a pleasing color as well.

In the distance he could see the mare, her mouth full of leaves and grasses yet she was not chewing. Instead her head was erect, ears perked and her stance reflected a sort of surprised look.

The mare wasn't sure of this predicament. She could only make out a figure standing over the water on a hill of sticks and mud. Up until now the chain of events over the last days had proved difficult. She had been through narrow forests, the trunks of trees so close they squeezed her saddle, nearly pulling it off. In swamps she sank up to her belly causing her to leap out of the slough. Rushing rivers had pulled her sideways as she franticly paddled across to find dry shores. Instinct beckoned. With the strange new vision in the distance she decided immediately that to avoid any additional hardship she would free herself. One pull on the rein to was all it took. With little effort the rotted leather from her bridle broke free, and recognizing a good thing she turned and started trotting back the way they had come.

From his perch at the top of the beaver lodge Mills watched the mare go. "Damn if she didn't bolt right off! Maybe a snake spooked her. Only natural here in this bayou."

Jumping the tangle of roots, sod and mud took some doing but he leaped down the side of the hill cutting the soles of his feet. Back across the floating marsh he ran, flying from island to island, using poor judgment about the stability of the weeds. Reaching the birch tree where the mare had been feeding Mills was relived to find that her hoof prints were recorded along the muddy shore. Through the narrow tunnels of foliage he dashed. He knew that the trip until now had been long and they were both tired. Why would she bolt?

He spotted her ahead in a small clearing. She had stopped for a bite of grass, but seeing Mills approaching, her head flew up and his movement through the trees sent a message, 'Time to leave.' Jumping back onto the trail the mare pranced off faster than before knowing that a predator was in pursuit.

Mills found no sport in this game. "I've not eaten except for that meal at Balut's. My diet has been wild onion roots, watercress and a few of last year's hickory nuts. No energy left for this. My feet are soaked from this trek through the swamp and blisters are growing on my heels having no sole left to protect the skin!"

Around another corner she flew, passing the first bog and only slowing down to check out the intersection of the place where the first dry path had met the creek. She stopped to put her muzzle down, sniffing the ground. This action caused her to catch a remaining rein under her other hoof. As she asked her body to move forward she discovered her head was planted to the ground. Pushing ahead her mouth seemed tied to her hoof. Panicking, she pulled harder.

Mills was quickly moving closer seeing that somehow the mare had gotten herself into trouble. Using this opportunity he shortened the distance between them but not in time. He heard the snap of the last rein.

The mare's judgment now took precedence over any training that she had had in the past, preferring her own instincts concerning this man stalking her. All of her senses were on as she remembered smells of companionship from much earlier in the day. Onto the main road she turned west galloping back toward the first creek that crossed the road where they had stopped earlier for a drink. Just to the right of the creek was an easy trail going east. Well used, Mills had passed it before but had missed it, only interested in the investigation of his new property.

Legs flying, the mare swerved right and disappeared.

Mills stopped to catch his breath. "No need to track her at this point. The forest's silent with no wind blowing through the branches. Gives me an opportunity to hear her hooves on the dry road. Damn I'm tired. Without food I'll die out here. Two thousand acres of nothing. Berries won't come 'til fall, nuts too. Apples, pears, still months away. Perhaps I'll could cook and eat the saddle. Right now I'm definitely in favor of eating that horse."

Finding the new trail was simple, the drive well used. Turning onto it he heard a sound far off, one whinny, then another. Different the second time, higher pitched than the first, telling Mills other horses were present.

"Great," he speculated, "Robbers to steal my horse and then shoot me. I don't mind being shot as long as they leave the gold coins in my saddlebag alone."

Stirrups flipping as she flew, the mare made it to the end of the path in no time flat. A boy grabbed her just before she cleared a fence to join livestock in the back pasture. Mills wasn't far behind. Limping, at times hopping, he entered a clearing with only a barn and water pump to show for the puny settlement. The boy seemed astonished that the man had made up the road in such a condition, and barefoot! Now winded, Mills was clutching his knees to catch his breath when a man of his same size, perhaps a few years younger, came out from the field to examine the new visitor and his horse.

"Lost your way?"

Mills tried to straighten up and appear less distressed but his pants and coat were torn and his hair was filled with sticks.

"Afternoon. Names Yobel." As the man extended his hand it appeared to Mills that the farmer had some wealth wearing solid boots and wool pants.

"Curran. Thomas Curran." Mills shook hands but was careful now, uncomfortable using his new identity.

A young girl stepped from behind the barn with an older girl, perhaps her mother? The boy who had caught the mare tied it and approached Mills pointing to his feet, "Pa, he's bleeding."

"So he is. Ya know its easier to ride 'em than try to catch 'em."

Yobel and his son began whooping up a laugh and the ladies both smiled big. The younger of the two ladies swished over to Mills horse and began petting it, even giving it a hug. Mills was glad he did not have a gun at this point or he would have shot them both.

"Better soak your feet. Do you have anything in your pack to wrap 'em? Do you own any boots?"

Mills explained that his boots were too small and that traveling without shoes had been the situation since early morning.

"Good news, Pa!" his son grinned, "You could trade him for those boots you bought last fall. They're too big for anyone here."

"Come with me Curran." And the two big men walked across the yard and into the family's quarters inside a barn. Entering, Mills thought it a good size, twice the size of a cabin but small for all the uses intended. Cows stood at the rear separated by a fence under a shed to keep out the rain. Overhead in a loft were the chickens and pigeons with a small bed for a child. Geese were here and there. A goat rose from the dirt floor to greet them as they entered. A woman old enough to be dead twice sat on a cot sewing and smiled as they came in.

The walls were of milled cedar planks, closely joined and sealed only with spider webs. There were no windows, yet the hovel supplied plenty of sun in every direction. Mats were hung from pegs on a wall and several tree stumps served for chairs and tables.

Digging under the cot Yobel dragged out a pair of large leather boots. Shaking them out a mouse fell to the floor and scampered away. "Bought these cheap. Needed the leather for harness. I'll trade you for the small ones you have."

With the deal done, Mills let Yobel know that he was going to homestead on land west of their place, "Guess I'll be living across the way now, for only a short time. Not sure if farming will suit me." Just the word 'farming' made Mills cringe so it was easy to suggest leaving this hellhole soon.

Yobel asked, " Are you of any particular faith Mr. Curran?"

Mills was caught short. What had faith got to do with anything at this moment? Making up a fast lie he answered, "My family is from Christian descent but until

109

they join me I'll be starting the farm. Won't have time to do a lot of churchin".

"OK, needed to check." Yobel spit on the ground, "Here on our place we follow a Mormon tradition and some in these parts of the south don't always agree with our philosophy. It's best that we stay partial to one another, stay peaceful. You understand."

Mills felt like dancing at the news as this guy was hiding out, too! He relished the possibilities, 'Yobel and his family are keeping a low profile and that suited me just fine. Except for that damned horse now things are looking up!'

Back on the Curran land for the evening Lew Mills laid down to consider his dilemma. 'Neighbor has a couple of cows, a goat, dogs, chickens, an axe. I have lots of money and so there's a chance of buying a few animals from them. There might be about 30 coins left. Sparingly, they could last for years but the coins could be traced back to the Brother Jonathan in California. Rare twenty-dollar double eagles could cause talk. The law in Crescent City may have men out trying to find me. If I had a match I could start a fire and melt one of the gold coins back down turning it into bouillon." He dug around in the hackensack he had absconded with near St. Louis. No luck. The dead guy he ate was too cheap to stock up on the necessities that Mills would have preferred such as cigars, rum, blankets and extra matches. 'Miserly bastard.'

In the moonlight he turned the coin around in his fingers feeling the texture from the image embossed on each side. Both were different. One side had an eagle looking out from behind a shield. Turning it over there was the image of a woman. "Liberty" in her curly hair, stars surrounding her pretty head. Standing up he kicked around until his foot bumped a rock. Picking it up he carefully set the coin directly on the rock's rough surface. Finding a second rock he placed it over the coin and slowly began grinding. Rubbing and filing he opened the stones occasionally to check his progress in defacing the gold currency.

It was late. The sun had been down for a very long time and he badly needed rest and food. Putting the money back into his pocket he laid down to sleep.

The next morning he woke to find that although he had hobbled his horse's front legs the night before it still had managed to hop its way across the pasture to look for any new shoots of grass among the old withered weeds. He cursed at her from afar, and hearing his voice she turned to hop in his direction. There must have been a serious need for her to want to return to him and Mills felt that water would be her request. Knowing her better now Mills figured she would have found the creek long ago but for the rope around her legs. Walking toward him, she stopped and waited for release.

Together they headed down to the water. Both thirsty, immediately the mare dropped her head and quietly sucked for a long while. Mills dropped to his knees and scooped up the water, pushing it into his mouth then slapping his neck and face. His feet still ached from the day before. Remembering the chase he glanced over at his companion. The mare returned the look, raised her muzzle and snorted back at Mills, covering his hair with her snot.

Chapter 9
FREED SLAVES

So Lew Mills decided to build a cabin, very small compared to the lavish plantations across Campbell County since the war. He started with a fireplace of rocks picked from the fields. Choosing a size of his liking he would load them onto a gurney behind the mare and drag them back to the flat area where the cabin would stand. The fireplace was primarily to hold up the wall of sticks attached to it.

"Like killing two birds with one stone, clearing the pasture while at the same time making a chimney. Someday someone will arrive, a stranger, and do this work for me. Then it will become a property of value, more than just a place for whitetail deer to graze."

After that first meeting with his neighbor, Ben Yobel, he had made a list of supplies he would need to live: an axe, more matches, rope for that loathsome horse, dried pork, eggs and more clothes. Using the unidentifiable coin he acquired the items and now had them in his possession. The two men had agreed on additional supplies coming later from the same coin, as gold was extremely scarce. Since the war business between farmers consisted mostly of barter in the small town of Alexandria, but Mills had nothing to trade.

Standing back to review his accomplishment so far Mills shook his head. Walls of the cabin were a poor attempt at piling logs together. He added stones to plug large holes and watched them fall back to the ground as the wind wished it. Lew Mills had no idea what made a shelter. Winter would eventually set in to find him patching and mending this crude hovel each day.

The roof was another matter. Branches were lifted and dropped onto the wobbly frame. It provided no cover except to keep out the sun. Everything else came in; birds, spiders with an occasional squirrel. Some of the cuttings still had their leaves. As he pulled them from the forest they seemed insulted to be used in such a course manner but Mills never claimed to be an architect. The limbs revenge was to wait for rain. On those nights in his wet cot Mills considered that he might have been better off just standing outside under a tree.

"Oh, God, to be back on the boat. Any boat. Under the pilot house or warm in a berth next to the boiler room. Each day here in this world of weeds, trees and sweat there is no anticipation of a pleasant day. No visits with lady friends, not a moment of dry comfort to look ahead to."

To forget such thoughts Mills keep to the task of completing the cabin. Each new log, each new stone moved him further away from his despair.

His empty stomach was a problem of its own. Small snares and holes were used to catch a different meal everyday, sometimes a squirrel, fox, or possum, other times a rabbit or a bird graced his menu. Hardly enough to survive.

This land in the commonwealth was new to many, settlers or slaves. The Indians had left sometime ago and now this land had lain empty. His solitary life drove Mills to lead his horse out each week acquainting himself with his property and locating neighbors. Using the saddle to carry tools he tacked up the mare and unrolled Thomas Curran's map once more trying to make sense of the lines and markers. He planned to find neighbors, meet them, but not encourage visits.

The days drifted into weeks and the cabin became less damp. Even the worms visiting after each rainstorm had stopped crawling across the cabin floor. Holes remained plugged after numerous attempts with mud became more successful. Rain was being diverted as more branches were thrown up on the top of the crude structure's excuse of a roof.

Eventually the first limbs collapsed on to the floor in the middle of the cabin. Mills dragged out the branches and burned them to keep warm. Now it was May 1868, and the first snows of a Kentucky winter could arrive as early as October. Mills thought of the steamer Magnolia last January. They had experienced gales of snowflakes so large as to block the Captain's view and send the ship aground. That memory helped him stay focused on the nights ahead. Caught wet and cold in his bed he considered what more he could be doing during these summer months to avoid discomfort later.

Picking a warm sunny morning in July Mills once more set out to explore. This day he would again walk, still leading his horse outside the perimeters of his property to seek yet another contact. On a trail heading northeast Mills knew that he was heading towards the Ohio River yet to his best recollection that was off by a distance of about nine miles. Scrapping through the brush he discovered a sign of occupancy on a tree. A crude sign fashioned from twisted vines to form the letter C, he moved forward detecting just a small settlement made up of three buildings. A loafing shed for a bull, several corrals for horses and a well near a windmill. Down the narrow path he stopped his horse. One of the buildings was used just for the animals and silage, the other was for the family. A loom was standing under a tree, as was a butter churn. Herbs and tobacco hung from branches. Mills had found another neighbor of value and he wanted what they had, this home with food and warmth.

Sorting her reins he tied the mare to a fruit tree nearby and went to search for the family. The front door of the house was latched shut so he headed toward a garden he had spotted around the back of the cabin. Walking closer he saw a melon and some beans.

His large body had never been this thin. "I wonder if I'll have to kill anyone to get food today."

"Hello, hello there." A broad shouldered boy stepped out from behind the cattle barn waving to make himself seen, "Best to you sir. I'm James Craft. And you are?"

"Thomas Curran. From just south of here."

"Good. That's good to hear. Seen any Indians your way, slaves?"

"Haven't seen either, why do you ask?"

"They're not so bad these days, Indians I mean. Used to be they walked up to the house each night looking for a benefit, something to eat. And the slaves! If you see them, shoot them."

116

Mill's life on a ship had been spent among every race and nationality. Since death held no prejudice he did not understand this boy choosing which race to eliminate. "And why would I want to shoot slaves or Indians?"

"My Pa says to shoot 'em. They'll eat anything growing, worse than the deer. Garden grows a little, than it's gone."

"I've already solved that problem having no garden. But I do have some turtle shells here that I scrapped to make bowls. They're strong and hold up good for crushing nuts."

James examined them. "We would be glad to have 'em. There's only a small crick here, not too many turtles. You probably live down by the bog. We fish that. Or did. If you would let us keep fishin' there we'll split the take with you."

"Done. And so, these shells, what could I get for them? Is there any food that you might spare?"

"You can stay for lunch. My Pa and brothers will be here shortly. We'll pack you some jerky and bread to go home."

So he spent the afternoon listening to the Craft family talk at him. As a guest he nodded in agreement often but mostly kept to himself. A danger always followed Mills wherever he went. Rumors off the Brother Jonathan and his false ownership of the Magnolia made him a wanted man. As he studiously watched one of the boys working butter he thought back to the fact that somewhere Grim Reapers were missing his contributions to the game they played. The score keeping from catastrophes amongst themselves never ended. Somewhere death and destruction were happening at this very moment, far from this peaceful farm.

Thinking to himself he considered, 'The Reapers will be talking, exchanging assumptions as to my location. At some time I'll have to reenter the game and play or suffer the consequence of waking up on the wrong side of the River Styx.'

⟡

"Indians, ex-slaves, trespassers, not worth my consideration. Reapers of Death are another matter. For millenniums before this we have challenged each other in games of death and over time I've chalked up some pretty impressive numbers. Volleyed scores of fatalities from the sinking of the Greek city Helike to hosting the Black Death in Europe during the 1300's. Why, I wonder would other 'players of the game' even bother to find me now? In the short time I've been in this Kentucky wilderness the peaceful atmosphere would repel other Reapers. Fear seems miles from Campbell County. No surprise. The worst local catastrophe might be a swarm of locusts or maybe a flash flood off the Ohio River. Anything on that scale would be ignored by the 'fans of destruction' who otherwise only cheered on large events such as earthquakes, forest fires and pandemics. Yes, Reapers are elsewhere."

Pulling the mare along by her reins his feet began to ache in the boots he had received from Ben Yobel. "Time," he muttered, "to order socks when Yobel goes to town again. Shit, socks! Hell, I should have stayed on the

California coast dodgin' the sheriff's bullets rather than be stuck out here with sore feet and nothing to eat."

As he trudged along he thought that eventually he would have to ride the mare. How hard could it be? She had a saddle but Mills only used it to carry bundles of branches, food he gathered on the land or his newly acquired axe. Too lazy to lug anything himself he valued this ease of transporting goods as well as the opportunity to take revenge on the mare.

She seemed pleased not to carry him considering his size. He towered over her 14-hand height, Mills measuring just over six foot four. If he did mount up he knew that it would cause her to sour more on him than she did now. Glancing back at her she pinned her ears and angrily tossed her head. If Mills ever picked a nemesis it would be his horse.

Back at the half built hut he noticed that branches left across his trail had been moved. Tying the horse to a tulip tree he sensed intruders lurking somewhere. Calling out for acknowledgment he received no response.

'This is no contest.' thought Mills as he walked into his shelter then out again bringing a bowl of nuts. Leaving it in the center of the yard he bid the hidden refugees good night and went back into his cabin to sleep.

Later that same evening Mills heard a shuffling of feet and then a crack. Mills jumped out from behind the pole shack and screamed, "What's going on here!"

Three men had been unsuccessfully trying to crack nuts with their teeth. Shocked with Mills sudden appearance they tried scrambling off into the woods, but failed with having one of the men crippled, they only traveled a short distance. The two called back for their friend to follow but with defeat they returned to his side.

Yelling "Where you from?" Mills waited but received no reply. They were paralyzed with the fear of death from this large white man. Ex-slaves all, they were now prepared for the end.

"I could shoot you for stealin' those nuts!"

Mills now examined his captives. Thin and weak they were in worse shape than he had been earlier after leaving the Magnolia. Carrying no food, all barely dressed and no shoes. The bony black men together would have weighed less than him. Feeling no threat he made an announcement, "I got a gun. If you're here in the morning I'll put you to work. If you don't work then I'll kill ya and throw your bodies in the swamp."

The largest of the men nodded 'yes' and Mills went back into his cabin to sleep and enjoy his lie about the gun.

The next morning there was a small fire going in the yard but the men still had no food. Mills gave them his newly adopted name of 'Curran' and asked them theirs.

"Jefferson. That's my Christian name.' The largest man answered. 'This here's Riddle and my poor friend there is Simon."

The man speaking was the fittest of the three having a tall straight back, full beard and strong arms. He appeared to be perhaps thirty-five in his long torn trousers and oversized cotton shirt. Riddle seemed to be about 30 years old dressed as he was in tight-buttoned pants and a crude hemp jacket. Simon was pathetic. Sickly and unable to stand he could have been left for dead long ago.

120

Bald and having few teeth, Mills wondered what the man lived on.

Mills immediately put them to work directing them to where his traps were hid in the forest. Later that day the three men returned with a catch of a one thin squirrel and someone's dog that had died in a snare. Mills was disappointed in the small take so he supplied them with wire and a shovel for worms, some string and told them to try their luck fishing at the bog that evening. The trip provided both fish and berries. Returning to the cabin the men found some hard biscuits by the same fire they had made that morning. Having no interest in the company of refugees Mills had retired for the night to his cabin so the three men dined alone on fish, biscuits, squirrel, berries and dog legs. It was a decent meal.

⚭

It was now late November 1868. Jefferson and Riddle had buried Simon in August but still discussed him like their own kin. They had put him to rest on the backside of the Curran land in a field where wild roses bloomed.

With the arrival of the dark men the farm had improved with every day during that summer. The cabin finally stood on it's own. Mills used Jefferson to go and collect a cow with a calf from Ben Yobel. The black men had put a shed across the yard to hold chickens but during the night a fox would tear into the coop. They decided to get a dog.

Mills sent Jefferson with Ben Yobel to Alexandria with an order to get nails, salt, flint, a newspaper and a slut lamp for Mills cabin. Mills instructed Jefferson to keep alert and catch any loose dogs in town. As Jefferson walked down the trail to meet up with Yobel for the ride he turned to bid good-bye to Riddle who was tied to a tree as insurance that he would return.

When the buckboard was loaded with supplies bought in Alexandria Jefferson tied the dog they had caught to the wagon. Ben Yobel clicked for the horse to head home. The dog let out a yelp and struggled fiercely to escape the rope dragging him. After only a few yards it appeared that the dog was too frightened to follow and just as Jefferson was untying it, two black women approached the wagon with something to offer.

Both young but no longer girls, one offered, "We'd be obliged to help you move this dog. We'll lead him behind that wagon to whatever farm your traveling back to."

Jefferson explained, "Ma'am, you don't want to walk that far today. Its cold and there's not much on our place. No bed when we get back there, just our crib next to the chickens."

The older of the two women, a black lady of maybe twenty-five, wearing only a dress and shawl with wooden soled shoes said, "We have no place to sleep here in Alexandria. This hound can sleep with us tonight and we'll move on tomorrow."

In a low voice Ben Yobel advised Jefferson " I wouldn't recommend more human traffic on Lord Curran's land until there's proper accommodations. That man has one angry temperament. He won't like the idea of more mouths to feed and people to clothe."

It began to lightly snow. The two women stood huddling while Yobel and Jefferson sat on the buckboard's wooden bench seat contemplating their decision. Yobel's gelding pulled on it's harness wanting to get back to the farm and into his shed before the snow became too deep. The dog, now tired of struggling was sitting at the women's feet keeping warm against their legs.

"Guess I'll catch hell later." Jefferson said, "I'll boost you two into the wagon and throw the dog on top. Think of what chores you can do before we reach the farm. Maybe that will keep my master from shooting all of us when we get back."

Nights at the farm were now Jefferson and Riddle, the two women from town and the new dog they named Zeke. The social life in this wilderness of Kentucky consisted of small luxuries such as a deck of cards with all 52 and perhaps some cider. Living better than most already that autumn the three neighboring farms shared melons, gourds, pumpkins and persimmon flour. Nuts and berries had also been stored away for the season ahead with a small amount of loose grass for the horse.

'Lord Curran' was the title the workers gave to Mills, who kept to himself. There was never any discussion between them except for orders of work to be done or food delivered to 'Lord Curran's' cabin. The only trace of Mills presence on the farm was the yellow glow Jefferson and Riddle could see from the pork lard lamp in his pole shack at night. He never asked them inside. The two men huddled together with Zeke and the two women on those cold November nights under straw blankets next to the chicken coop. That was their shelter. While they never enjoyed a comfortable alliance with their employer, gratefully there was a steady supply of food that would provide through that Kentucky winter.

Lew Mills did not discuss the presence of the two black women until December. Cold weather kept him in the pole shack, out of everyone's way. In that short time the four workers had collected enough stones to build a fire pit near the center of the coop. Round, it measured about twenty four inches tall and served both for heat and as an oven. With the spring melt they would add a tabby mortar to seal the stones but for now at night they each simply found a place on the sides to sleep, and most nights they would also allow a space for the dog. The result of this arrangement found the chickens each morning pressed against the heated side of their shelter gratefully creating a windbreak.

As December 1868 came to a close the Kentucky farm found one warm day. Sun shining, the four adults had spent the morning hunting in the snow for turkey tracks when out of the woods stepped the owner, Lord Curran, leading his horse.

Feeling a tension, Jefferson walked briskly across the withered grass putting himself between the master and the women. Scaring the birds from the trees Mills roared, "They've been eating food here, better be from your shares in the cellar."

Caught off guard Riddle remained speechless but Jefferson interrupted, "We've been blessed by these two ladies helpin' hands." He pointed to the older of the two women and went on, "This is Emma. She's been pickin' greens and nuts. Can find pig tracks, too. We tracked one, a stray hog, drove it back into our snare. Got it smokin' now near the coop."

"Rebecca here," Jefferson pointed to the smaller of the two women who stood stock still with fright, dressed only in a man's coat that covered her old dress. "She works the milk to buttermilk and cream. Carried some yesterday to Ben Yobel's. He's trading us for cheese."

Lew Mills was growing impatient with this talk. His horse had had enough as well, pawing the ground to leave. "How do we know they're not wanted for crimes in New Port or Louisville? Wandering loose in the countryside they may bring the law to my farm, get me arrested."

"No, no sir!" Riddle and Jefferson stepped closer to Mills' horse and cried together, "These ladies are good people. After they were set free from their farm, having no home now, they've been teaching us. We're finding more food growing on your place, more to eat. Remember that butter fried chicken? Rebecca cooked that. That was one of our hens."

Mills silence confirmed the fact that he was thinking of that meal now. He eyed all four of them to let them know of his displeasure before he spoke, "If I sense or see any local lawmen trackin' on my place," He pointed at the two women, "I'll tie you to a tree and burn you as witches. The law will be on my side!"

Pulling his horse around, Lord Curran left. Jefferson and Riddle shook their heads in bewilderment as the ladies bodies shook with dread.

Jefferson was brave enough to move fear aside and search in his mind for an answer. 'How could a man that had always known freedom, owned land cared for each day by his indentured servants…how could his man be so hateful?'

Riding back through the woods Lew Mills was grinding his teeth. "Damn thieves, all of them. And these cold nights with no good food, just acres of trees and not a decent bed for miles. No saloon for cards or women to swive. This is one pathetic life."

Reminiscing he remembered centuries before of dining in palaces on lamb, overlooking arenas where gladiators died by the dozens in one day! He enjoyed afternoons watching floods that wiped out towns and homes, with citizens and livestock washing away. If everyone died on this Kentucky property it would count less than the fingers on his hand.

As his horse trudged along the path behind him Mills felt a great self-pity. "Not since the steamship Brother Jonathan had life gone my way. I miss those memorable voyages along the California coast. Warm rooms, large beds to borrow, time to breath, little to do. When will I return to such an existence with so many pleasant fatalities? Maybe I'll get lucky and this place will burn to the ground."

Chapter 10
The KENTUCKY FARM 1868

Mills had been practicing riding his horse. No small task but he wanted to go it alone, so saddling up he headed out on a snowy afternoon. He walked the mare down the old deer trail that he had traveled months earlier. Finding it pruned it now allowed passage for travelers without hooking ones stirrups on passing trees. Heading toward the bog he surprised a group of ex-slaves resting. Crowded around a fire they ran off after seeing Mills approach on his horse.

They had been cooking some fish and crawdads. "Fish and crawdad's from my lake!" He grumbled. Kicking their fire over, Mills threw their pot into the water. A few had run off into the woods and from what he could make out their group consisted of a couple averaged sized men, a small girl, an older man with a limp and two young ones that had left so fast that he didn't get a good look.

"Listen up! These are my fish and this is my land! If you plan to eat my fish and sleep on this spread than you must work. I shoot anyone loitering on my place. It's my right. You all think on that."

Arriving back to the farm he found Riddle and Jefferson working at their chosen jobs, one with the cattle, one cutting wood for the fireplace in Mills cabin. Locating Jefferson he tells of the new discovery.

"Seems we have squatters on my place out by the pond, fisherman. Slaves comin' here faster than sailors to free booze. Crazy bastards lose their way and end up on my place. My horse stumbles over them, sleeping everywhere like locust. Either they work or we run them off. I'll shoot the sons of bitches, eating my fish for nothing. Humph." Mills spit on the ground and scratched his bearded face, "Jefferson, tomorrow morning you head out there. If they're gonna' fish then they must bring me as much cooked fish as I need for this winter. You tell them that."

Jefferson nodded understanding and walked quietly back to the shovel he needed to finish his hole, "That man is so selfish, why doesn't he see the benefit of all these free blacks camping, arriving on his place. He considers it a curse. All these folk want is a safe haven."

That afternoon Jefferson walked alone down the half-mile path to the bog. Some of the campsite was still there but the bedding was gone. Jefferson moved around the lake kicking stones and making himself visible to anyone or anything. Eventually a rustling from beyond the trees made him pause. Not looking in that direction Jefferson waited, standing very still, until from across the lake another rustling branch let him know that he wasn't alone.

Now he turned, facing in the direction of the lake but not stepping forward. Waiting and from his position he spied a smaller dark man standing still in the trees across the bog looking back at him. Jefferson lifted his hand and waved the man out, showing with this movement that he was not packing weapons.

They approached each other and it appeared to Jefferson that the man was only a large boy, maybe in his early manhood, not quite marrying age. Thin as a rail, Jefferson pictured this man as he had been not 3 months earlier when he'd first arrived on this property, hands calloused from the farms, teeth rotting from bad food and no care.

It surprised both of them when Jefferson extended his hand in a genial way toward the young black man. He had become a bit of a gentleman with trips to town acquiring a certain etiquette that reflected his dealings while doing business in Alexandria. Carefully the young man shook it and waited for the verdict.

"The Lord Curran won't let your people stay free. We need meat, fish and hands on the place. You can eat what you catch but first bring all we need each day to the yard up the path. Any extra must be smoked so we can all make it through this winter. Nuts and berries, too. Don't leave them on the bushes cause if Lord Curran sees them hanging and not on his plate he'll sure shoot you and beat us too."

The young boy whispered, "How many are there on your farm?"

Jefferson considered this question, not wanting to give up to much information, yet looking into the empty eyes of this man caused him to feel shame with any wrong assumption, "We have two women, one extra man and Lord Curran. He carries a gun that's always loaded. Note you don't want to meet him twice. Whenever you see him it's never good. I'm doing you a favor saying that if you can't find enough meat to bring each day than you'd better move off."

The boy nodded and extending his hand they both grasped in solidarity of faith. The boy turned to leave as Jefferson spoke again, "What do they call you?"

"Virgil."

"That's a kind name, I hope it sticks".

With that the two parted.

Later that day a small plume of smoke rose above the elm trees in the direction of the ponds that was noticed by the two men in the yard working on a new shed. They didn't say anything to Lord Curran or even each other, not wanting to put a hex on any agreements made. It seemed best to just wait and see.

The stray fishermen had not traveled far to reach Lew Mills farm. Walking north from Bowling Green their previous owners had sent them off with only their clothes. Four days had taken all they had to give, what with the older man, Winston, having a serious limp caused by the wheel of a wagon which had happened over him just a few months earlier. Then there was the other young man besides Virgil named Isaac who believed that he had been born just a year before Virgil and that they might both be coming close to twenty years old.

A girl figuring to be about 11 years old traveled off the farm with them. They called her "Salem" after the name of a town. She didn't seem to object to the name, preferring that to her own which she never shared. She never offered to talk about family, work or any of her past. She just came along helping with everything that needed help and the men adopted her into their group hoping to have no trouble later. Since Bowling Green they had been so tired that finding a path in any location of Kentucky was good luck, and finding a hidden lake was a blessing, or they thought.

After Jefferson left Virgil and Isaac cracked a hole through the ice on the pond and strung some meat to drop in. They drove fish into the fabric from their shirts creating a seine, trapping them. Flopping and jumping, the men tossed each one upon the ice. Salem had found a stick for the spit and Winston was working to make a fire.

As instructed the next day they walked the cooked fish up the path. As they arrived on the far side of the yard from behind the shed the help stopped to examine the new group, a mirror image of them just a few months earlier and pitiful to see. Sally and Emma crawled under the rail to meet them, having no fear of these strangers delivering food. They took the fish, that had been placed on a long piece of birch bark, and set it on a stump nearby. Then the two farm women took Salem aside to get acquainted.

Jefferson told Riddle, "If these folks have brought the food then there must also be trust."

Virgil, Isaac, and Winston extended their hands but did not speak, having nothing to say, simply glad for this moment not to be driven away or shot.

The group stayed together that day visiting and working together on a fence. Lord Curran was not about, preferring to smoke cigars in his cabin, making the day go easy. At sunset the new group said goodnight and moved off to sleep at their camp by the bog.

Later that week Mills didn't see the new comers working and asked Riddle about the disappearance. "They stay by the lake. Fish. Do some hunting. Might still be there, I'll find out." Curious, Mills rode out to the bog and found the group huddled around a fire. Because of the cold December day he had no desire to linger long enough to beat them so he turned his horse around and riding back to the farm told Jefferson, "They don't have enough to do just fishin'. Get them saws and send them off to the back of my land. There's an old stand of birch back there and some cedar as well. Have them start cutting trees for more fences."

"The group told me they'd done only cotton and beets on the last farm they worked."

"Well, if they could figure out how to catch my fish then they can figure out how to build a fence. Tell them that!"

So Jefferson and Riddle walked along to the lake. Arriving at the campfire they let the new group know of Lord Curran's request. He had also told the workers to send Salem back as insurance on the tools. She would be working with Rebecca and Emma that day picking eggs and milking. That night with the return of the men Mills would count the tools and Jefferson knew from experience Lord Curran would beat Salem if any were missing. Jefferson made sure every tool was returned.

∞

Spring 1869

Trees were coming down around the Curran Farm. There were fish to catch and flowers to pick. Even the neighbors to the northeast, the Craft's, stopped by to see the progress from what they had earlier thought was just one man. By now most of the neighbors knew that Thomas Curran had ex-slaves working his farm. Other farms would have wanted such a blessing except that even with their abundance of acres they still could not afford to feed any additional mouths. Little did they know that the gold coins Lew Mills hoarded, originally stolen from a boat that sunk off the coast of California, had been the main support to create the farm. Nor did anyone suspect that the Curran land had been a free gift off a dead man whose body still floated somewhere down the Ohio River.

Throughout the winter months the men had collected a large assortment of pelts. These were tanned and dried, ready to trade in Alexandria. The cabin Lew Mills had built when he first arrived was now twice the size with a buck stove and a fine bed nearly seven feet long. Mills watched the progress on his residence during the winter, saying nothing. The men did not discuss the improvements done in the small cabin but hoped that with the work it would insure for them a home on this land. This place had become their sanctuary. Salem was learning from Ben Yobel's daughters to spin. She had designs

on getting sheep of their own some day with the traded pelts. Winston was still limping but the cows found
him soothing to the touch so the milk flowed well. Even
the dog, Zeke, had not left the farm as first anticipated.
Spending most of his time sleeping, he was still valuable
if they parked him to sleep next to the chickens and the
new gaggle of geese.

Virgil and Isaac were the strongest of the workers.
Improving the sleeping quarters for everyone was their
first priority. Although the chickens would miss the heat
they had been moved to a location closer to the cows and
that first coop was changed into a bunkhouse. With the
original fire pit still centered there were cots for the men
on one side and women on the other. The stones collected last fall were now filled between with a tabby mortar.
Virgil had traded wild turkeys for Ohio River shells, lime
and sand to create a sturdy mix.

Isaac had the gift of building barrels. His previous
owners, the Parkers from Bowling Green, had been coo-
pers, so he'd known since childhood how to put a barrel
together. From any tree on Lord Curran's land the staves
could be cut, soaked, beveled and fitted. Ben Yobel was
paid in chickens to bring back rivets from town. Those
were used to hold the wooden hoops in place. Different
trees were cut for different barrels, some types to hold
dry goods, others for wet goods.

Rebecca served as Isaac's assistant. When he had the
staves cut and beveled to his liking she was instructed
to tie the staves on to the mare's saddle and take them
to the bog. Laying the pieces along the pond she would
sink them below the water's surface. From a collection

of rocks that she had piled on the shore Rebecca placed one on top of each stave to keep them from floating away. The process was slow but later the pieces would become soft enough to bend.

Rebecca had not been looking to find honey but there it was. A black bear near the bog would not let her pass with the staves and more than once the mare had chosen to spook, causing pieces of wood to fly from the saddle and Rebecca having to fend for herself against the bear. Reporting back to the yard the others listened to her describe the incident with a sobbing voice. She had bravely run the bear off with sticks and rocks twice but the men decided to investigate.

Marching down the trail Jefferson and Riddle lead with a rifle followed by Isaac and Virgil with rakes. Winston carried a crop. Along for the adventure were the visiting Craft brothers, James, Gill and Henry.

Emma, Rebecca and Salem stayed far behind, occasionally calling ahead for reports. Sure enough the bear had returned to the area to climb up into a tall coffee tree, having discovered a honey hole just out of it's reach. When the men had first spotted the bear they had all agreed, "The fur and meat will be good to sell. Rebecca's problems will end if the bear is destroyed. Although the bear is high into those branches it should easily be in range to shoot." Regrettably, Jefferson apologized to the large beast before aiming true, then he shot it down. Branches of the ancient tree cracked as the large animal crashed to the ground.

Additional discussion arose once the bear was dead. Winston suggested that the honey in the coffee tree had value. "Some bees have hives in the same spot for years, sometimes a hundred years. Could be a real find to get it out."

The men agreed to have Virgil, Gill and James walk back to the yard and fetch saws, axes and a rope. The warm spring wind and wildflowers kept the girls content as the men worked to fell the tall tree. Far enough from the bog it was wedged to fall along the shore after which the crew discussed splitting it for firewood. Larger than they had imagined and after much effort the tree began to wobble so everyone moved off for safety.

With the activity from the workers below, bees were spotted by the Craft boys leaving the tree. Yelling loud warnings to the others they turned and bolted for home. As the tree hit the ground the entire swarm flew in the same direction out toward the bank where Winston, Emma and Riddle had been watching from a distance. The bees came out fast. Having no time to run Emma and Winston were covered. Rolling around, hands and feet flying to avoid the onslaught, the two victims screamed in a panic. Riddle turned back and began dragging Emma toward the water. The swarm had crawled into her hair and clothes. Other workers still present grabbed her arms and started to run with her toward the lake about 100 feet away. Winston was getting the worst of it, covered with the bees he struggled to reach the muddy shore but his bad leg made it impossible. Gill and Jefferson ran to the rescue actually picking the old man up and heaving him into the pond. Treading in behind the two men supported Winston's body with their arms while knowing that now the old man was unconscious.

Emma had been plunged into the water where she stayed for only a minute before surfacing with painful screams. The two men beside her were wet, shaken and badly bitten, yet they tried franticly to wipe the drowned bees off her skin, from her hair and off the fabric of her thin garment. Floating her carefully to shore they placed her swollen body gently on the muddy grass to rest. Her body seemed paralyzed as she lay on the shore. Feeling the soft breeze pass from the pond's surface across her body Emma tried to open her eyes but they had become only tiny slits. From a blur on the water's surface the motionless bodies of the winged creatures floated like tiny knots on a quilt, drifting across the ponds surface into the distance. A crawling feeling on her skin remained up her back, her neck and into her head. Too weak to resist, a haunting message accompanied the pain, creeping into her mind, *"The bee's lives have ended. Their last assault on this world proved to be the root of their destruction. Now dawns a new beginning. Be aware, Emma, for you and your children, from this land begins a new era that will carry into the next generation and beyond."*

Chapter 11
The REAPER BREEDS

Unseen at first, Lew Mills rode out on the mare to the pond. As the group took part in the rescue Mills laughter from the trees caused everyone to turn and notice the big man on horseback hooting and slapping his knee. Curious about the activity that day Mills had decided to investigate his workers and discovering the mayhem with the hive he found the event hilarious. His loud laughter mixed with their painful cries. Riddle moved forward wanting to lunge out of the water and kill the man but Jefferson grabbed his arm, whispered a comment and Riddle pulled no more.

Finding no one to join in with the joke Mills frowned with disgust. Turning his horse around he began once more hooting through the forest, waking the dead with his laughter as he rode back to the farmyard alone.

Winston and Riddle were in bad shape. They had several bites that covered their backs and faces. Emma had fainted and they were thinking that she might be dead. Jefferson pulled bees from her hair and clothes, with Riddle too exhausted and Winston barely moving. A small request was heard from the old man's lips asking, "Leave me in the lake."

The next morning some of the group returned to the boggy pond and with Jefferson in charge they lit bundles of grass, leaves and sticks, throwing them toward the hole of the tree. Most of the bees had left but there was still the fear of another attack. Smoke and small flames licked the bark around the entrance eventually driving the last of the bees away. Hours passed and the workers kept a vigil on the beehive entrance and Winston. It was early afternoon before anyone could approach the coffee tree so they decided to leave for the day and return to their chores.

Even with the abundance of honey it was a sad crew now. Emma had been badly hurt and was now unconscious, resting on ferns under a cherry tree near the crick. Winston's eyes were swollen shut and he was unable to walk. Isaac's welts festered even with the mud packs brought fresh from Salem for his burning skin.

The hive entrance was only big enough to reach a small hand through so the next morning they took axes and chopped an opening the size of a man's head. Gathering all the milk buckets and leather bags they could find they had a plan to store the honey in the root cellar. Rebecca made baskets lined with leaves and found some wooden bowls. Using a large metal spoon they had bought for stew, the workers dug deep inside the tree finding additional honey. Salem took sticks from the back of the tree and dipped them as far into the hole as she could reach. This produced candy sticks for the men, and they never remembered anything so sweet.

After three days Rebecca met with the men, "Emma's not doing well. Her face, arms, most of her body is swollen from the stings."

Isaac had a thought, "My mama used to take mint leaves and mud. She'd grind them together between stones, make a mash we'd lay on like a poultice." Using that remedy they painted Emma's legs and back with as much mint and mud as they could find. They also tried moving her into a position of comfort but to no avail. "Burning, burning!" Emma cried out, so they carried her once more to the cool pond. Isaac and Jefferson helped too, taking turns floating her there. As they watched, her eyes closed and she would find peace. Soon the workers began to think about Lord Curran flogging them for spending too much time away from their chores so when she fell back asleep they would quietly carry Emma up to the beach covering her with leaves and branches and head back to their tasks.

Winston died. Unconscious for days he had been bloated with bites, too weak to improve. Taking him in their arms they carried him past the two ponds and up a hollow to a place where the ground was soft. Using the farm spade to dig, Virgil, Riddle, Jefferson, Gill and Henry took turns moving the dirt away until they all felt that it was deep enough to cover the body. They laid him there carefully making him a blanket of leaves and re-turned the dirt to the hole. Gill and Riddle covered the mound with branches while the other men found rocks nearby and laid them on the grave hoping to keep the coyotes and black bears from disturbing it.

After many nights much had been done to save Emma but keeping her with a guardian down by the pond any longer was becoming a risk with coyotes stalking closer to the cherry tree each night. They moved her to a shelf that they had built on the back wall of a barn on the far side of the yard. Used as a place for milking during the day it was a cool and dry, out of the sun and close enough to be watched.

And Mills was watching.

People were making trips back and forth from the old shed each day. He knew Emma was not up and working since the tree had fallen so he surmised that she must not have recovered from the beestings. Last he had seen of her, she was being dragged into a lake.

So he waited and planned.

Rebecca and Salem made trips each day into the dark building. They confided, "We have berries, milk, corn mash and honey. Emma tries to eat but it's so painful for her to move. Her body's frozen from the swelling around her joints. Pushing food into her mouth, dribbling the milk and honey past her tongue, that seems to help. This is a good sign. The men are hopin' that Emma will soon be part of our family again."

After five nights of watching the parade, to and from the barn, Mills wanted to be included. Waiting until all of the fires were out and the men had retired to their lodges for the night, he opened the door of the cabin, gazing across the long yard from left to right to spy any movement or catch any noises made from men still awake. He pulled on his boots but didn't bother with a shirt, the night being so muggy. Crossing the yard he strode directly toward the shed.

Emma saw him coming. The moon created a long black shadow that approached from the cabin. The sound of the door opening had caused her to swing her head around, maybe for the first time since she'd been moved to the wooden slab. A terror rushed through her. With each step it seemed a countdown to her fate. She turned her face back toward the wall putting her head deeply into her hands and tried to make herself as tiny as possible. Squeezing herself far into the crack between the self and the wall she wished now that bees had killed her.

Mills didn't say a word. Walking directly up to the end of the board where her tiny knees pushed against the wooden wall he grabbed her feet from beneath her skirt and pulled her toward him. Throwing the paper-thin fabric out of his way he pushed his way inside. She never saw him or anything else as she kept her hands tightly over her face. The pressure made her think that she was being torn in half. Biting her lip she became dizzy with the pain and fear. Before she could think to scream it was over.

Mills pulled away, dropping her ankles and backing away. He pulled his pants up, tied his waist string tight and left.

Tears of anger began to find their way from under Emma's hands but she was too weak to even whimper. Coming to this farm she had hoped to be away from the plantation of slaves that before had held her captive for so many years. Her dream had been to find a place to live peacefully and survive. But Hell had followed her here as well.

Two nights later Mills returned to the barn once more.

Chapter 12
MILLWHEEL PLANTATION PROSPERS

Lew Mills had chosen to name the property 'Millwheel Farm'. A play on words at best, it incorporated his former name with the addition of a lumber business along his crick. He also felt that naming the farm would add stability and significance. His privacy was at risk since discovering the growing population along the shores of his ponds.

"Millwheel Farm is off limits to the homeless. Refugees from the war need not stop here or they'll be shot!"

Regardless of his ranting and raving the farm was becoming prosperous. The men were felling more trees than anticipated and crops of wheat were already in the ground. The addition of the millwheel for cutting slabs and grinding corn seemed obvious decisions for the future of his estate.

At first Lord Curran was suspicious of the request made from his workers, "We need to pay a blacksmith to forge a saw. Than we can cut planks, build stronger sheds and sell whats left." Jefferson and Virgil were ecstatic. Lord Curran wasn't concerned about this new industry on his place, entertaining at best, as he reminded the men that he was leery of any visitors asking questions about him or changes to the property.

New barracks had already been built since August, one for the men, he counted eight of them now and the other for Sally, Emma, and Salem. "Just as well", Mills figured, "the baby would be arriving this winter so it would need a place to sleep. Just a warning," He said sternly to the farm workers, "I better not hear any crying in my cabin at night. That will not be tolerated."

The Millwheel crew had been trading lumber from the farm for cattle and fowl and finding additional horses to pull the new wagon. Mills' mare was stubborn and not fond of pulling anything from behind. She kicked until the single-tree, dash and shafts had been turned to kindling. One man suggested, "This might work in our favor to bust up firewood in the fall!"

The trees were difficult for the men to handle and quickly they found dragging the logs behind a horse to the mill slow and difficult. Locals asked to buy the lumber directly off the property, except that proposition caused Mills great discomfort. Privacy was Lord Curran's main concern. He showed no interest in Emma's pregnancy or money concerns, the crops or even if the sun would rise tomorrow. Still, Jefferson took it upon himself to set up a spot on the main road for lumber transactions, keeping the public off Millwheel Farm property. As it drew cold that winter of 1869 there where split cords of wood, numerous shelters built for the livestock, rail fences surrounding the property and before the first snow any additional lumber was traded for oil, food, or bullets.

With the spring flooding the mill blade turned quickly while workers pushed hundred year old trees down the carriage to trim off the slabs, preparing the trees to become boards.

The winter had been mild. Consumption, dyspepsia, influenza and smallpox had all passed by Millwheel Farm. Ex-slaves passing through that winter reported to Jefferson that they were heading northwest, perhaps as far as Canada to find a new life that would accept all men equally. Still, unknown to Mills, many stayed and Millwheel became their port in the storm. Word spread. Men, women, children, many came, stopped and worked. The war had been the end for many, even the strongest.

Emma had found herself wondering, "Will I be strong enough to carry on? The baby arrives in February. I hope it's a boy. Wesley is a fine name. But I'm frightened. Lord Curran has not visited once since my sickness with the beehive or during my pregnancy. A small kindness of any kind would have been welcome. Instead he stays cloistered in the cabin playing cards or pouring bullets."

He also read. Jefferson has been given orders from his boss, "With each trip to Alexandria I need newspapers from both Louisville and Cincinnati purchased from the post office."

Ben Yobel greeted the opportunity to scan the chronicles as he and Jefferson traveled back from town. "It's no doubt your master would be asking for the paper." Yobel noted to Jefferson, "Never any good news. Always articles concerning sunken ships, crimes and deaths."

Jefferson couldn't understand why Lord Curran didn't enjoy daytime on the farm. Sun shining through the birch trees created the appearance of leaves made from gold. The wind would pick up causing tiny waves on the pond, imaginary diamonds floating across the surface. Jefferson, now considered the farm manager, found it all breathtaking. Each cloud that swept across the sky might bring a call for rain, filling the fields with more grass than they would need to feed the 30 head of sheep, 20 cows and 6 horses that had been acquired since the first day he had arrived on the land almost three years before. The hands at Millwheel couldn't figure out why anyone would find pleasure in the shadows of a small cabin stuffed inside a grove of trees. Who would want to miss days pretty as these?

Walking along with Isaac Parker and Virgil, Jefferson had to once more listen to their assumptions, "He might be making spells in there. Maybe something worse. We know he pours his own bullets. Maybe he has women in there we don't know about? Maybe he's a wizard, makes black magic, that sort of thing."

Stories and gossip passed between workers. Jefferson frowned on rumors that might get back to the landlord and stir things up. "Best to just let things lie. Let's reflect on today and thank the Lord for this property and all it gives. Master Curran's like a storm, not here very often, thank God. Let's be content with that."

Necessities were met. Lately, the workers were trusted with their time. If they were hungry they ate, tired they slept. When sick there was someone there to care. Somehow the farm thrived considering the lack of leadership

148

and authority that would normally be the responsibility of the owner. Even with the knowledge that a mysterious proprietor was amongst them, there was no place else these freemen would rather be. Their bellies were full, new babies were fat and in the evenings there was a small fire to heat up some coffee. Then the workers would rest because the next day they would have to go out and do all the laborious chores again.

But pry they did and it was often asked why the "Lord of Millwheel" would not come out of his dwelling long enough to see the success that this small group of men and women had achieved.

"We've finished a fine fence that will stand in any weather. Where's Lord Curran? It's good to boast today." Riddle went on, "We have opened a road that circles his land, cleared the bog to find a pretty lake and cut the trees. Beautiful wood to mill, hickory, black gum and walnut, we have it loaded to sell in town."

"Don't rant on." Jefferson pleaded, "Just enjoy your deeds and hope the sky doesn't fall on us."

With the new baby the women would pick eggs and milk the cows. They found in each other the gift of security that in the past could not have even been considered. A bond. For each man and woman that by some accident had found this new property they had also brought with them a history of abuse, loneliness and loss of kin. Just a few years before as slaves the torture in the fields could have been enough to cause a man take his own life. This new freedom joined the entire group, and with that had created a family.

Jefferson knew every man's name and they all knew his.

"Go see Jefferson, the big black man on the place. He's wearing a new leather hat and a green vest. He'll find you a bed!" Advised Isaac and Virgil to new travelers. Yet freed blacks wandering in were warned, "But you must work hard and don't go near that cabin in the woods. Just do your job or move on."

One family from Nashville had stayed during the heat of the summer and had with them a blind man. Salem's new responsibility on the farm was the tending of the sheep so secretly she considered this man a prize. After his breakfast each morning she would bring him two fleece cards and a large pile of wool. She discovered that his capable hands could clean out any clumps from the fiber, tease the wool, lay the pieces out, and while humming a song he would comb all day. Hour after hour he combed the large piles of fiber brought to him, not only from Millwheel sheep but the Mormon's fleece from across the road as well. Salem made a contract to put away any extra wool, selling it during the cold months for other purchases.

"I call him 'Stropshire," Salem proclaimed, "after the sheep Jefferson found from Virginia. Now that we raise 'em here, guess we can name the sheep and that nice old man, too. Anyway, he seems to prefer 'Stropshire' more than any name he had in the past."

Chapter 13
The MURDERS 1875

'I'm pregnant again,' thought Emma. 'Curse Lord Curran and his needs. I have two babies now and Rebecca has one of his also, eighteen months old. The Master has started a breeding farm of our babies.' Emma began to cry softly wanting no one's attention, 'He even wants it on the Sabbath. I pray in the morning and he comes at night. He's the devil but my babies are the angels. Someday they will grow strong and survive.'

Now it was Sunday. Mills routine would be to come out before the sunset and look for Rebecca or Emma. They always knew why he was there. He would just walk up and either pull one of them into the shed or his cabin. Sometimes they were tired, with no energy to fight. Master Curran would just drag their bodies away, his needs tended to first. If possible, the ladies would hide in the hay or the forest but then guilt would overtake them. As his concubines they knew that if he didn't take one then the other would do. Sheepishly one would volunteer to save the other from the pain. "Best to get it over," Rebecca sighed. With her baby Elizabeth now walking and new teeth coming in the tiny girl pulled at her mother's dress for answers to the pain. "Hope I have time to nurse you before the Master gets here."

Curran was already stalking around the place looking for his prey. Rain the night before had left him ornery, with holes in the cabin roof making for a sleepless night. Curran first checked the ladies bunkhouse only to find Emma nursing her baby boy, Westley, "You know what day it is?"

In a tiny voice Emma pleaded, "He just hooked on and he'll be asleep soon, then I'll be there for you."

"Shutdup! Where's Rebecca? I need to find her. She's as good as anyone, makes no difference to me," he snapped as he walked out.

Rebecca had gone to the sycamore tree with baby Elizabeth. They called it their secret place by the woods. Isaac Parker had built a swing for them there hanging off a branch on the large tree that overlooked the hills beyond Millwheel. From their perch mother and child could rock back and forth as she nursed, viewing the pastures that gently unfolded before them. The crick flowed below and if quiet they could watch deer come to drink. Elizabeth had been cutting teeth for weeks and irritable. Rebecca had saddled the mare and, having Riddle help them up, she placed the baby in the front and rode out. As she swung and nursed in the shade the mare grazed nearby and she could hear the singing of the Millwheel workers from deep in the woods. They were taking down a large white oak today. Isaac's business was flourishing and they needed staves to build more whiskey barrels. With the distant song, she followed the melody, humming to help Elizabeth sleep. She thought of Isaac. He was always sweet on her but she would never let on having Master Curran to answer to. The owner would kill Isaac if he thought there was a connection between them so she hummed along from a distance knowing not far off Isaac was sharing the same song.

Lord Curran's manhood was annoying him, which made him angrier. "Where's that woman gone? I've searched the barns, the holding pens, nothing. Baby's gone too, probably with her. My mare's gone. Saddle's gone. Guess I'll walk out and check the fields." Tramping along the trail he could hear singing from deep in his forest. The path ended on the top of a hill where just beyond he spotted Rebecca with her child swinging under the sycamore.

He yelled before reaching her, "You know the day. Where have you been?"

The surprise of his voice brought terror to Rebecca's eyes. As he reached them he grabbed her arm causing Elizabeth to fall from Rebecca's lap and onto the ground.

Back at the cabin Emma had had a bad feeling in her gut. After Mills had left the cabin a strong message of danger caused her to step outside into the farmyard. Suddenly the feeling became unbearable and finding Salem she yelled, "Watch my babies. I need to find Rebecca and warn her. Master Curran's off looking for her, I got to go...."

Emma knew that Elizabeth was teething and remembered Rebecca's swing under the sycamore tree. Running as fast as she could she was already too late. Lord Curran had Rebecca on the ground, her dress half torn off. Fear had caused baby Elizabeth to crawl away to safety behind the sycamore's large trunk. Her eyes wide with horror she watched as Emma ran out of the woods to her mother's side. Lew Mills saw her coming as well. As Emma flew up to the bodies struggling on the ground Mills swung back his huge forearm catching the small woman on the side of her head above her ear. With a crack of bone Emma flew through the air landing about ten feet away in the tall grass.

Although Lew Mills was pinning Rebecca to the ground she screamed, but only once. His body pushed against hers and any breath seemed to leave her body. For the last time she watched as the men ran toward them crushing down the golden oats that just that spring she had carefully helped them plant. Mills rose up pulling Rebecca by the neck. "If you come any closer I'll kill her! You know I will! I'll kill you all, don't matter to me. Come closer and she's dead!"

All the men stopped where they were, a terror on their faces. Lew Mills tightened his hand around Rebecca's neck but she was gone. A lack of air had stopped any further struggling, her legs and arms falling limp to her sides. The workers could see she was now dead, yet Mills caught them off guard with his next move, "OK, now I'm gonna' kill this baby!" Dropping Rebecca's body he took two long strides toward the tree. Grabbing the tiny child he pushed it up above his head, "I'm killin' this child now, then I'll kill all of you and your folk…"

BANG

A shot from the woods hitting Mills directly through his side.

BANG

A second shot smashed into his shoulder.

Dropping his arm Mills released the baby girl and she fell to the ground wailing. Now crawling, the injured man tried once more to reach the child but with the second shot the men from the field had started running and reached little Elizabeth first, pulling her to safety.

Lew Mills stopped moving.

Gill, James, and Henry Craft stood over their neighbor's body. Even with the rumors they'd heard over the years of their neighbor's evil ways they had never realized that the wickedness was real. Now Isaac had arrived to pull Rebecca into his arms, hoping to spend one last moment with this kind woman he had loved from afar. His tears were late, their solemn romance over as he asked himself, "I always knew, but failed to step up to the danger and take her from Millwheel. She would be alive now had I removed her from this place long ago." With that he pulled her body closer and cried in despair.

After seeing Emma run off the farmyard and down the trail Riddle had arrived, short of breath but found he was too late as well. She lay in the soft bluegrass, motionless. Virgil Parker had been able to reach little Elizabeth before Mills. Cradling her now in his arms he calmed her sobs with cooing noises. She was bruised from the fall but the sores would heal. Now she needed safety and Virgil would promise her that.

Jefferson walked out from the woods to approach the murder scene, rifled musket in hand. Evening was near, the sun slowly drooping down below the trees. A meadowlark hidden in the tall summer oats sung a last song before finding for its nest for the night.

As Emma lay motionless on the ground and Isaac held Rebecca in his arms Jefferson noticed Lord Curran's body twitch. The others saw this also and their fear returned. Jefferson chocked the rifle, "Do you want to end this? Call the law or hang me for what I'm about to do, but I love you all and I can't let this man pain us no more! Leave here now if you want and don't be a part of this, but to save the farm I need to end this evil!"

Jefferson's face was wet with tears as he loaded another ball, aimed at Lord Curran's chest and fired. The Craft boys turned away, never before having seen a man killed. Gill Craft, suddenly realizing what had happened to his neighbors, forced him to fall to the ground and crawl away.

In the twilight quiet sobs were heard as Jefferson spoke once more, "Since the first day I came to this farm an evil's been here choking us." Quietly he whispered, "We need to take care of this tonight." He paused in thought then straightened up, "A couple of you need to go back to the barns. Virgil, Riddle, collect some shovels." Using his arm to push some of the wetness off his face Jefferson counseled the men, "We'll not tell Salem. She'll be asleep with the babies but may have heard the shots. Let her know in the morning. Let her rest. I'll stay here. Men, bring back some blankets, rope too."

The Craft brothers were scared but James Craft walked over to visit Rebecca and Emma once more, kissed them and walked home with his brothers through the woods. Dark now, the sunset had painted the trees black against the night sky. Crickets and birds hidden in the shadows were the only sounds.

Jefferson had a plan. Virgil and Riddle returned with all the tools and clothing. Just down the hill from the sycamore swing was a flat place that in the spring would be covered in crocus but now was grassland. The ladies were wrapped carefully in blankets and lovingly covered. Three graves were dug. A hole for Lord Curran was dug, but filled in again empty. After the ladies were buried it made the appearance of three finished graves.

Lew Mills' body was half gone. Jefferson, Virgil and Isaac loaded what was left onto the mare's bare back. Guiding her up high past the crick through the trees they came to the top of a ridge far from where they farmed but still on Millwheel property.

"Thunder and lightning will keep him company up here." They all agreed.

Digging a shallow grave they tied the rope around the dead man's hands tightly. After that they tied his feet together. Dumping the corpse in, dirt was thrown over then branches and rocks. Virgil remembered the damage from the rifle shot, "If he ever had a heart, it's gone now."

Isaac thought about their fate, "What if hunters find this place? Dig it up?" Jefferson's spoke calmly, "We hunt this land. Live here. We'll work this land and keep it ours, for the children. No one will come up here again for years. I'll make sure of that. By then this body will be as rotten as the man that used it."

The mare's back was red with blood so the men took her to the pond and Virgil rode her through the water several times, scrubbing her back with his hands. In the back pasture she dropped down to roll the dampness off her back, erasing any traces of the murder.

That morning the men returned to the farm barracks finding the children and others asleep. Riddle snored as Virgil and Isaac laid down to rest knowing that sleep would be hard to find.

Jefferson would not sleep until he entered Lord Curran's cabin one last time. It had been a number of years since he had been inside. Entering, he was not surprised to find it dark even with the morning sun breaking through the forest. Without guilt the tall black man began tearing the shelves down, kicking tables, pulling at blankets. He knew what to look for, the double eagle gold coins.

"Thomas Curran had come to Kentucky with plenty. More money had been earned over the years from our lumber, the barrels and wool." Swinging a log around the room it landed against the buck stove, collapsing it in half. Ashes spilled out onto the floor. The bottom held a grate and hidden underneath was a metal piece box. Jefferson had seen one used by a coalminer to hold sandwiches. He opened it and found four stacks of twenty-dollar double eagles. "But there's still more." He thought.

Sorting through dust and battered furniture he came up empty but at the back of a drawer was a map and deed of the land Jefferson knew as Millwheel Farm. "Better," he said examining it. "Except the name Thomas Curran has been crossed off and someone named Lew Mills was scribbled in. Strange. When I find that guy I'll kill him too." Under the mattress were some green backs rolled up along with drawings of ships, steamboats and newspaper clippings. Jefferson had no time to investigate the meanings of these finds, but folded all of the discoveries together for keeping, then scoured the room to find a match.

The flames caught with little effort. Licking into the morning sky the smoke could be seen from Ben Yobel's farm and as far away as the Craft place. The wind blew the sparks east and a black cloud of smoke draped over the high ridge at the top of Millwheel Farm.

Chapter 14
PART 2—
OCTOBER, 1998

The wide river pushes from east to west past her, not blue like the sky, but a vast moving sea stained by the henna rock and silt that lines the shore, descending to the bottom. Moving along the bluff India takes in the afternoon. The colors, mahogany from the maples, bronze from the oaks and gold from the birch across the Ohio River take her breath away. This river in late autumn finds the foliage coloring the surface as it glitters away toward ports north to Cincinnati.

The bank falls below onto a spongy beach. Over millions of years the dead remains of gray driftwood bodies have littered the shore half buried in sandy graves waiting to be exhumed again with the next spring flood.

Tempter feels the warm push of a breeze and wants more of it as he stands erect beneath his rider, India Curran. A wind from the northeast causes him to brace his long body, which measures nearly eight feet from nose to tail. Feet planted he throws his head up and down, then shakes his head hard causing the quake to move down his neck to his chest. His whole body shakes in frenzy, all for nothing more than to satisfy an itch. Leaning forward he scrapes his soft nose against a lower leg, satisfying yet a different itch.

India ignores these activities from her horse. Reins rest in her hands like faithful friends, her saddle safely bound to the beast. Twelve hundred pounds of muscle under her can move and shake, stand or rest. Sitting over Tempter seems very secure and predictable like a port in a storm. There's no place that India would rather be this Friday evening. Glancing up the river a gathering of yachts and houseboats arrived to tie up to the cottonwood trees along the beach for the weekend. They sit right off the bank to rest in the shallows. The trick is for the captains not to come too far on the sand and ground out. Their boats would founder and be impossible to move back out again on Sunday night.

One of the boaters spots India from far upriver and waves. She's a bit of a novelty but it all ties together, the river community, water, boats, horses, all meeting by coincidence on this balmy afternoon.

With the tiniest suggestion India barely moves her hands to the right setting into motion the earth beneath her. Tempter already knew. With just the turn of India's head and a slight shift of her weight it signifies to the aging thoroughbred gelding which course to take. Moving upriver they follow a slim path carved through the Kentucky bluegrass, down to the beach.

Across the field to the east rest century old homes, occupied now by bats and sparrows. At one time the rock buildings housed the slaves that had worked these fields, their families and the families before them. But the buildings became weak and the years cracked the mortar between the stones evicting the residents to more sturdy dwellings, not necessarily better.

The fences are also a testimony to the years. Combinations of old fragile posts, bent metal pipes, all lazily holding up a combination of wooden rails patched with wire. Two hundred years ago grand draft horses grazed there bumping away an occasional sheep or goat with their thick legs. Slaves used this pasture, perhaps walking the same shoreline on an evening such as this. They inhaled that same sweet wind that pulled the warmth of summer south with winter they knew was only a breath away. Slaves had been the builders of these rock residences that sit across the field from where India rides. At the time of construction it seemed that these cottages would be far enough from the shore to avoid rising floods each spring. But the farm managers and surveyors then did not have the knowledge to read what was already written along the land. The Ohio River valley is strewn with trees and waste that had climbed up and over the banks, sweeping inland with the spring tides. Long reeds and grasses drape over the treetop branches, some twenty feet above the ground. Had those early builders known what to look for they would have built those first structures another half mile east, up the bluff, further from the Ohio River.

Sharing her thoughts with Tempter was nothing new, "It's a good afternoon to leave Millwheel Farm. I need some time alone to think. Sometimes I can't fathom the responsibilities of being the youngest owner of the largest breeding establishment in Campbell County. Lately I've had to invent ways to sneak off and ride each week. But this is the best way to organize my thoughts. Final decisions need to be made for the next breeding season of 1999, and what better way than to hash them out here riding this pasture than sitting in my stuffy office at the farm. Any comments, Tempter?"

The gelding answered by tossing his head to avoid the deerflies.

But the sun was setting and it appeared to be getting very dark in the west. Heavy black clouds were pushing the sun below the horizon sending a message for India to return home for the day. Far in the distance lightning slapped against the hilltops, then waited patiently for a snap of thunder to follow. Back at the two-horse trailer she rushed to throw a blanket over Tempter, not even bothering to unsaddle him. Her short black hair tingled with the electricity in the air. Looking into the rear-view mirror as she backed her rig, India saw the weather changing right before her eyes.

In less than an hour she pulled up in the yard at the estate. Flip Dodge, the farm manager, had been waiting for her and worrying. "Did you check the weather Miss, before you took off on us?" he complained.

"The day started out so pretty, I couldn't resist. And its good to get out. Tempter loved it. Tomorrow I'll catch up on all the things I missed today."

"We're all glad your back just the same. Next time take your cell phone and call before you head for home. That way we will know you're OK."

India rolled her green eyes and thought to herself, 'What a mother hen,' With that India Curran, Mill-wheel's owner, lead her old equine friend into the barn to be stalled for the night.

No one could have contemplated the storm, a deluge of rain like no other. During the darkness of the night they all slept while across the bluegrass of Campbell County disaster reigned. It washed the rolling hills, inducing barns to cling to foundations and birds to branches. Mud slid south filling holes and covering drains. Roots of ancient trees came loose and with them trunks, branches and nests fell, crashing into the mud below.

The torrent caused tombstones to sink closer to their owners, an unexpected visit to loved ones below. Other graves without stones, just crudely placed cairns, welcomed the tempest. Movements of the squall above shifted the rock and ooze across the bones of the dead and forgotten below. Although the rot and smell had dissipated years earlier, energy now activated from beyond, causing the reawakening of an immortal heart.

Raindrops became cascades turning to waterfalls. Lakes appeared where creeks once flowed and shallow oceans spread across fields. Logs, waste, all floated to new locations.

At Millwheel the morning rose with surprises. Branches, lawn chairs, rusty buckets, even part of a car chassis had come to visit the property from creeks beyond. Those things would all be easy to remove over the next few weeks, most with little effort. Other surprises from the storm would prove to be more difficult, if not fatal.

Damien Alva's Law office was located on the west side of Main Street in Alexandria, Kentucky. Seedy, it had at one time been a family's small one story rambler before they were evicted.

Sally, Mr. Damien's secretary had been working on her resignation letter since arriving that morning when the tall dark man opened the front door allowing the cold October air to sweep inside, blowing the papers off her desk.

"Geez," Sally said as she ran around the room retrieving papers, "Close the door!"

After a moment she collected herself and sitting back down at a desk she asked, "Are you here to see Mr. Alva?"

"Why yes, but I don't have an appointment."

"I'd ask you to take a number," Sally said swinging her arm around to exaggerate the empty room, "But instead I'll just tell him you're here."

The man remained standing as Sally stuck her head inside a door, there was a murmur and then she announced, "He'll see you now."

Damien Alva was a short man with a weight problem and a face the color of vanilla yogurt. That, and his social history, gave him a free pass to let all the boys at the Elks Club know he was 'sexually challenged.'

The waiting room guest could overlook any lack of qualifications, wanting only to set the stage for the takeover of a Kentucky estate.

"And you are?"

"Mills. Lewis Mills."

"With any new client it is my duty not to discuss any of our conversation outside of this office. How may I assist you?"

"It appears that a property that I am under contract to purchase does not hold a clear deed and may need further attention to guarantee that all of the land in the purchase is accounted for."

Alva asked, " Didn't you have it surveyed?"

"It would be that easy if recent boundaries were marked," Mills went on, "But the process grinds to a halt without the original markers from 1868. Frustrated with the property, most buyers have taken their business elsewhere. I believe the land is cursed!"

With that they both laughed.

Alva was now curious, " What is it you do for a business, Mr. ah, Mills?"

Before answering the visitor Mr. Mills glanced around the room at cabinets and bookshelves lining the walls making note of the fact they appeared excessively scratched and worn for a law office.

"Lately I've dabbled in racehorses, just as an owner of course. The thought of a "hands on" responsibility I find disgusting. Then there are the ships. Seems I'm able to find older yachts and make a profit reconditioning them. Several under contract as we speak."

"Good, Good. Keep money moving, that's the American way. Buy, sell, trade."

Alva was getting to like the way this conversation was unfolding, no bumps yet. *'Uncovering the original deed for this client at the county clerk's office should only take a single afternoon,'* thought Alva, *'I'll make a note to keep a careful record of time spent.'*

The attorney inquired, "And your residence at this time?"

"I have a post office box."

"And what has your deed search come up with so far?" Alva asked, although was already becoming bored with this petty questioning. In any event, it had to be done.

"The only deed discovered so far was written in 1868 to a Thomas Curran residing in Saratoga Springs, New York. It appears he bought the land from Benjamin Van Cleave after the Civil War and traveled here to set up a farm and homestead. The realtor only showed me the plot east of Persimmon Grove Pike, about 800 acres. With discovery so far it appears that the land on both sides, including the north side of Lickert Road, should remain together. I have acquired a copy of the original 'Metes and Bounds' for you to examine."

Alva groaned thinking to himself, *'This would involve the record of patenting, then finding the warrant, then the entry written in 1868. After that a new survey and patent would need to be applied for. Clearly this client is stating that he has obtained the original grant and that may be enough to get started, but it would still be necessary to have a large portion of earnest money up front.'*

"Are you aware Mr. Mills, that the property you are alluding to on the west side of Lickert Road is the old Millwheel Estate? It's been in the Curran family for over 130 years. India Curran and some of her relatives still live there. A few are buried there. It would seem that their boundaries would be marked and recorded."

" The investigation so far has discovered no proof the property ever being separated. I understood it to be one large parcel containing 1800 acres. It stands in my favor to purchase the entire estate, and I'll kill to get it."

Alva was now feeling the bumps. Needing to get things underway he lied, "Well, this investigation sounds fairly easy then. Should be a breeze. Leave whatever documents you have with Sally out there and I'll get started next Tuesday."

(Alva made a personal promise never to start anything new on Monday's allowing for his passion of boating the Kentucky River on those days.)

"Have you stopped to visit with Miss. Curran? She would be happy to share any knowledge of a deed with you now that you plan on becoming her neighbor. I even believe that over the years she's been running cattle on the old Parker place and for that dispensation her family paid the taxes. Seems like everyone was happy, don't you think?"

The meeting completed for now, both men stood and confidently shook hands. Before stepping out Mills said in a voice tinged with menace, "Its important for you to find that these acres are still one parcel. Keep in mind that I do not want to be disappointed."

Chapter 15
LAWYERS, GHOSTS and DEEDS

"Hello?" India yawned into the phone. "Millwheel Farm, India Curran speaking."

"Hey, Sweetie. Sorry to wake you up, but the floods from that storm aren't the only big news you'll hear about this morning."

"Who is this, and what are you talking about?"

The caller answered, "This is your shoer, Tony Wallace."

"Ferriers don't get up this early and if they did it would only be to cut the hooves off of dead horses to re-use the shoes."

"Well don't hang up. I got news. Did you know the Parker Place has been bought?"

India sat up now, scratching her short black hair with her free hand, "What? That's impossible. That family hasn't been heard from in fifty years."

"Guess they found 'em. And the buyer must have had a lot of dough seeing that it's what, eight hundred acres give or take."

India was silent. This conversation didn't make sense. The Parker place had never been for sale. The only known relatives had put it into a trust long ago.

Tony went on, "It might be developed for big fancy houses or a subdivision. What if it goes into storage buildings or a landfill?"

"Oh, for the Christ sake Tony, stop trying to scare me. Who bought it, do you know?"

"No one local. The Alexandria Newspaper would have been all over that information. Probably a huge overseas corporation. You should get your butt out of bed and call a realtor, get with the new owner."

India shuttered to think of an office park or warehouses right across the road from her beautiful farm. People have always commented that Millwheel is the prettiest estate in Campbell County.

Tony spoke once more, " I'll keep my ears open and try to find out what I can. Hey, think about this—it may just be a breeding competitor, someone with bloodlines even more valuable than yours."

❧⚓❧

With the anxiety of the Parker's property still on her mind India Curran set out later that morning to check on Jeff Taylor, one of the tenured Millwheel employees. His job had been to disk a field on the east side of the farm. Walking, it took her twenty minutes to spot his tractor in the distance. As she traveled across the fields the birds made such a show, flying back and forth trough the trees with such speed that she was certain that they would collide.

Jeff's tractor was just turning to make another pass across the dirt. Slow and sluggish, it kept the pace with

painful lurches. This field never flattened out. Some places always too wet, others too dry. India struggled up the
rise that followed a tree line separating the fields. Hidden along the way deep inside the branches and bushes
there were still traces of the farm as it had been when first
established. Old wire, wooden posts clumsily holding up
the fallen cross rails, remains of fencing that at one time
had held the livestock in place, at least until thunder or
hail would drive the animals through the barriers and
onto the neighbors land.

Passing a huge tree perhaps 50 feet high she noticed
some stones stacked carefully at the base. They had been
picked from the field over a century ago and laid there to
rest for eternity. For an instant she could picture the slaves
still holding them in their strong hands, each carrying a
stone and setting it in the secluded spot so it would not
slip into the field and chip a plow blade.

Lifting each muddy foot she was almost within yelling distance of the tractor when she spotted a movement
from inside the treed fencerow. Hearing noises she wondered, 'Kids, children, inside the brambles playing? Did
they have a fort? With so many thorns it seemed silly that
they would find more fun here than in the yards of their
own neighborhood.'

It appeared that they had spotted her as well and instantly became quiet, froze for a minute and then slipped
out of their lair onto the opposite field, running as fast as
their bare feet would take them.

India loved it. She had obviously become their imaginary monster and it delighted her.

There were three of them about six to eight years old, but tiny and thin. As they raced further from her she noticed they had dark complexions and strange clothes. Baggy pants held up with string and no shoes. One of them, a girl, had hair resembling the brambles where they had been hiding. Already too far off to call, India was disappointed. She would have loved to meet them. Lately she only had brief relationships with the children that arrived for riding lessons and even then there was little conversation. The students were always so focused on climbing onto the saddle that India was never able to develop any friendships. 'Well,' India thought, 'maybe the children will return later.'

Still curious, she crawled into their small fortress in the trees where they had been playing. Tucked deep inside she spied a doll made from burlap, strings twisted around it to create a waist, with arms of sticks. The eyes were knotted thread and the skirt on this doll was painted red from the waist down, reminding India of the paint on an old corner post not far down the field. India looked around. There was also a type of slingshot, two wooden swords again using bailing twine to hold the handles on. 'How quaint,' she thought, 'Kids taking the time to fashion their own toys.'

Jeff had noticed her, shut off the tractor and was waving. Leaving the fort as she had found it India slogged up to him, "Did you see the kids?" she asked and then pointed in the direction that they had run.

"Hard to take my eyes off the row Miss. If I do move off the tracks with this machine it will mess up the whole field for me."

174

India elaborated, "Some kids, looked like they've been playing here for a while anyway. Nice to see kids outdoors and not stuck inside watching TV."

"Well, if I see them in the future what do you want me to do?"

"Nothing" replied India, "Just keep an eye out so you don't run over one of them. And be friendly, that's always good. You know I've always encouraged trespassing on our place." Jeff smiled, knowing that all of the employees at Millwheel, neighbors too, loved walking the property even during the winter.

"You bet. Well, anything you need from me?" He took a swig from his canteen.

"No, just checking on how much further you had to go up here. I'm hoping that you can still drag the arena before you go in for lunch."

Jeff started the tractor up and nodded yes as he put it into gear. He also liked to see the arena sand pulled smooth each day groomed like a Zen Garden. Each of the drivers wanted their designs in the ring to be the prettiest and the riding instructors appreciated it, too.

Walking back to the yard India passed her two round pens, each holding a stallion. The two studs would be worked separately in their own discipline and then sent out into large holding pens far away from each other so they could strut around, tails erect and call to their girlfriends.

Entering the house she kicked off her boots and went directly to the fridge to grab a can of anything available. Opening the refrigerator door she stooped to consider her choices, "Soda, juice, water, and what's this?"

She pulled a ceramic pitcher from the shelf and peered down into it. "Milk. Why would milk be in here? Maybe a carton had broken open again. Figures. Best to drink it up before it goes bad."

She poured a small glass and noticed that it was thick like a cream. "Probably sour." She smelled it. "Yum, smells good." With no odor to make her pour it down the sink, she took a sip. "Someone brought us some cream today. Wonder who? Need to find out what it's for, maybe a whipped cream for dessert?" India shuttered at the thought. It was all she could do to stay around 120 pounds. She now considered skipping lunch.

"So what else, any vegetables?" On the bottom shelf was the usual yogurt, an old square of Colby cheese, bacon and next to a cartoon of eggs was a bowl of brown eggs. Something else special, she cringed, hating the thought of saying 'no' to something sumptuous.

The phone rang. India closed the refrigerator door and moved to answer it. Just before she touched the receiver she felt a chill, a flash of a premonition that this call was different. She picked up the receiver and said hello.

"Good afternoon, and to whom am I speaking?'

'Great,' she thought, a sales call at two in the afternoon. 'I thought these people usually called during dinner.'

India returned the question. "And whom might this be?"

"My name is Damien Alva and I'm calling to contact a certain India Curran. Is she home?"

"This is she".

"Good. Good", He went on, "My call, Miss Curran, is to bring to your attention today that a certain party I am representing has filed a formal inquiry concerning your property."

"What type of inquiry?"

"It seems that my client purchased the land on the east side of Persimmon Ridge Road, also known as the Parker Farm. This includes the property on your side as well. You may have already been notified of this action".

'What, are you nuts!' India screamed inside of her head. Burying her anger she took a deep breath, remembering that her parents would be deeply disappointed if she totally forgot her manners.

"Sir, you must have a wrong number. This property has been in our family since 1868. Our graves are here. We have never even had any thoughts to consider putting it on the market."

"My dear," Mr. Alvin arranged the facts to his advantage, "It appears that from our investigation that the farms on both sides of the county road are one single property and always have been. The Parker farm extends from Mell Road, around Barr Road and includes your land."

"Who are you again?"

The attorney stubbornly repeated his name.

"Well, Mr. Alva, you are terribly wrong. You can ask our neighbors where our property lines are. Some of them have been here longer than us. Some since before the Civil War! I'm afraid this phone call is just a ruse to stir me up today and you're probably a crank caller."

"Ms. Curry, do you have a current survey of your property?"

That stopped India.

"Why would I? The county surveyed our property in 1868 and since that time our family has never moved off of it. Someone, in fact dozens of relatives have always been on this place, living, dying, reproducing and I know that the Parker Farm was only a part of our land in the beginning. Way back when, maybe 1877, 1880, something like that. A road went through you know as Persimmon Ridge Road splitting our 1600 acres."

India was almost out of breath. "Anyway, who is the buyer of that land?"

"I am not at liberty to give out any additional information concerning my client". He answered.

"Well, you tell Mr. Mystery Man that he has an old deed from before the Parkers owned it. He's the one that needs a current survey done."

"Is that all Ms. Curran?"

" I believe that's enough Mr. Alva"

He went on, " We will be contacting you again soon. All correspondence from you or your family concerning this action must go through my office or your attorney. We are looking to you to supply my office with a current survey or binding deed for your land or we will be seeing you in court."

Chapter 16
ADVICE and LOST JEWELRY

"Who the hell does he think he is?"

India was livid, not needing any additional anxiety at this time. Leaning against the kitchen stove she pondered which way to go. Relatives such as her Aunt Ginny were still around. Maybe she would have a copy of the original deed. How about a neighbor? As land changes hands over the years it would seem bordering farms would have needed a record of Millwheel's Metes and Bounds before purchasing their properties.

She started to bite her nails. "Stress is kicking in. In this condition if I were to jump on one of those thoroughbreds right now, it would buck me off. First this morning there were little kids running loose in the fields, then strange food in the fridge, now an eccentric attorney. What a day."

India paced across the yard, and opened a door to her pickup truck to allow Maggie, her German Shepard to jump in the back. She waved good-bye to Flip just coming from around the barn to find her. With no time to talk, India was off to see her Aunt Ginny.

Following up the mile long gravel road it seemed a while since she had found the time to visit her mother's sister but her aunt liked to keep distant of the workings going on around Campbell County. Having raised 5 kids in the past fifty years it would seem peace was well deserved.

Letting Maggie jump out to roam around on her own India stopped to take in the view. Ginny's ranch style home was directly on top of a high ridge that overlooked several miles of Campbell County. It had once been part of the original Curran estate but so much of the 1860's property had been sold off over the last 130 years or divided between other kin, eventually India felt her farm would sink into the ground and disappear forever if not protected. She needed to say vigilant.

Facing north, India spotted another ridge she was also very familiar with. Now part of the Parker property it rose higher than where she stood. Noticing a movement in the trees India wondered if a deer or something else was feeding there today. The figure seemed larger than a deer as it passed behind the trees. From such a distance it would be impossible to make out the object. Suddenly shivering, she thought, 'Looks like Big Foot's living up there. Think I'll have a nervous breakdown before the end of the day.' Turning toward her aunt's house she decided, 'Nay, I'm too busy even for that.'

Ginny was just finishing lunch when India walked in. A lady in her seventies she still stood straight and moved quickly around her kitchen wiping up the counters. During Ginny's lifetime India believed she had never changed clothes, always sporting the same loose 'Muumuu' type dress, corset beneath and tights worn in every season of the year. She displayed another eccentricity by having the only pigeon in Campbell County living in her kitchen.

His name was Piccolo and he produced a growling noise from far inside of his breast at anyone other than Ginny who approached him.

"So, what say you lovely lady," Ginny purred.

"I come from afar to rescue you from your secluded life on the top of this hill." giggled India.

"So be it. I will move down to the 'Palace of Mill-wheel' and you can wait on me hand and foot forever, or until I die. Which ever comes first."

With a tired smile India fell down onto an old couch. "Why not? I have 40 horses I already cater to, hand and hoof every day. What's one more mouth to feed?"

Ginny sat down to join India. Curious at this surprise visit India's aunt knew staying silent would weed out the reason from this young woman faster than.........

"I received the worst phone call from the most hideous person who tells me he wants a current deed to Mill-wheel Farm because some guys buying the Parker place and thinks the two properties are connected but he's nuts and I need you to tell me what to do!"

"Is that all?"

"And, I have lost kids playing on our land with hardly any clothes on and mysterious people leaving strange foods around in my kitchen and I think I spotted Big Foot. Is this a normal day or am I just crazy?"

"The county should first have sent a notice to the neighboring farms that border the old Parker place, if for no other reason than to make people aware of the purchase."

"You would think." India threw her feet up onto the coffee table receiving a disapproving look, "But I get a phone call and right now it seems pretty difficult to just rush out and start a new project."

"Everyone in Campbell County knows you India. Trot down to the historical society or the land office in New Port. Everything is documented. And you'll love it. The land we live on is very historical. From the time of Noah people have wandered across these fields, hunting, sleeping. Indians may have fished from your lakes and there are records, not many, but letters proving slaves once stayed here! You will be fascinated by what happened before you were born"

"Yes, well that's all very romantic," sighed India, "but on the way here I figured that the thing I need is an agreement between two parties that states the land was divided at some point. The Curran's had over a thousand acres in 1870. It seems that a simple contract would be lying around somewhere. Would you be a dear and help me find it?"

Ginny painfully stood up and turned toward the backdoor heading outside, "You'll not find a contract here. But you might go to the other spots I mentioned or that Jesse Southgate over on the west side of your place. He's old but he's not dead yet. Check with him. After that you could try exhuming a few of the bodies in that old cemetery you have on your hill next to the Sycamore tree. Beneath the dirt one of our relatives would possibly be clutching the paperwork you're looking for."

"Very funny" India moaned following the woman outside.

Ginny began pulling towels off the clothesline, "What do you know exactly about our ancestors?"

"Well, I know they got here around 1870. Thomas Curran had a bunch of wives who died on the same day. It's on the stones in the cemetery. What was that about, do you know?"

"Two wives, Emma and Rebecca that we know of. Three children from them, Westley, Elizabeth, and Joseph. And then they had children who were your grandparents, then your parents, then you."

" Knowing that our family had always lived on this land that I ride everyday keeps me thinking about their lives, what they did, how they survived. In the spring I still stop and put flowers on their graves. I always hope that they might be watching from somewhere close and I'd like them to know that we'll always be family."

Ginny finished folding the towels and walking off she mumbled, "They might be closer than you think."

❧

"What a nightmare. And why now? Pregnant mares in the barn, holidays around the corner?" Making her way past rows of farm equipment at Millwheel, India was pleased with the suggestions from her Aunt Ginny. Soon she would attack the historical society, then the land office in New Port. "Pen, paper, cameras, what else?" thought India, "Only want to do this once, get that damn attorney off my back then move on to important things."

Inside the smaller of the barns she took a moment to check out the tack rooms, "Haven't looked for any signs of mice for a while or bats, brrrr, yuck."

While sticking her head inside of a grain bin she considered, "After hitting the society in Alexandria and the Land Office it would be good to visit some neighboring farms, too, but no reason to be making a pest of myself right away. Maybe something wonderful will happen like the new owner of the Parker Place will die or something."

The only shame she felt now was the fact that she had lived in Campbell County her whole life and never stopped to look up anything about her property before. She would have to make time to do it. This fall was supposed to be her best. Healthy horses and foals, good grass and farm help comfortable with their jobs. Who could ask for more?

She knew it was too good to last.

Ernie had worked on Millwheel about 6 years, having the job of caring for the largest barn himself. It had box stalls for 40 horses, 20 on either side, with an enclosed riding arena in the center. At one end of the barn there was an upstairs office with an observation area overlooking the ring. In the center was Ernie and Flip's apartment. Small, it only had a bed in the main room, another in the back and a small shower, which had been added when the horse wash was installed below on the first floor. They had worked to make the living quarters cozy by adding a Lilliputian sized table next to the refrigerator and calling that the kitchen. Flip was second in command helping Ernie move horses, muck, wash, repair, feed and everything else involved with running a good sized barn such as this.

"How is your day going Ernie?" Asked India.

"Fine, although more rain is expected, both tomorrow and Wednesday morning. Mares arriving this week will have to be backed up to the barn opening and unloaded as close to inside as we can swing it."

"Good, good, best not to bring in any shipping fever." India said.

"Joseph is still out there in the field sinking fence posts"

"I'll catch him when he comes back in and put him on something else. He can watch for Bernie and the hay to make sure it all goes right inside. Keep that dry at least. Bernie's so lazy, he'd love the help tossing those bails anyway."

Quietly following Ernie around as he worked, she finally asked, "Say, Ernie, you've lived in Campbell County all your life, right?"

"You know it. Except I always wished my blood was as blue as the grass. Wouldn't need to work so hard. What's going on?"

Hands in her pockets, India kicked the ground and began explaining the attorney's call and demands, looking for someone to pour herself out to and hoping for a little moral support.

"Don't worry, there's a way to get that attorney off your back. He's crazy anyway. Got his facts all wrong. Sounds like he's being lead along with false information by a land hungry client who only wants to open a huge can-o-worms for his own benefit. But I'll ask around. Feed store, you know, see if anyone has any poop on this guy, get you a name."

"Thanks. At this point I'm just calling him Asshole".

Digging into his jeans Ernie asked, "Do you have a lost and found here on the farm?"

"Depends on what it is." India replied.

"Your Morgan, Willie's stall here. Mucked it and found this was lying on a ledge. Pretty isn't it?"

Ernie placed on India's palm a locket, gold or brass, on a chain. "I don't remember your horse wearing jewelry. Someone accidentally must have left it."

"Inside Willie's stall? Weird. Maybe it dropped out here in the aisle and with Willie out in the pasture they figured to just place it in there close by. Someone will ask about it. Tell everyone that we have found a locket so it can get back to the owner. I'll put it in my desk, right hand top drawer, Ernie. If you find the owner just go get it. And let me know who's it is, OK?"

India carefully dropped the locket into her coat pocket and started back for her office in the farmhouse.

Chapter 17
INDIA INVESTIGATES

The following morning India was already in Alexandria having coffee after first stopping at the bookstore, the drug store and, she thought, a hundred other places. Now it was a waiting game since the Campbell County Historical Society did not open until 10am.

From the coffee shop she could see the building across the street that once was a courthouse built in 1837. A compact car pulled up in the parking lot and Mike, a Society volunteer, climbed out. Walking around to the front of the building he unlocked the tall white doors under a portico supported by four gothic Greek columns that rose up 40-feet to meet a soffit above.

India stood up, digging into her pockets to find money for the coffee and glancing up noticed another car pulling in to the Courthouse parking lot. A dark gray Mercedes parked and out stepped a very tall man, dark hair, wearing a long black coat.

"Seems the historical society appeals to undertakers, too." She thought, pushing open the café door.

The dark man entered just moments after Mike.

India dropped cash on to the table and started across the square. Pulling open the heavy doors she trotted up the long set of stairs to the second floor. Behind old wooden cabinets Mike was just settling in. Years before the room had been transformed into a library-research

center of sorts. Shelves covered elevated walls support-
ing old books, maps, boxes and dust. Narrow windows
climbed up from the floor to the ceiling supplying what
appeared to be the only source of light since any bulbs
served only to light the ceiling.

He looked up, "What can I do for you?"

Mike looked to be about 70 years old with short salt
and pepper hair, dressed casually in a flannel shirt and
khaki pants.

Before India could speak Mike reached back and
finding a knob, turned on an old radio sitting on a cre-
denza next to a window. Loud music blared out, a 1940's
style India guessed, detonating the huge room with
sound. She was surprised the speakers were still capable
of the task.

"What kind of music is that?"

Mike smiled, "Big bands. Love it, can't get enough
of it!" He needed to yell his reply to answer. "So, did you
need to find something?"

Afraid of eventually getting a headache from the
noise India got right to the point inquiring about land
deeds.

"What have you done so far?" asked Mike.

"This is the beginning of my search. I'm looking for
a contract, hopefully a current one written for my farm
south of here."

"Oh, you have a long way to go. But just to inform
you, all we have in this library are records of families,
several hundred loose copies of Metes and Bounds, in no
order at all and lots of cemetery records."

Raising her voice India tried to be heard above the orchestra, "We have owned the land since 1868."

"Good, knowing the year helps. Hope you're aware you're not the first owner."

India's face screwed into a questioning look, "Why not?"

"What?"

A little louder India repeated, "Why not?"

"Cause after the Indians and the Revolutionary War parts of Louisiana were given to our soldiers as payment for the battles they had fought in. This was all Louisiana at that time. Anyway, where's your property again?" Mike yelled.

India told him Millwheel's location.

"Oh yah, the Curran place." Finally admitting defeat Mike rose up and turned down the radio. "Before 1868 there were already settlers here, or there, or where you said."

India rolled her eyes, then looking around found a stool to sit on.

"It all started with Major David Leitch. He came first, awarded land grants for service during the war about 1780, 1785. His salary was paid in land. Pretty nice, huh?"

Wistfully India smiled at the thought, "Sounds wonderful."

"It was okay if they didn't mind land filled with poisonous snakes, wild animals, lots of bad weather and Indians running around everywhere hunting or trying to kill each other."

"True, but it must have been magical."

"Yes, and that's probably why people stayed. After all the sicknesses and diseases it was magical."

"So do I need to find a deed from David Leitch?"

"Nope, try either Benjamin VanCleve or Thomas Lindsey. They were in that area where your farm is now about 1810. Things get a little dicey during then. David Leitch dropped dead of pneumonia. His young wife at the time married his best friend General James Taylor."

"Humm, cozy."

"Nice for her. She was too young for Leitch anyway. Seventeen. Keturah was her name. He was thirty-seven when they married. So after Leitch's death Taylor took over, got the girl, the land, the whole kit and kaboodle. After that he had thousands of acres and started selling off the land mostly to attract more settlers, get people to stay. The offer was, stay, clear the land and get 100 acres free. It helped a great deal. Kept families from leaving, got a few more people to populate the area. About then he sold the land where your farm is to either VanCleave or Thomas Lindsey."

"But don't you have any deeds here?"

"Nope. Only what I said. Deeds are available though. Next stop for you is the Administration building in New Port upstairs in the Land Office. They will give you a number that represents your farm property. Find that number and you can go backwards to find the person that owned the land before you. He'll be the guy that sold your farm to your ancestors. There will be a deed record of that previous owner who passed the property to, who?"

"Thomas Curran"

"The deed, measure of the land, neighbors border-ing your place at the time. Something should be lying around. Then any additional contracts are recorded af-ter that in the same book. From there any further trans-actions will be listed as well."

India gave Mike a hug but was certain that she had her work cut out for her. Hoping for more help before she left for New Port she asked, "Are there any other vol-unteers here in the building?"

"Today I'm the only one here. Why do you ask?"

"After you arrived at 10am another gentleman walked right in behind you. Big Guy."

"Maybe he was lost. We don't get many visitors as you can see."

True, in the hour she had spent with Mike no one else had stopped in. She thanked him again and walked across the square back to the coffee shop where she had left her car. Unlocking the door she couldn't help but notice the courthouse door open and the large man that had entered after Mike came out, walked around the building and a minute later the charcoal colored Mer-cedes left the parking lot.

'Damned if he wasn't in the building the whole time!' India thought, 'I wonder if he stopped to talk to Mike after I left?'

Starting her ignition she thought, "Mike was right, that guy really was lost."

New Port, Kentucky was about 45 minutes straight north. About the time Thomas Curran had arrived in the commonwealth steamboats were traveling up and down the flowing highway and flatboats moved people back and forth between shores. His journey crossed India's mind as she turned her car into the Administration Building parking lot. Taking the elevator to the second floor and finding the Land Office door she moved directly inside and up to a receptionist behind a tall desk.

"I'm looking for a number."

"A winning lottery number, I'll bet." replied the receptionist.

"I wish...no, I need to find someone to help me find the number for my property."

"Hold on," the woman said to India and picking up her phone punched in a four-digit number and waited. Listening, she asked, "Are you in the middle of anything?" There was a pause then, "OK."

Hanging up she looked up at India to relay the message, "Mr. Able will see you in about two minutes. If you would like you may have a seat right over there." And she pointed with a hand heavily covered with rings toward the chairs along the wall.

Sitting in the car had been enough for India. "I'll stand."

While the receptionist went back to her duties India shuffled around the room killing time. Glass windows separated the other offices next door and across the hall. A sight stopped her cold. The man she had seen that morning in Alexandria driving the Mercedes, it had to be him. Close, just in the next room he sat on one of the waiting room chairs against the wall and was reading the Courier Journal newspaper. As she watched him he slowly turned a page and from where she stood it appeared to her that he was reading the obituaries.

"Mr. Able will see you now."

India jumped.

"Just go right through that door."

Thanking the woman she walked into the office of James Able. He did not stand to greet her but that was understandable as India spied a cane hanging from the handle of his chair. Through his Santa length whiskers he smiled, "Looking for answers? Land questions? Trying to find out where the bodies are buried?"

India laughed at his charm, "It has come to my attention that I have land but no current deed. Squatters are pushing at the gates to get in. Can you help me?"

Chuckling, he pushed aside formalities, "Call me James." And he extended his hand across the desk.

Reaching across to accept it, she took note of his long white hair pulled behind in a short ponytail and his sweater that could be worn skiing. Not so out of place with this cool October weather.

James asked, "Did you lose it in a fire? Did it get washed away in a flood? You're supposed to hang on to those things. Good to have when greedy relatives come knocking."

"Unfortunately my parents died and I never had an opportunity to see it. My great, great, well, too many to count, grandfather came to Kentucky around 1868. In our cemetery we have his grave and the graves of two of his wives, their children and grandchildren."

"Why do you need a deed now?"

"In the past few days a mysterious person is claiming my farm is still connected to a large parcel of land across the road known as the Parker property. I know for a fact that the two properties were separated around 1880, 1890, something like that. A county road runs between them! I would love to find a written copy of the contract from when the Curran family sold the Parkers that half of Millwheel farm. Hell's bells, until now I've never even seen our deed or a map of our estate!"

James was already online targeting the Curran land on his computer.

"Here is your place, an aerial view. Now, if I draw closer we can pick up the streets bordering the property and this program gives me the two numbers we use to list your land in Campbell County. This first number here indicates the book you must find. The land library back in Alexandria has records dating back to 1786 and that book. The second number here," And James pointed it out on the screen to India, "is the page number. Easy. And this page will have Thomas Curran's name on it as the purchaser and the seller's name. You can go back as far as you want. Follow the trail to the man who owned your land before that man and so on. You get to see history happening, the history of Millwheel Farm."

India was in awe. Before she was born on her land, even before her great grandfather lived there, events had been taking place. Her mind reeled. 'How much had happened while Thomas Curran lived there? From that time in 1868 on that farm where I live what must their lives have been like?'

"Sometimes its kind of interesting," James went on, "And maybe your research will help you discover why there are questions about the Parker property."

India stood and shook James hand once more thanking him profusely. Leaving his office she once more looked across through the glass to the office next door. Just as she suspected, the chair was empty. The man had vanished.

Diving south again to Alexandria India glanced into her rearview mirror looking for a spooky gray Mercedes. "What was the point of following me?" India thought back to Damien Alva's threats only a few days ago. "This wild goose chase is entirely his fault."

It was 3pm and she wanted to eat but this mission would have to come first. Food could wait. Better to finish this now to eliminate any wolves howling at the door. Pulling into the parking lot of 'Deeds and Documents' India jumped out, locked her truck and checked for any dark foreign cars with creepy guys inside. Finding the coast clear she headed in.

A simple one-story brick building it apparently held secrets within that she had not been aware of. Before, she would have stopped to renew her driver's license at the front desk but now she as walked further she discovered a clandestine library in the rear with rows and rows of the most beautiful books she had ever seen. Hundreds of them both along the floor and reaching over her head. Ginger in color, they looked to be leather, the size maybe 24 inches tall and a spine width ranging from 5 inches to 9 inches. She contemplated lifting them figuring the task could not be more difficult than the bails of hay she hoisted each day.

The first set of numbers James Able had given her was 138. Returning back to the front desk she asked a man there for advice in finding the correct book.

"They are in order, the one you seek is between 137 and 139."

He quickly dismissed her by going back to his files. To India this was a slap in the face compared to the last places she had visited but she was tougher than that. Feeding off her inbred tenacity she asked in a stern voice, "And where might 137 and 139 be located?"

"Back of the room, by the exit door" he replied without looking up.

India turned and marched away toward the back of the room in search of her book.

Across the shelves she counted 130, 133, 135, coming to 138. It slid easily but than it fell into her hands like a boulder. Lugging it to one of the tables in the room she flopped it down with relief. Taking a breath gave her time to notice that there were others in the room clearly doing the same ancestral legwork.

At another table a pair of older gentlemen were happily involved in discoveries of deeds and relatives new to them. Noticing India's stare they piped up, "We didn't realize our great grandfather had so many wives! Signed land over to each of them. He was both generous and a gigolo!" With that they both began laughing.

She shared in their bliss with a smile and a nod.

On another table behind her a woman was quietly speaking into a tiny tape recorder. Shaped like a fireplug the lady had not one, but several of the large tomes open in front of her. Glancing up at India she gestured a grin and went back to her inquest.

Book 138 rested in front of India. Pulling it open she discovered every page had been written in long hand. Ancient calligraphy penned in ink for each certificate of ownership written long ago to finalize the agreements between men now long dead. Finding page 87, the agreement on the deed was between a Thomas Lindsey and Thomas Curran but her grandfather's address was Saratoga Springs, New York. The year was 1867 and the contract had been recorded in New Port. The land encompassing 1904 acres had been sold to Curran who had in this agreement listed himself as a sheep farmer.

The cosigners were people that India had no knowledge of, 'Probably, just witnesses of the proceedings that day.' She thought, 'Thomas Curran is listed here, and a wife Elizabeth, and two children, Isabella and Winston. That must have given his family some insurance that they would inherit the land in case of his death. But that doesn't make sense. They are not the names on the graves in the Millwheel cemetery!'

India read on finding descriptions detailing trees, rocks, creeks and lakes used for markers along the edges of the land, with noted smaller tracks of property listed as appurtenances.

So, thought India, 'Thomas Curran did not grow up in Kentucky in the 1800's, but then not too many people did other than Indians.' Scanning the deed she now searched for any mention of the Parker family. Her investigation today had brought her so much closer to her roots but not solved the question of when her great grandfather had split the land for the Parker family to purchase.

'When was this done?' India thought, 'And who were those women in the cemetery? Had Thomas Curran been a Mormon? In the graveyard their tombstones showed him and his wives dying on the same day.' She closed her eyes and tried to envision their deaths, making her heart pound.

Chapter 18
A DEATH at the BREEDERS CUP

A cold chill lay across Kentucky, late October mornings opening with a gray overcast rather than the warm blue skies of July and August.

Speeding across the fields the young foals found that racing would warm them, so race they did. From the barns the workers watched hoping that common sense would stop the colts before the wooden fences did.

India was studying the results of last summer's Bloodstock sale when the phone rang carrying with it the voice of an old friend.

"Next week, November 7th, where will you be?"

It was India's childhood friend Abigail Culver.

"Oh brother," India replied, "I supposed here at home watching the big race. You'll be at the track no doubt. Lucky girl."

"Finally, its back in Kentucky! Breeders Cup is wonderful, but in the last few years I've been following my trainer to a lot of cities with weird hotels, then sleeping in campers and cots, from Hollywood Park to Woodbine."

"Its good news to have you back in town. It must be crazy at Churchill Downs with the Breeders Cup race in what, ten days?"

"About that. Say, I talked to my trainer Tie Anderson about you. Told him all about your breeding farm in Alexandria. Wants to meet you, said I could invite you to join us on the backside if nothing goes wrong before then."

"Holy cow. That's fantastic! How long has it been? Two years? I haven't seen you since that yearling sale at Keenland."

"Three, and it will be so nice to have you to experience the day with. Of course we'll be working."

"Of course." India knew that there were no free rides for a groom on Breeders Cup day but she was excited to help out just the same.

"I can't leave the horses to meet you. I could leave your name at the guard shack. Security will be very tight. I'll be on the backside all night so come early. Do you think you could find your own way inside to join me? It will save time."

"Don't worry about me finding you," Boasted India, "I have my own ways of getting inside Churchill Downs."

The Breeders Cup races had not attracted India Curran in the past few years. Her schedule would not allow her to venture off Millwheel Farm to witness those fabulous race days taking place in such majestic locations as Hollywood Park, California, or Woodbine racetrack in Canada. It would have been exciting, no doubt, but traveling was impossible as the farm called for India's full time attention. This year it was returning to Kentucky and she swore to go down and visit the backside of Churchill Downs and take in the entire day with her friend Abigail. Only the Kentucky Derby attracted a larger crowd.

Growing up, Abigail Culver had been her partner in crime. Both girls had been raised on the bluegrass, covered in horses. Their lives revolved around the sounds of speeding hooves, the feel of the saddle, even the smell. What a great smell. Abigail once told India that horses smelled like love. India's mother did not always agree. While shampooing the ratted black hair in the bathtub her mother would remind her young daughter that equine sweat was not considered a perfume.

For the past five years Abigail Culver relished the title of 'Head Groom' for one of the leading trainers at Churchill Downs. After their phone conversation she wanted India to show up, no excuses, even Fed-Exing a jacket for her to wear. Working for trainer Tie Anderson, Abigail had responsibilities of overseeing ten mounts each day. On that Breeders Cup weekend one of Tie's four-year-olds was running in a stakes race late on the card, the turf mile. Even with so much to do, Abigail was thrilled to be sharing this race day with a fellow equestrian such as India Curran. Bosom buddies, horses, hay and harness equaled heaven.

So they agreed to meet early.

Abigail said, "Be there about 4am to help feed and water. Then there will be legs to wrap, some grooming, saddling. Riders need to breeze a few colts. There's only a short time to watch any of the big races, but we will definitely need to catch the Classic at the end of the day."

That Saturday morning India entered the backside of the track with a local veterinarian she knew as a friend. Security for the track was always an issue, and this race day included thoroughbreds that had arrived from around the world to participate. As they drove past the backside security booth India just smiled and waved at the guard shack. This would be fun.

Finding Abigail was no problem. The long barns were marked with large numbers. India glanced across the grounds noticing the Twinspires. They stood as always, sentries of this racecourse since the spring of 1895, keeping peaceful surveillance over the historical grounds below.

Large massive bodies crossed the alleyway blocking India's path. Like giant athletes with coats sleek like gun metal, each animal had the strength to travel 42 miles per hour on a straightaway. She considered each a work of art.

Although it was sunup, the backside was already a circus of television cameras, interviewers and commentators surrounding the trainers for their stories, predictions and exaggerated opinions of their entries. The girls found one another. Each wore the racing jackets representing the owner's farm. Red with yellow amulets on the sleeves and a big yellow star on the back, a smaller version of this jacket would be worn by the jockeys later that day. Both also sported blue jeans making the two female grooms look identical, with their short dark hair and lithe frames. While hugging, some of the racing team commented on the girl's similarities.

Abigail included India in the day's chores immediately. "This chalkboard lists everyone's jobs. We still
need to send the bugboys out for a short breeze, then get
the coats off the rest of these horses. Also, I have a rank
five-year-old that I could use help with when the ferrier
comes."

Behind their stalls on a grassy area Tie was being
held hostage by a group of racing paparazzi. Everyone was
asking questions fast, scribbling notes. Abigail needed to
ask the trainer about a missing can of a drawing salve
called Ichthammol, but stood quietly with India near the
chaos. The dawn brought out sleepless owners, their colts
drifting on and off the track, and breeders watching to
see how their offspring were performing. Mixing with
the monoliths on four legs it was easy to miss the large
man standing under the oaks. Hands in the pockets of
his long black cashmere topcoat he sported sunglasses
and a fedora. With the cool sunny weather that morning
his attire did not attract any attention.

Chattering to the crowd, Tie Anderson was puffed
up over facts surrounding his colt, "He did five furlongs
in 100.20 earlier this week and has not done that well
since the spring meet at Keenland!"

But Abigail was on a mission. She needed to ask about
the misplaced medicine, so pushing through the crowd
she whispered to Tie, he answered, and she slipped away
glad to be away from the madness.

"Did you find out?" India asked.

"Yes, someone never unpacked it. Still in the box."
Abigail stated as they marched back to the stalls.

Behind them the tall man had waited to distance himself before following the two young women.

"I'll be ready to wrap this colt soon so lets get those leggings rolled, wash the old medicine off and wipe on the tar."

Opening the can India coughed, "That stuff smells like gasoline!"

"That's for sure, and its hell to handle, very sticky."

The treatment they were administering to was inside the stall of a 2-year-old colt nervously experiencing his first time at the track. Having been hit by another colt's back legs out of the shoot the day before, the impact had broken some skin. The girls spoke gently, but consistently, letting the colt know their position inside the stall at all times. Leery, his head high and eyes wide, he was uncertain of these two strangers who might add to his pain.

The tall dark man stood down the aisle-way, placing himself in the shadows and contemplated his chore, "Because of my occupation this endeavor was simply a matter of course. It would be less trouble if I knew which girl was which...then I wouldn't have to do this twice." He could hear the girls dialog from where he stood, their quiet demeanor to pacify the colt's restlessness. A boy in a similar racing jacket stepped close and the tall man, catching his attention asked, "Do you know those two grooms, the young ladies attending to that colt down the way?"

In a broken Spanish the boy answered, "Abigail Culver, our manager and a friend, that's all I know." With that he grabbed a halter from the wall and sped off.

"Not very helpful," Thought the Reaper, *"But it's a fifty fifty chance to satisfy my needs. At the end of the day I'll know*

if Millwheel has the same woman presiding as its owner or if there's an opening for new leadership!" He grinned, listening to the activity around him, smelling the sweat, oats, and leathers.

Abigail made a request, "This tar is so firm in the can, I can't get it out with my fingers. India...go back to the tack room. You'll see a spatula there. That would help to smear this crap around on his cannon bone."

Leaving the stall India set out in search of the tool. Entering in the tack room she found Tie Anderson lifting a tiny racing saddle from a peg. He asked, "How's that colt's leg, any swelling?"

Before India could speak a horse's scream came from down the aisle. Bangs, exploding like shotgun blasts, several times against a hard surface from the same location.

With no thought India was running, the trainer on her heels. They were back at the stall in seconds. The colt was circling, throwing his enormous body against the wooden walls, panicking, pacing to escape. Where was Abigail?

Tie threw open the door, lunging at the colt to grab the lead line. Several other grooms were already running to assist, pushing past India's small body knowing that this stallion could eat her for breakfast.

As the colt jumped out of the small containment, Tie was already down on his knees in the corner, saying nothing. India stepped in to see where her girlfriend might be hidden.

Blood covered most of the body, the yellow amulets and star now matched the red of the jacket. Bone, teeth, and skin could be found hanging from the wall and across the straw. Legs spayed out and her arms crushed, little of the young woman was left to destroy.

❧

Recipe for Death;

Take one Sociopath
Mixed with a large portion of Grim Reaper
Add Natural Disasters
Human Error
Sprinkle with Disease and War

Serve at Room Temperature

A funeral was not necessary. Rather a memorial service was planned for the following Wednesday. Cremated, Abigail's body would be scattered the following spring along trails that she had loved riding throughout her life.

India had left the track long before Tie Anderson's colt ran. Like a darkness, the change in morale covered the entire racing team. Even their 4-year-old entry knew. Being led by the wrong groom from the backside to the paddock, saddled by the wrong attendant and the depression of the jockey made the colt edgy, producing only a fifth place showing.

Arriving back at Millwheel was only a momentary relief. Climbing out of the car India had forgotten that she was still wearing the racing colors sent to her from Abigail to wear on race day. Removing the jacket she opened the truck of her car and tossed it in. "Deal with that later."

The news of the accident had reached beyond the track. Bits of information had trickled off the news stations, so as she slammed the trunk closed her farm personnel instantly surrounded her. The group was in sympathy but India wanted Abigail's death put aside for now.

After a hug from Jeff she asked, "Any problems here?"

Her green eyes were still red from the tears shed on the return from Louisville. Wiping them once more she listened to the farm manager's uneventful report. "Okay," India whispered, "Sounds like things are peaceful here. For that I am grateful. Now a walk would be good, help me sleep tonight."

Away from the barn area long gloomy shadows spread across the fields and hills. Only the tops of the leafless trees on the ridges reflected any light left at the end of the tragic day. Wanting to catch a glimpse of any riders coming in late, India walked off, calling her dog, Maggie, to join her.

Coldness traveled over the pasture driving black birds from their perches to fly in unison to more sheltered roosts. The brittle air caused India to wish she had a scarf for her face. So close to the night this short trek out may have been a bad idea. Her feet were beginning to freeze, the consequence of still wearing the same shoes she had worn at the track. With the dampness of the ground rising up her thoughts jumped back to Abigail, dead.

"Are you out here with me tonight Abigail, or have you already floated away?" Tears fell as she remembered the two of them as kids. "Wherever you are I know your riding. Along creeks, through deep fields into the woods.

I want to be with you. I want to gallop away and laugh out loud with you again. Manes in our faces, strong legs flying under our mounts, we should be together. Don't ride away. Please, please, wait for me. The horses we had as children are waiting. They're pawing the ground in anticipation of our return. Lets saddle them again together and fly across the fields of our youth, you and I."

India could see her warm breath leaving her lips as she spoke into the emptiness.

The darkness of evening was almost complete, but a movement far off held an image that was possible to see if she squinted. Only a shadow, the sinister form floated effortlessly from the Sycamore tree swing toward the small family cemetery down the hill. Maggie turned and trotted back for the farmhouse alone. India was startled. Her dog had never left her side before. Turning back toward the graves she watched the apparition solidify, becoming more opaque. It appeared to walk a few steps, then stop. India couldn't remove herself from observing this spectacle, regardless of the danger. She had never felt a supernatural presence on the farm before. Shifting a few feet over, the figure seemed to pause once more. Time seemed to stand still. It now had turned to face India and the farm. Halting for a moment to take in the view, it then dissolved.

Chapter 19

NEW YORK, GOLD COINS and CAMELS

Tall windows of the history class faced north on to the football fields. Trees edging the stadium had been without leaves for weeks now and the cold autumn weather demanded players wear extra warm-ups, gloves, and hats. Students attending late afternoon classes taught by the history teacher, Nicolas Curran, tended to pay more attention to the activities out on the field than inside his room. He was not surprised to see them wanting to be out there. He had the fantasy of running away as well.

"Today we need to move along with this session on Ancient Roman—Greek religion and superstition. Next week we will be covering Roman wars and Greek tragedies. Perhaps the tales of torture will peak your interests? Lots to go over."

Of the 30 or so students in the room, mainly juniors, only a few of his pupils lifted their heads to regard him. Mr. Curran strived to interest the kids with exciting historical accounts each week. Sometimes it worked. Or not. "So lets start, take notes, you will be tested on this at the end of the quarter."

He turned to face the blackboard. "Charon's Obol" taking the chalk he scribbled 'Charon' on to the board, "Was believed to be connected to death between the 6th and the 4th centuries B.C. After a death it was customary that the family or someone present would place a coin, metal leaf tablets or a gilded cross over or into the cadavers mouth, then the burial could take place. Why you ask?"

The only response was the sound of girls talking in the corner. Mr. Curran waited until they finished, gave them a dirty look and then carried on with his lesson.

"Glad you asked!" He smiled, "Charon was the ferryman that took souls to the 'other side'. The recently deceased needed to travel after death with Charon on his ship across the rivers Styx or Acheron. These rivers divided the world of the living from the world of the dead. But there was a charge to make the trip. The fee, so to speak, was the coin. Typically called the 'obol', lifting his chalk Curran wrote the word on the board, "Charon, as the ferryman of the dead, delivered souls to King Hades. So during these cultural times for the Roman's and Greek's, Hades was otherwise known as the place for the dead, or also known as the underworld."

A hand went up, "So where's heaven? They get hell and no other options?"

"Heaven is from the Christian religion. That came much later."

A girl in the front row spoke up, "And what happens if this procedure doesn't happen, say a guy dies away from his family or something, like at a war somewhere?"

"Good question! The historians and priests of that time believed that if the fee was not paid than the person could not become a passenger on Charon's ship and the passenger would be doomed to go back to the world of the living, wandering for another 100 years."

The girl interrupted, "So whats so bad about that? Some religions believe in reincarnation. We learned that last quarter, remember?"

Rather than discuss her rudeness Mr. Curran said "And I'm glad you were paying attention! A returning soul did not travel back to the earth as the same person, but instead roamed or haunted the world as a lost spirit."

Curran hadn't noticed the time until several students were closing notebooks and searching the floor for their backpacks.

"Thank you all! Students that asked questions today will be noted." He began arranging papers on his desk for the next class as students made their way out the door, pushing past him with bumps and chatter, "Hang onto your notes, and read those last two chapters!"

Holding the mash of homework papers in front of him he glanced around, and it became apparent to him that he was shouting to an empty room.

That had been his last class for the day and even though he wanted to escape there was still more work to be done. Parents needed to be called this evening unaware of their children's poor grades. Curran would get to that later. His neglected answering machine was an embarrassment. Important messages ignored. Alerts shouting, "Call back now" overlooked. He remembered his students and their shortcomings, finding the ugly comparison a reason to groan. A few teachers were asking about field trips and one message from the principle was asking when was he going to call back about the field trips. Great.

One phone message that could not be identified was from someone named India Curran and she left a return long distance phone number. It appeared that she was inquiring about a deed or something about a Curran family in the New York area during the 1800's.

Nicolas made a face, "No wonder she found me with only a few Curran's in the phone book. Geez, my schedule is too hectic. I'll put off calling her until next week." He sighed, "But she did seem a bit anxious. How should I handle this?"

Nicolas Curran sat down at his desk in the history room. He began struggling through answers to student's tests hoping to make a dent in the stack of homework. At the same time he was trying, to no avail, to ignore the message left from one 'India Curran'.

The following Friday he found his afternoon class mostly deserted. Handing out a short written test he approached one of the students, a soccer player with high grades and asked of the young man, "Would you mind keeping an eye on things while I run to the office?"

"Easy squeezy, lemon peasy" replied the student.

"Great- be right back." With that Mr. Curran shot out of the room.

Entering the school office it appeared as empty as his class. Already the Principal and Vice-Principal had left for the weekend. Scanning papers from his mail Nicolas was trying to stay ahead of the game before next week by checking for any changes in the schedule. Finding nothing in his "In Box" he started to head out the door when the last remaining member of the office staff, Patty, summoned him, "Mr. Curran, Mr. Curran! You have a Fax. Just came through. Haven't had time to put it in your box."

Curran turned back to retrieve it.

"I hope it was OK. A lady called this morning. Knew you where a teacher here. I hope I didn't step on anybody's toes. Figured that if she was sending it here and not your home, I sort of thought it would be okay, so, I gave her our fax number."

Rolling his eyes he thanked her and took the paper. Walking back into the hallway he stopped to examine it, finding photocopies of coins on the page. The hallway began to swirl around as he instantly thought of his twin brother Nathan, before his disappearance. A cold sweat covered him. Three years earlier Nicolas' brother had sent glossy pictures of the same coins. Those coins had been the reason why Nathan needed to dive off the coast of Crescent City into the Pacific.

Nicolas sat down on a bench close to the drinking fountain. Feeling hot all over it was impossible not to think back on the conversation they had then, "How come you want to go down that far?" Nicolas begged at the time, "Just for a couple of coins? I can loan you money if you need it. This is a bad idea brother. You could get a job at a dive shop, steady wages. Much safer."

"This is my moment!" Nathan jumped in, "I've been working to get to this point with Jeremy for years. We've done the homework, researched the wreck of the Brother Jonathan, practiced and prepared for this. We can't stop now. I'm not worried and neither should you be."

There had been silence before Nathan added, "People are afraid to die only if they have not lived enough."

Nicolas could hear this conversation in his head as if it were yesterday. The last comment had hurt, the two of them disagreeing as usual and gaining nothing as usual. Now he held a fax showing coins just like the ones that Nathan had mailed about his discovery of the 1865 shipwreck. Nicolas relaxed his fist that was crushing the paper.

"Why now?" He wondered. "With Nathan's death I lost half of my soul and in the last three years I'd been struggling to rebuild myself...With this women's investigation will I be able to hold things together, keep moving away from the pain?"

Since the drowning he had stuffed everything from Nathan away. Nicolas had found a large box and shoved his brother's items into a downstairs closet. It held a few rugby shirts, some shoes, a yearbook. Nathan was the jock. Nicolas was the geek. Their dreams and ambitions had been so different yet they had always remained close. Nathan had dubbed his twin brother the 'King of Common Sense,' which at times caused Nicolas to wince. Nic never took chances, unlike his crazy brother who saw nothing odd about running across train trestles while whistles blew, or climbing through windows of abandoned houses. That was Nathan all over. A happier kid couldn't be found. Nicolas had every reason to be gray before the age of twenty.

Saturday morning Nicolas barely remembers dialing the phone to locate the woman from Kentucky. In his head were only pictures of the faxed coins that she had sent. Although it was early he had no appetite for breakfast so this seemed a good time to get things straightened out.

It was early, 6:30am, when the phone rang. Eventually a man picked up. "Millwheel Farm, Jeff speaking."

Nicolas wasn't sure if this was the correct number but he needed to ask, "Is there a Ms. Curran there?"

"Yes, but she is out in the field. Would it be possible for you to call her back on her cell phone?"

Nicolas wrote down the different number, and dialing it waited through several rings until it was answered by a more familiar voice, "Oh, shit…this is India Curran."

"Have I got the right number?"

"Oh boy, sorry about that. My foal heard the phone ring, spooked and ran off. I thought she'd be ready for a trip out today, guess I was wrong."

Nicolas did not quite know how to respond to that but he asked, "So you're the one trying to contact me?"

Although India had never spoken to the caller until now, she felt correct inquiring, "Is this the party I have been trying to reach in New York? If it is, thank you for returning my call."

"Curiosity drove me to do it. I forgot about the difference in hours. Did I find you at a bad time?"

"This is mid morning on a Kentucky horse farm. We'll be having lunch by 10am."

Nicolas' own equine experiences growing up in Saratoga reminded him that horses slept little. It would figure that a farm crew would have a sleepless schedule as well. "Are you doing research into genealogy, of Curran's that may be in your family tree?"

India giggled, "Not like that exactly. My family name Curran goes back to 1868 in Kentucky but there seems to be a land deed problem here and I'm having some difficulty finding what I need. While nosing around the archives in our area it came to my attention that the name Curran was originally from your area of New York. Is that true?"

"Any skeletons in the closet are still hidden at my relatives. I have never been aware of connections to Kentucky from here in Saratoga, except that in my profession nothing surprises me."

"Yes, I understand that you're a history teacher there. Fascinating." An unexpected smile grew on India's face.

"My expertise is in global government, cultures and their leaders over the centuries. I teach a type of "Historical Domination" class, you might say."

"I'm impressed. We could use more leaders." India hesitated, wanting to know more and hating to change the subject to something as dismal as Millwheel's predicament. "Unfortunately, my problem rises from a legal issue that could badly affect our farm. It appears I have found a link between a man named Thomas Curran from Saratoga Springs and here. He signed our legal deed back in 1867 in the city of New port, Kentucky and apparently he began negotiations from New York, but did not arrive here until later, in 1868. Have you any knowledge at all of this transaction in your family?"

"I have some older relatives that may have information."

Nicolas then became silent, thinking about the intrigue surrounding a man, almost 130 years ago traveling west alone to claim a new land. At the same time Indians lived across the Commonwealth battling strange illnesses, a lack of food, and new settlers. This member of his family had been a sort of leader, one brave enough to travel nearly 800 miles across the country perhaps even with a wife and children just after the Civil War. That had leadership qualities! If his school could see this as a trip of value then perhaps the Principle could allow him a few days to do research of his own. Bring it back to the students as a "Historical Fact Finding Mission?"

For an instant his thoughts skipped back to his brother Nathan and the coins, but he knew not to go there now.

Provoked by his peaked interest he said, "I will do what I can from here and send you in the mail anything that I can find. Later, if possible I might spend a day or weekend in Kentucky, but that would be a long shot."

This was more than India had hoped for. After the attorney's call and Abigail's death a light was now shining from the end of the tunnel. She told Nicolas that she would keep in touch and with that bid him good-bye.

The young filly had disappeared after the buzzing from the cell phone. India grumbled, "She'll be back at the farm by now screaming for her mother and tripping over her lead rope." Starting the long trek up the field she hoped that the foal had not broken its neck. Up since 4am, India had wanted to beat Flip, Jeff and the rest of the kids from bringing out the stallions. That activity would have caused greater anxiety in the foal. Mares too would be pawing the floors of their stalls for release wanting to take their offspring for a romp. India chose to handle the foal on the ground long before the farm woke up. Reaching the knoll that overlooked the barn area India could see all of the crew, about 8 people, gathered near the round pens. She started to run, panicked that the foal had stepped on its lead and perhaps broken a leg. Out of breath India was now able to see above the six foot fencing that made up the corrals what all the interest was about.

"Camels!" she huffed, "What's going on? Escapees from the Louisville Zoo?"

Then she remembered, "Where's that filly? Did anyone see her when she came back?" The fact that the filly was out of Jewel Princess by Storm Cat made the well being of the expensive foal her number one priority. To hell with camels.

Jeff answered, "We grabbed her coming into the barn. No problems, although she was hot so we threw a sweat sheet over her."

Looking at the exotic creatures standing quietly in the round pen convinced India that the farm crew was capable of more than loose foals. Bewildered, everyone turned to their boss for answers.

"Don't look at me! I was up at dawn and there was no trace of zoo life when I walked across the yard. Is one of you starting a camel racing club?"

Now back to staring at the two massive animals everyone snickered. A camel in each pen, the crew of employees found them surprisingly peaceful. Tall and shaggy they chewed on grass found growing along the cracks of the inside wall. Each a dusty brown with one lump and droopy chins, they were both quite beautiful in an alien way. Seeing no crisis looming India walked closer and stepped up upon the observation shelf around the outside of the pen for a closer look.

"Do I know the owner of these things? Does one of our breeders have some sort of agreement with Millwheel that I'm not aware of? Anyone, speak up."

A stable-hand, Jeannie, knew India well enough to interject, "Regardless, the stallions were scheduled to be worked as usual in these pens before lunch. You'll have to make a decision on who goes where."

Flip spoke up, "Guess the boys have the day off. Can't take a chance on some unknown germ carried by these camels that might spread into our breeding stock. I don't know about Dromedaries but our vet might have a hard time curing a desert disease if one of the stallion gets sick."

India answered, "It looks to me that they don't want to run off anytime soon, so throw them a little hay and fill some water buckets. I'll make some phone calls." With that said, India walked to the mare shed to check on the runaway foal.

Chapter 20
MILL'S FOLLY

'Skeletons in the closet. Nicolas Curran had mentioned that in their phone call earlier. With history changing so rapidly over the last 150 years right here on Millwheel soil, it would figure that ancestors might have been killed, died strangely, drowned in one of the ponds, or burned to death in a fire.' India's mind was reeling as she took the time to carefully examine the legs on the Storm Cat filly. Gratefully she found not a scratch and promised herself that in the future to have Jeff or Flip walk along with a second lead to steady the young foal.

Right after the attorney Damien Alva had first contacted India, Aunt Ginny had mentioned visiting their old neighbor Jesse Southgate. New information might be available, but if her neighbor solved the deed problem now then might that stop Nicolas Curran from visiting Kentucky? She hoped not. He sounded sweet. Maybe too sweet, sort of a "Melvin Milquetoast" type.

"Oh God, I wish I had the time to be fickle!" She sighed.

Putting the morning's camel dilemma on hold India drove over to Jesse's old house on Woeste road.

Now, about 9:30am it was still early and getting colder. India pulled her leather jacket tight as she and Maggie spun around the far northern side of Millwheel, turning left onto a road that trailed along the edge of the crick shared with her farm.

The old colonial brick home stood alone between the cottonwoods and sycamore trees. Behind it ran the stream that meandered both across his property and Millwheel's. The home, built in the early 1800's by slaves, showed each stone to be still tight in place. To find a chink of missing mortar among the thousands of carefully laid rows would be difficult, even today.

Windows were tall and narrow. Starting from just a few feet above the weedy lawn they reached up to the second floor, then after a few rows of brick began climbing once more nearly to the eaves. Scruffy patches of grass edged with bushes of blackberry, forsythia and taxus made up the landscaping. The bur oak trees shadowing the house would have been just sprouts when in 1803 Lewis and Clark had first crossed the land to meet each other for the first time in Louisville. A towering canopy of gnarled branches scratched at the pitched roof in the morning breeze.

India knew better than to knock, knowing that her neighbor was hard of hearing. Stepping in front of the heavy oak door she simply pushed it open enough to call inside. "Jesse, are you here?"

She spotted his wheelchair turned away from the tall south facing windows. Fast asleep, India entered and stood a distance away to beckon him once more, "Jesse, are you reading?"

Opening his eyes with a jerk, he took a moment to recognize her. " Yes. Just trying to finish this book. Its on deep sea diving, you know." Straightening up he adjusted his seat and went on, "Wanted to get through it before the library accuses me of stealing."

Moving the chair into the middle of the room he asked India, "Open that door. Its hotter than hell in here. The families that built this house, worked the land, needed to keep the heat in here for later, after dark, not now." He squirmed his body in the tiny-wheeled chair until his thin frame was more upright. Rubbing his face he looked around his desk, finding a glass of water, "Where have you been? Haven't seen you in forever. Thought of calling you though. Got a son-in-law, has a colt with a bowed tendon. Was sore before a race, now the horse could be lame for good. Looking for a place to lay-up. Any room for him over there at your farm?"

"I'll have to get back to you on that." She looked around and found an ancient yew wood-bow back chair to sit in. "Have a problem. Maybe you can help me. Your family had 300 acres on the Licking River back when they settled here. Did any of them visit out our way, at Millwheel I mean?"

"320 acres, and it was September 1857 when they came. Southgate's were everywhere, on both sides of us. Owned more land than what we had and lots of riverbank. My family's cabin floated off twice back then. They say our property flooded often, so they came live here. Learned our lesson. I doubt this old place would ever float away."

India smiled, with both of them sitting inside the massive brick fortress she felt secure. Around her the walls were built with Flemish bond bricks. This house would out live him and her as well.

She interjected, "Seems the Parker family living across from us years ago, they owned that parcel. I'm trying to find their deed, a deed separate from ours. Their graves are there. I remember Virgil, Salem, an Isaac Parker? All have stones with their names. But the only existing deed found by some slipshod attorney shows our two properties still connected."

"They didn't live there long. Died, you know in a fire. That's all. On the same day, too. Then everyone left, skedaddled. Don't know why." Jesse took another drink of water, "I used to hunt that. We all did. Turkeys, beautiful birds, all over the Parker place."

India shook her head in agreement. "Maggie and I have followed behind gangs of turkeys, to fat to fly. On the ridge they walk in front of us until becoming annoyed, then they'd run away into the forest to hide."

"Been to the top, of the hill I mean? Sure you have. That ridge has another grave." He said opening his eyes wide. "Not a Parker. It's a shallow grave, rocks, some dirt. Ever seen the knoll on the top? Grass is different, too. Might be Indians. They have graves that stand up from the ground like that. Maybe it was a body with disease. Someone who the Parkers or your family wanted to keep away from the other family members.

"I've ridden past that little pile of dirt all my life. Did just last month." India replied. "Perhaps a long time ago it was a place someone started to build a home, began digging and then quit."

"I don't know where the Parkers went or where they put their deed but my Grandfather and I used to hunt that when I was a boy. He told me that the dirt pile was a grave. Gave it a name too. Named after a person, that pile."

There was silence in the room as they both considered the mystery. Jesse's thoughts traveled back to a day spent 75 years earlier with his grandfather, chasing down birds, both enjoying the forest together. India let him stay in there with his memories. She envied Jesse who at one time had lived with three generations of Southgate's on this land.

"Mill, or something." Jesse whispered.

"I'm sorry, did you say something?"

Looking up at India with his pale eyes he repeated, "Mill. That was the name of the dirt pile. Mill something. Two names my grandfather used to call it. Not windmill. No. Not sawmill either. Haven't had to think about this for a long time."

"It must be the name Millwheel, of the farm, or the lumber mill that had been there for a time." She answered.

"Nope. Had something to do with the grave." He rubbed his head and asked India to get him a fresh glass of water. While she was in the other room she could hear him speaking to himself and she hoped he had not been too weak for a surprise visit such as this. Thinking to leave soon she carried the drink back to him. Reaching up his bony hand he said, "Mill's Folly."

"Pardon?"

"That was the name of the dirt pile, or grave. Grandpa Richard used to refer to it as 'Mill's Folly.'"

Heading back India remembered that she still had to deal with the camels in her round pen. Arriving at her farmhouse she needed to find the owners so she planned on making phone calls from her office. Just out of curiosity after entering the room she went directly to her desk and slid open the drawer on the top right hand side. The locket was still there.

India stopped.

So were several other pieces of jewelry. A puzzling collection. She counted two watches, which looked to be gold, a ring, a pillbox with a fragile enamel lid and a silver bracelet. Ernie had found the first piece a few days ago in Willy's stall.

"Is my horse becoming a kleptomaniac?" India sighed, hoping her bad humor would help the situation.

She held the bracelet up to the sunlight of her office window. "With 30 boarders on the farm I'll need to leave a large notice on the tack room wall concerning these items." She studied the jewelry carefully, "These were keepsakes. Long ago families would have given these as gifts. This beautiful silver bracelet, it would have been very dear to buy, expensive even today."

She looked it over remembering no recollection of any guests wearing items as lovely as this when they rode. "Anyone at the farm would have warned a rider against wearing something this rare."

The tiny chain was made up of an innumerable number of woven links to make the piece almost resemble lace. The connecting lock was made up of two small flat silver leaves holding a hook. On the leaves were engraved the letters CVS. "How lovely. But where had these pieces come from?" She became curious about the rest and reaching her hand down to investigate the others,

SLAM!

With a loud bang the drawer flew closed nearly missing her fingers. India jerked back and, losing her balance, fell flat on the floor.

❦

As a rule the Millwheels farm ran according to the needs of the animals. Before sunup the horses were fed massive containers of grain that went in the front-end at 6am and by noon came out the backend. Then the cats. They were easy to find near the grain. Camped out with tails twitching they stayed glued in place with a mandate on the mice that tried, but failed, to steal what horse feed would drop onto the barn floor. Dogs ate next, then people.

India had no time for any of these chores today, having others to run the farm. Soon Nicolas Curran's plane would be landing in Hebron, Kentucky. The young history teacher had called back explaining to India that the Principal had found a flimsy reason to allow the young educator permission to travel to the Bluegrass State.

Nicolas explained over the phone, "And holding his head high while waving a finger in the air Principal Swiggert announced, "Your family's legacy remains a puzzle unless you research the trail that Thomas Curran traveled. We'll be looking for you to return with a chronicled saga to share with your class. Or else."

227

India pulled a brush through her hair, then lipstick, mascara, socks, jeans, a sweater and jacket. Moving across the compound to her pickup truck she called "Maggie!" and opened the door for her dog to jump in.

Arriving on time she stayed in the truck and waited near the exit doors marked 'Arriving Flights.' Nicolas had been informed that she drove an old Chevy three-quarter-ton, hunter green. As he came out from the terminal she was pleased to find him easy to look at. Smiling, he spotted her right away as well and throwing his suitcase into the bed introduced himself through the window.

"India? I'm Nic." He said quickly, extending his hand across the bench seat.

Waving him in she said, "Glad you could come. Climb in and we're gone."

Adjusting his seat belt, Nicolas was surprised by his first kiss.

"Maggie, we just met him. Now go lay back down. Sorry about that."

"Not at all. Cold and wet is how I like my kisses."

Chapter 21
STEAMBOAT HISTORY— JEFFERSON'S RETURN

From the Airport India described the situation so far with the attorney Damien Alva. Nicolas remained quiet, listening to her dilemma while at the same time taking in the scenery. Kentucky seemed to him much like Saratoga Springs with mossy green hills that rolled up and over the land, falling into a hollow to meet water, then climbing back up again toward a soft blue sky.

As they traveled Nicolas noticed large birds feeding along the roadsides. Freaks of nature, turkey vultures congregated as content carnivores tearing at their dead meals, stopping only to hop off the pavement with just enough time to avoid becoming road-kill themselves. In the moment Nic couldn't resist, "We have those in New York State too, although ours are better looking."

And he smiled at her.

As Maggie remained asleep in the back seat India blabbed on as she often did when nervous, about the farm, her family, local history and just about everything else. As she drove the conversation became increasingly one-sided so she stopped talking long enough to see if Nicolas was still in the car.

India thought to herself, *'He's thinking about the situation concerning Millwheel or the problems with the farm deed. Maybe the students in his class at the high school? What else would he have to think about on such a pretty morning as this?'*

Coming into Alexandria India knew of a corner tavern that served great Red Beans and Rice. Spicy fare for 11am but Nicolas had mentioned that his early flight had cancelled any plans for breakfast so she pulled in. They slid into a booth by a window, ordered and India decided to not speak any longer. She considered her theory, *'Eventually he'll have to say something or I'll have to kill him.'*

Fidgeting with his drink, Nicolas finally got the hint and began, "Doing a little research of my own." Quiet once more he waited to be saved by India's curiosity but she refused to take the bait. Sitting silently for a few minutes until the food arrived he knew he was licked. "Contacting my Great Aunt Louise I found a few old notes. Seems that our family had been in Saratoga Springs from the time that Thomas Curran had arrived on the boat from England across the pond around 1852." Nicolas cleared his throat, "He had started out in wool. With the Civil War ending our ancestors had built a small mill in Saratoga Springs."

He took another spoon full of the southern fare thinking that it would be easy to get hooked on the stuff. "Since 1788 the British had considered any wool mills built by the colonists illegal." He took another mouth full, "Following the war if 1812 the settlements were free to open their own mills and flourish. My grandfather landed in America from England at just the right time."

"And you being a history teacher, how could I guess?" India gave Nicolas a cute little smile.

Feeling brave he continued, "So the land around New York was becoming valuable, too precious to raise sheep on. That may have been what drove my great grandfather to go west. Apparently, he was looking for cheaper land. Anyway, with some research I found that sheep, like rabbits, were mass-producing in Indiana. In the year 1868 there were over eight million sheep in that state or about three sheep for every one person!"

India laughed out loud at the thought of white balls with four legs roaming vast fields like snow and leaving not a trace of grass. "So, assuming that the progress of the city pushed your Grandpa to leave, he still had a mill in New York or Saratoga still operating, and he had a wife and kids."

"It seems. Her name was Elizabeth and she had two kids, a boy and girl."

"Yup, Isabella and Winston." She boasted.

Nicolas was pleased, "How did you know that?"

"Found a copy of the Metes and Deeds in Alexandria."

"So we are partners in crime! That's good. Anyway, like I was saying, before he disappeared to Indiana or Kentucky other relatives had moved to Saratoga from England and that must have been a reason he could run off and leave his family like that. If his wife had been alone and helpless perhaps he would have stayed at the mill in New York and taken his chances."

India speculated, "People first coming to America from across the ocean back then were already savvy gamblers. Thomas Curran had crossed the sea for wealth and with the success in Saratoga he may have wanted more. I don't blame him for the vision of buying property in the west."

"But," Nicolas stated, "There's more. Elizabeth had saved a long letter from her family in England. Yada, yada, some lady talk, and then the writing became sympathetic, mentioning how bad to hear that Thomas had not returned from his trip west. There were questions about investigating to locate his whereabouts, even involving the military along the Ohio River at Fort Washington. Nothing, unfortunately beyond that."

India was surprised. It seemed that in the few days Nicolas had before this trip to Kentucky he had really done his homework.

"You've found out quit a bit. This information is wonderful."

He stood, stretching his long body to settle his meal. India tried not to stare but it was nice to see a man in shape. Better this than having met a different man from the plane, 105 years old and 200 pounds over weight. Lucky.

"Shall we go?" Nicolas grabbed India's hand and they left. As they pulled out of the parking lot a gray Mercedes Benz left as well.

Their first stop was not Millwheel but instead the Campbell County Historical Society. The sunny day and long afternoon ahead found them both full of new energy. Running up the long staircase to the second floor they could hear the big band music ahead. Once more she discovered Mike, the only volunteer, turning down the radio as they entered.

"Hello, India" Mike smiled and approached them both, "Still digging?"

"This is my friend Nicolas Curran. Nic, Mike." The two men shook hands as India pet a cat sunning itself on the wide windowpane.

"I'm glad you came back," Mike stood and carefully crossed the room to a shelf covered with stacks of paper, "Found this first, an old newspaper article about the explosion of the Steamboat Magnolia. The article was written the next day after it happened, in the New York Times." And with that Mike handed the copy to India.

"And why do I want to know about a boat that blew up a long time ago?"

"I had a thought about the year, 1868. Lots happened back then. Started looking at disasters, illnesses. Tragedies happened around every corner. So I had a hunch. What if your 'Thomas Curran' had gotten caught up in some mayhem that would complicate his trip to Campbell County? The division of Thomas Curran's land from the Parker Property is the treasure we seek, but your problems may have begun well before he arrived on his land."

"Mike, he's buried on our farm."

"You say he is, but after opening our computer file, I typed in his name. This article jumped up and as you can see he was injured on the Magnolia in March of 1868. How badly? If the boat exploded in 1868, how did he get to your farm to die years later?"

Nicolas asked, "What's the date on his stone?"

"1875," she answered.

"So, I got lucky," Mike stated as he handed more notes to the visitors, "After finding the manifest, or what there is here recorded from March 17, 1868, the Cincinnati Enquirer tells a story. A lot of speculation as to how many people were on board, with the 'Times' saying that there were 120 passengers, the 'Enquirer' says only 100. These were packet boats, like city buses, they went up and down the Ohio all day, delivering mail and people to different ports. Hard to say who was onboard. Lot of kids snuck on back then, wives tagged along next to their husbands, never signed their names on the register. But here under "Saved from the wreck" your grandfather is listed as 'slightly injured.'"

"See," India piped in, "He was probably fine. Maybe just burns or a bump on his head."

"But further down he's mentioned again. Seems he was carrying notes. A local gentleman named Doc Able found some papers, receipts. Your grandfather's name was on those items but your grandfather was nowhere around? Shouldn't he be walking about, looking along the shoreline for his lost documents?"

Nicolas wanted to know, "It says here that Thomas Curran was from Daver, Kentucky. Where's that?"

"Probably a misspelling," India corrected, "That must be Dover, on the Ohio River by Higginsport, but that's south of Alexandria.

Mike explained, "Staying at an inn I suppose. Left his clothes in Dover while he traveled to New Port Land Office. There, he would have picked up his deed papers with the Metes and Bounds. Then he turned around, got on the packet boat Magnolia to go upriver and next thing you know, it explodes! Happened all the time. Over 500 river steamers sank between 1850 and 1870. By the way, I have a copy of Kentucky Land Laws from the 1850's if you want it."

Nicolas was beginning to look a little worse for wear, having caught a plane out of New York early that morning. He excused both of them saying, "I believe we may have to take a rain check. I am still looking forward to seeing Millwheel and maybe getting a look at the family graves before dark."

India and Nic said their good-byes to Mike and headed for her old Kentucky home.

❧

Nicolas Curran never made it to the graves, a cemetery or even dinner. As they pulled into the yard he had already excused himself from any evening activities. Later when Ernie was sent to announce dinner he found only more proof of their new guest's exhaustion. "Dead to the world. He passed out with all his clothes on, even his belt. No shoes though, which is a good sign that he was conscious before he hit the bed."

Seated around the table the other employee's shared the humor with India.

"Could be worse. He could have fallen asleep in the truck and we would have had to carry him upstairs."

Jeff smiled, "More food for us!"

India sympathetically pointed out "He was a very tired man. Counting backwards, I figure if I picked him up from the plane at 9am, he had flown, what, an hour and a half, so he got to the airport about 5:30 to get on a 6:15 flight. Left his place to get to the airport on time, say around 4am?"

Sitting across the table from India, Jennie said, "I'd say you were lucky to get him as far as the Historical Society in one piece."

Their boss was still disappointed. "I so wanted you all to meet him. He was very nice and had already done a ton of digging to find out more about Millwheel's history. I've learned quite a bit. We should all be grateful. This could be the missing link that keeps the wolves from our door."

Jeannie swooned, "Did he talk much about New York? I've never been and it must be incredible."

"From what I could tell, he spends all is time in Saratoga Springs. It must be an engaging profession, as a teacher. And although I've never visited there either, he did say that the buzzards are better looking in New York State."

About 2am Nic's eyes popped open. He had to use the facilities but quickly came to the realization that he did not have any idea where the bathroom was or anything else for that matter. "Okay, I'm in Kentucky, on a horse farm...and I've been asleep." Looking down at his rumpled clothes he judged, "Or I may have been kidnapped, who knows?" Finding a dark hallway he dragged the wall with his palm searching for a switch. Ahead a door opened and the light from that room lit the area enough for Nicolas to keep from stumbling over a man that stepped out. Dressed in a green vest and old shirt the tall black man lifted his hand to pinch the wide brim of his leather hat in a silent greeting.

"Hello....I'm Nicolas Curran and I'm sort of new here, I mean in the house. Well, everywhere I suppose. Is that the bathroom?"

"No, it's across the hall, that door. Do you always walk in the dark?"

Nicolas chuckled, "I'll be better by morning. Right now I'm sort of getting the lay of the land. Have we met?"

"Not yet, no, but I'm not always at Millwheel. I move around quite a bit."

Sleet was hitting the windows at the end of the hall and wind whistled between the glass and pane. There was no moon, so blackness was the only view from the hall into the night outside. Nic shivered from the cold wanting to return soon to his bed and covers. "Hey, thanks for the help," Nicolas said as he followed the man's directions. Moving around him to open the door Nic asked, "I didn't catch your name...."

"Jefferson. Just Jefferson. Hope you like it here at Millwheel. Stay as long as you can. And, don't worry.... you'll get used to the dark.

Chapter 22
A GRAVE MENACE

Nicolas Curran tossed under the covers causing a cat sleeping by his feet to open its eyes and yawn. More flipping and the cat hit the floor at a run. After witnessing the escape Nic ran fingers through his greasy hair then across his cheeks to find short bristles had invaded his face during the night. Time to move. Rolling out of bed he made his way back to the bathroom starting a shower. Before stepping in he first looked down the hall to check if someone might be about. If India appeared would he ask her to join him? Slapping his own face, he turned to enter the hot water alone.

Once dressed it took but a moment to figure out that everyone was gone. He stood on the cold front porch listening for sounds. From a weeping cherry tree cardinals were listening as well, screaming in defiance to make him aware that any dried berries found were treasures already spoken for. Voices from a barn across the yard broke Nicolas's exchange with the birds.

Exiting from the building Flip saw him, waved, and after introductions he asked, "How was your night?"

"Great. You didn't wait dinner I hope."

"Naw, I ate yours, then mine."

"I suppose that I missed breakfast, too."

"Got that right, but lunch is at eleven so you still have that."

"Where's India?"

"She's tied up with a colicy mare in there," and Flip threw a thumb over his shoulder, "I'm waiting for the vet but you can go inside. Listen for the racket down that first row of stalls."

As he approached the wooden 12x12 boxstall he could hear unidentifiable noises waft out. Skylights above provided filtered sun down into the small space where three workers plus India moved around a mare that seemed unable to stand. "On the count of three..." They all pushed their hands under the huge body and together attempted to lift the mare onto her feet. The mare would have no part of it.

"Nicolas, walk over here by me, grab her under the butt. Jeannie, don't let your hands slip from her chest. Keep it moving up at the same time. Okay, one- two- three!"

As the mare sensed the new pair of strange hands her natural lack of trust plus the agony in her abdomen caused her to stand and protect herself from any additional pain. Once up she introduced herself to Nicolas by pinning her ears and showing her teeth. With pushing and pulling they finally moved her on to the cement aisle.

"Let's get her outside to a spot under that tree. If she goes down again well, at least she won't be so confined."

Nicolas waited until India had a moment for him, "I wanted to walk out to the graves with you but I guess you have your hands full."

"You go. I'll be along after the veterinarian pours some mineral oil down her throat. Probably need a pain-killer, too. So, you go. Over there," India pointed across the yard to the open field beyond, "If you walk about a mile to the right. Look for a tree line, then up on a hill is an old sycamore tree. It's just below on the slope."

It took Nicolas about twenty minutes to reach the small cemetery. A short black iron fence skirted numerous tombstones planted around the site. Trying the rusty gate seemed useless so he stepped over the fence and inside. He could view the stones from outside of the enclosure except that he found the etched names so shallow from years of rain that the writing was nearly illegible. A few names carved after 1890's were easily read;

Jeanna Marie Curran Born, 1892   Died, 1939

Franklin Harrison Curran   Born, 1898   Died, 1927

The cemetery was divided into sections of graves. Three more were to his right:

Riddle, Died 1881

Winston, Died 1869

Jeff son, Died 1885

Nicolas considered the stone, "Young boys dying so soon as to carry no last name but only identified as a man's son. Sad." Next to those a flat stone held the small statue of a lamb with the name 'Stropshire' carved beneath. Nic had a vision of a baby buried there, for a lamb on a tombstone usually represented innocence or a child's marker. "Stropshire is a country bordering Wales," Nicolas figured, "This baby comes from the right neighborhood for our investigation." But then he noticed two wool cards embedded in a cement stone below, "An important keepsake, perhaps? Maybe someone planted dead sheep here." Moving around through the brambles brought him close to a rock wall covered with thorns that kept the field dirt from washing down into the cemetery. The names on these tombstones were difficult to make out so he used his fingers softly to feel the indentations,

Emma Curran, Died August 8, 1875

A center stone read, Thomas Curran, Died August 8, 1875

And on the left, Rebecca Curran, Died August 8, 1875

He stopped to contemplate that this was the man who started the wild goose chase bringing him from Saratoga to Campbell County. The two women India had questions about were laid next to him, Rebecca and Emma. But how did Thomas know them? There was no mention of 'husband' or 'wive of.'

To the side of Emma's stone were two with writing;

Joseph Curran, Born 1872 Died 1911

Westley Curran, Born 1870 Died 1914

To Rebecca's left were laid two people under the same stone;

Elizabeth Curran Hansford 1873—1926

Wife of Barry K. Hansford 1870 - 1920

Movement caught Nic's eye. A swing hung below a large branch off an old white Sycamore on the hill above. The wind had caught it, moving it gently back and forth with the breeze. A squirrel pushing his nose through brown grass focused only on his hunt to find a nut that was buried beneath. Nicolas pulled up his collar and then shoved his hands deep into his jacket pockets. Reading the cold stones had made his fingers raw and cold.

As a history teacher he understood the deaths recorded all around him, but there was so much more to uncover. "Beneath this shared ground lay the first settlers. This land is their legacy. No wonder that India is frantic to protect her home. Everyone since 1868 worked to guarantee that this farm would always survive for generations of Curran's in the future."

A last corner of the cemetery produced graves under a old apple tree. Wilted, it held no leaves or fruit. Nicolas stepped carefully to read the carvings,

Della Louis Curran,   Born 1890   Died 1954
Andrew Marion Curran,   Born 1895   Died 1955

Two more stones were lost under wild roses that had fallen down hiding the message. Nicolas bent lower to see,

Andrew Curran II,   Born 1917   Died 1983
Judith Curran,   Born 1920   Died 1983

"Those are my parents."

"Whoa." Losing his balance, Nicolas fell onto his knees. Deep in concentration he was unprepared for the voice behind him.

"They died when I was sixteen."

He stood up finding his jeans soaked with mud, "I didn't hear you sneak up on me."

"Come on. You knew I was here."

"No, really." Nic brushed off the clumps as best he could with his hands, "You caught me off guard."

India stood outside of the iron fence and asked, "How does it feel to see your great-great-grandfather's grave?

Nicolas walked back to the spot, "Is it him? Could it really be my relative from Saratoga Springs? Seems remote even with the document you found at the license bureau with his name, seems queer somehow."

She pulled her toboggan down around her ears and said, "Don't you think he made it this far? If not, then why bury him here? Or better yet, who would this guy be? Maybe it's an imposter." India laughed, now getting the squirrel to stop and notice.

"Got me." He stepped back over the fence to join her, "If someone is buying your land or anyone else's in Campbell County then it's up to them to find the correct maps, boundaries and other legal shit. You live here! They have no right to harass you into anything."

"Thank you. I heard a speech similar to that from my Aunt Ginny. It's true they have no case but it still scares me. Just the thought of going to court to prove my family owns this estate makes me sick."

Nicolas's eyes jumped to India's face when she said that. Then it occurred to him. "Do I own Millwheel?"

Nearby, binoculars were lowered from dark eyes and stuffed back into a leather case. Pulling his fedora down Lew Mills walked back into the forest away from the two sleuths. "Thinks he may own it, well his grandfather thought so, too. That poor guy, wonder if he's still floating? Must have reached New Orleans by now." With a smile the tall man stayed a course going east on to the Parker property, "The competition grows. First, I can't run off my relative so easy and now this guy shows up and gets a wild hair. Like 1868 he reminds me of those damn vagrants coming out of the woodwork, eating my fish, building places to sleep, what next? I haven't had any fun since Churchill Downs. I need to send this guy packing. What to do, what to do…."

꧁W꧂

"You're very sweet to have come this far to help us. Have you any thoughts about the graves? The women buried on either side of Thomas Curran?"

As they walked toward the Parker property Nicolas stopped to pick up a rock. Examining it he scowled and threw it into the trees, "I suppose he could have re-married when he arrived. Seems foolish to us, giving up so much in New York, a wife, children, a woolen mill. Things must have been unbearable in the east to have made such a choice."

A crick ahead was shallow but far enough across that India could jump, "Perhaps his wife was a witch."

Nicolas laughed at her.

"No, I mean it. She could have been a horrible person, he may have been miserable. Comes to Kentucky, meets two Indians or freed slaves, maybe leftover Mormon wives," Now they were both laughing, "And he wanted to stay here. Yup, just like that. No more screaming, nagging. Could have been pretty nice, too. In fact, he may have jumped off the Magnolia, swam to shore and walked off to freedom. Never wrote home to say that he was still alive.

With Nic's big smile he just had to interject, "That may seem to you to have been the perfect con, to fall off a sinking boat and pretend to die but he still came to settle the land that he had purchased. Someone in New York had met him, took his money and signed the deed to transfer it."

They climbed a steep hill, both of them grabbing branches near the ground, pulling them to the top. India, although out of breath asked, "Your school is still in session. Have you a date to return? Have you booked a flight home yet?"

Nicolas ignored the question as they stopped to rest on a frozen ridge that overlooked the Millwheels barns far away.

He reached toward her to untangle a branch from her hair, "So, why aren't you married?"

"That was abrupt."

"I'm serious. All of the boys in Campbell County want to know."

She giggled at his imagination, "Hmm, let's see......" Thinking for a moment she answered, "I'm not as exciting as a football game." Nic nodded in understanding, "And I don't taste like pizza or beer. I would not want to have someone on a weekend decide between me and their ATV. And my clothes are dirtier than I am. There, now you know. My celibate life is by choice."

"I suppose there's something to all that. At least you're not a tease. Tell me, are your horses the only ones you flirt with?"

"You got that right. I don't have to worry about safe sex. The only protection I wear is a helmet."

Nicolas threw an unwelcome arm around her, but after a moment she decided to tolerate it. Noticing that she was uncomfortable with his embrace he assured her, "Enough of this loose talk! I'm starving and the only food

I've seen at Millwheel is alfalfa. What do you say we head back to the farm, put on the feedbag, so to speak, and wash it all down with good Kentucky Bourbon."

India swooned, "We can do better than that. Let's wash it down with juleps."

Chapter 23
NIC'S EPIPHANY

The next morning a veterinarian checked both the mare and camels, pronouncing everyone in good health. So, convinced that the farm could survive without her, India packed a cooler and joining Nicolas they headed down to the place on the Ohio River where the steamboat Magnolia had sunk on March 18, 1868.

They parked along the Mary Ingles highway, which skirted the river and noticed immediately that the wide current was traveling fast. Maggie jumped out of the backseat and headed directly for the water. "Maggie, no!"

The shepherd stopped instantly.

"She won't run off, will she?" Nic asked.

"Never." She assured him, "But she likes to go into the water up to her stomach and that's probably too deep. The undertow could pull her away from shore."

Ugly brown mud painted the bank that stretched for almost 60 feet down to the water edged with a lacey hem of ice that ran forever in both directions. As they walked the soles of their boots sank down into the ooze, nearly sucking them off. After walking for ten minutes following the freeway they spotted a driftwood stump under an abandoned railroad bridge and used it as a place to rest.

"See," India pointed in a northeasterly direction, "Over there is the Cincinnati California Water Works, built in 1893. That's a few years after the Magnolia sank. Those men that built it, worked on it may have never even known about the explosion and all the lives that were lost on that stretch of river."

Both quietly studied the beautiful renaissance revival style building on the far side of the Ohio. One wing was a rotunda shape, the other end square, both topped with a maroon colored roof and joined in the center with a walk through, certainly the work of an experienced architect.

India continued, "The waterway in front of us now is controlled by the dams and locks that were put in place during the 1900's. The river during the 1860's was not as deep as it is now. It could be anywhere from three feet deep to forty feet. Mother Nature was still its designer so it changed a little each day. Imagine in a dry summer it must have been impossible to get the steamboats up river through all that silt."

"And that accounted for the explosions." Nic said. "The boilers ran so hot pushing boats up shallow waterways. No surprise they were overheating."

"Or it could have hit a log. Deadheads lined the shores then. Men along the rivers cut down all the trees to supply fuel for the boilers. After a flood or hard rain loose logs would slide into the river and sink just waiting for a hull to puncture."

Maggie was tracking some river rat along the bank so India excused herself saying that she would join Nicolas later. "And don't fall in!" she warned.

Now alone, Nic walked downriver further from their car and sounds of the highway. Trees tight together, he pushed his way along thinking about India's comment that much of this shore in 1868 would have been a wasteland of stumps and slash. From the water he heard a whooshing sound and looked north hoping to see perhaps a barge that might be moving in his direction. Although still almost half a mile away he was delighted instead to see a steamboat plowing it's way upstream.

There were people onboard moving about or seated. Crewmen were working. A child was leaning for a moment over the upper deck rail but suddenly disappeared, pulled back by a woman concerned for its safety. Nicolas smiled, thinking that the kid had probably been warned numerous times about falling into the river and now his mother had stopped threatening and decided to take sterner measures.

"This is great!" Nicolas thought, "Having an event such as this while visiting." He stepped closer toward the river, "Although December seems a strange time for a cruise. I've heard of the Belle of Louisville and the Delta Queen. I'm guessing this boat would be about the size of the Belle."

Nicolas was ecstatic hoping that India could also see the boat approaching from her position on the river. As he searched for a sign of his missing companion it is clear that the shoreline had changed. The woods behind him were gone. A quagmire of branches and stumps littered the embankment. The Water Company across the river was not visible, but instead now looked to be an open field with sheep grazing. Even the swiftness of the water that earlier had seemed dangerously fast had somehow slowed to a crawl.

Suddenly smoke began pouring out of the boat followed by a large explosion. Then a second explosion. People were jumping from the boat, some are blown free of it, others were running along the decks on fire screaming.

251

Nicolas couldn't reach them. The boat was 1000 feet away and the shore was so deep with silt he was helpless to move any closer. Floating passengers in heavy coats or long dresses are shouting, screaming, disappearing in front of his eyes. From the paddlewheels the fire raced forward consuming the wooden hull toward the bow. A tall black stack on the upper deck slowly began to bend with the heat ultimately falling into the inferno, crushing the wheelhouse. Hats, chairs, baggage, other cargo floated north toward Cincinnati. Magically a small skiff appeared carrying two men franticly paddling across to the ship. Some swimmers reached out to the rescuers while other bodies silently floated past. Waving arms and smoky garments of burning victims begged the rescuers to move closer.

Pulling out of his boots Nicolas ran for a pile of branches. Grabbing a long piece he ran back towards the water's edge heaving it out into the stream. Turning, he made a second attempt throwing more limbs out to the swimmers. To his relief some scrapes of the boat are now floating and people are swimming toward them to grab on. The water catastrophe was now drifting downstream, the boat sagging below the surface as the water followed the flames up to the bow.

A few of the passengers had made it as far as the muddy shore and began pulling their wet bodies up onto it, grasping, tearing at the mud, hoping to rise above the water long enough to breathe.

Nicolas's attention was drawn to one small man whose luck had found him on the shore. His clothes burned, black from the soot of the coal and fire, he used reeds to wrench himself to safety. Rolling onto his back he gasped for breath. Feeling along his large coat into his pockets and around his waist the man seemed satisfied. He closed his eyes to rest, his chest rejoicing from the fresh air.

Nicolas couldn't take his eyes from the man until the paddling of another swimmer disturbed the water.

"Good," Nicolas said to himself, "A man following that guy to shore. Maybe it's a friend."

The newcomer was much larger and must have been much stronger, showing no effort exiting from the current of the Ohio. Approaching the resting burn victim the large man stepped up, grabbed the charred coat and spun the resting man over. Using his back as a dais, huge hands pushed the small man's face into the ground. Flailing arms and digging feet could not find release from the attackers grip and in a moment any power left to defend himself was spent. The man on the bottom ceased to move.

Barely dressed the large man tore the coat off the dead man then probed pants pockets, the waist and even the sleeves of the victim. Nicolas noticed a smile appear across the dark man's face that spoils had been found, a coin belt and folder of papers. Standing straight again the executioner shoved the bundles behind his belt and using the corpse as a platform he stood straight, black eyes studying the shoreline for a way out. Under his feet the corpse began to sink down and the large man began to teeter. Perhaps thinking to avoid discovery he lifted the body from its mud grave and flung it out into the sweeping current. As the body sank below the eddies the murderer paid no attention. Spotting a path leading to drier ground he marched up the bank away from the river toward an open field and directly past Nicolas Curran.

❦

It was becoming difficult for India to accept someone new into her carefully structured life. She enjoyed Nicolas's fresh humor and new ideas, his camaraderie among her employees, the easy way he fit in around the horses. All of this would have been perfect except India needed more space.

Brushing her teeth she surmised "I've never had such a concern for anyone on my farm in the past. I've dated, that was okay and should be a young woman's prerogative. But he's different, consuming. I'd love to ask someone around here what they think of Nicolas, maybe get an objective opinion but he doesn't seem to be a problem for anyone else except me!"

Friends had called that morning and invited both of them to stay overnight at a lodge located by a small lake. A beautiful farm, with pastured Saddlebreds across the pond that kept the banks neatly groomed for such weekends. India had thought that it might be a good idea, removing the two of them from additional research for a time except that in the past to such gatherings she had never brought along a male guest. The weather was questionable yet India told her friends they would attend and to Nicolas she cooed, "And you'll meet my best friends, old riding buddies."

Still somewhat shaken from their last excursion Nic agreed to go thinking, "I hope I'm not riding the Trojan horse."

About twelve riders, they were on trail most of the day, India on Willy and Nicolas on Tempter. By the time they returned to the lake it was already dark. Flip had a fire and campsite ready for all the arriving equestrians to rest and visit. It didn't take long to unsaddle, water and crosstie the horses.

Seated around the fire Nicolas quietly listened to new acquaintances laugh, complain and playfully pick on each other. There was talk of shows to enter, the price of alfalfa and the realization that it might rain. In the night sky distant flickers of light suddenly accompanied by wind suggested bad weather. Smoke curling around the fire caused the campers to jump up and move their chairs.

He could not stop looking at her. Everyone was talking, fighting to win the floor with crazy adventure stories to catch the crowd's attention. But he had to look at her. She was so confident with her coy smile and big laugh.

In the trees the horses begin to scuffle and fidget. India threw her head around, concerned, knowing that as lightning approached they might spook. Nothing worse than having to chase down horses in the dark.

Nicolas rose up to get a beer, making his way between the legs, smoke and assorted coolers. "Think I'll walk to the lake."

With the storm approaching the surface was choppy, glazing the top with flocks of tiny waves bordered by flat water on either side, soon to be caught by the breeze to join in the fun. Nicolas took a sip from the can and felt the first drops of rainfall on his arm.

Behind him the crowd had already begun rushing to grab towels, chairs, even the clothes still hanging from branches. Tied to the trees the horses rebelled, pulling and dancing, hoping to find a way to escape the pandemonium.

Walking up the bank he noticed India checking the knots above the horses heads. Moving among them soft words were whispered as to small children asking each to relax.

"I'll be right over there if you need me," she cooed, stroking their sides.

The horses quiet now she turned and noticed him observing her.

"We need to move inside now." India let Nicolas know as she walked past him to get away from the darkness and the rain. "Is there anything else you need to drag in?

He just shook his head.

"Well then, lets get going. I only wish that there was room for the horses inside too".

Nick followed her like a puppy.

The party had already started.

Stepping into the lodge India observed, "After riding all day, the trail had been too long for some, not long enough for others. Horses, dogs and those kids hanging off the back of saddles, good time for them to get some sleep."

Blowing around, the storm roared directly overhead. Oaks, maples and cottonwoods surrounding the encampment banged against each other with snaps and moans. India considered how it would have been smarter to leave the horses up the hill in the barn. It seemed miles away now. The dry empty stalls called for the horses to come back and fill the empty spaces. Sitting inside the lodge it had been poor planning not to have detected the squall sooner, making India feel sinful for having left her equine friends outdoors alone and wet now to fend for themselves.

Beer, chocolate cake, moist potato chips were being passed around the group. Each crack of thunder stopped the conversation, injecting shrieks, howls and jumps from the crowd.

India had been patient with the storm until now but a suggestion had been developing inside her mind, "Would anyone be in favor of letting the horses move back up to the barn?"

"Are you nuts?" Flip replied, "There's a gale out there and its dark! How do you propose to do that?"

Nancy, another rider who brought a stocky palomino for the weekend added, "I'm not stepping outside of this building! You couldn't pay me to ride anywhere right now".

"Hey, I know it's iffy but I know horses, and what they want right now is to be safe and dry."

Even Nicolas wasn't supportive. "I doubt that you'll get any volunteers to ride with you back up there. The barn's over a mile away and there's still the lightning to deal with."

"And," Nancy added, "If you take only a couple horses away the rest will go crazy with the group split up."

Defiantly India stood her ground," I believe from all of my best instincts that I can take those horses all the way to the barn and not even get wet."

They all chimed in, "So what do you suggest?"

"Nicolas and I will get the two sane horses, probably Tempter and Vicky Joy on long lines and lead them up the road alongside the truck. The other horses will be loose. All of them know the way and as soon as we start moving they are sure to follow or will gallop away and meet us at the barn. If any move off into the field from fear or darkness it would not be far. The headlights of the truck will be their beacon to follow. The older horses will most likely walk behind, knowing that they're headed back to the stalls."

Nancy doubted the idea, "Na, not smart. What if you got stuck with the truck and all? You can't walk back here leaving twelve wild horses loose and ask for a push!"

"It will be fine. I have new tread and four wheel drive".

Lightning hit once more but the thunder waited a bit longer before it echoed the message from far away.

"Well, I'm thinking that the horses will get there Ok," Flip interjected, hunting through the crumbs at the bottom of the potato chip bag, " Horses have been galloping in storms for millions of years, finding safe locations by instinct. Granted, they're not real bright, but it's only a mile and these horses are not aggressive. Should behave."

"Ok then, I'm off! Come on Nic!"

And before anyone could stop her India reached for her slicker, opened the door and was gone. Nicolas followed, apologizing to the group.

India untied both Vicky Joy and Tempter. Asking Nicolas to get in first he was handed the lead for Vicky through the window. His hands were ice cold but the heater from the truck was already beginning to warm up. India had Tempter close as she untied the other six horses. Jumping into the driver's side she had a long line connected to the aging thoroughbred. As they pulled away she said to Nicolas, "Tempter raced at numerous tracks years ago. I'm sure from those experiences that loud noises and movement won't bothered him."

Trotting along side, the gelding licked his lips in agreement. His head fell even with his withers sending the message to India that he was pleased with this decision to leave. The younger horses had sped away, gone in the night. Three other horses jogged behind the bed following the red taillights having no need at this time for tomfoolery.

Approaching the dark barn it was apparent from whinnies that the first horses had arrived safely. Nicolas jumped out letting Vicky find her own way and groped the wall in search of a light switch. The thought of first finding a Brown Recluse spider suddenly came to mind but Nic closed his eyes and got lucky. Flicking on the switch the room filled with a bright glow.

Fourteen stalls made up the alley. India knew that now was the most dangerous time with the horses excited and moving around loose. She swung doors slowly open, waited only an instant as a single horse pushed past and then locked it tight to seal off any intruders that tried to follow. Within five minutes all twelve of the horses were separated. On the stall floor they rolled, legs in the air to chase away any itch from the rain.

Around the barn the smell of the hay bales and saddles, mixed with the sound of the tempest rattling against the aluminum siding accompanied the stirring of the horse's hooves. This produced a symphony of music that only a horseman knows.

Nicolas swung a stall open, "Okay. Check this out. Hay stacked against the wall, perfect for a place to sleep!" he proclaimed, flopping down.

India peeked in to see what he was doing and just shook her head. "This is not going to do."

She left, returning with horse blankets found in a trunk near the water spigot. Twisting them around her she created a cocoon and fell onto the soft pallet along side Nicolas.

A soft echo was heard, "This is not going to do."

He moved off soon returning with another armload of blankets. Unrolling India he organized the bedding so they lay together tightly between the layers of quilt and flannel. She twisted some to loosen her arms as his head pushed against her neck. Just close enough. He smiled and kissed her there, just a peck to test the waters.

She flashed her eyes wickedly showing her distaste and tried without results to twist away.

He kissed her again and heard a venomous growl rise from deep inside of her.

'Good, it's working.'

To avoid a slap Nicolas placed his hands around hers keeping up innocent attacks along her neck and shoulders. Small kisses of no consequence, he enjoyed waiting for results. After a time her objections melted away with only sighs remaining between them as the two began to share. With their clothes pushed off a competition began between the lovers and the storm for attention.

Chapter 24
SEX and REAPERS REVENGE

Sex seemed natural and inevitable. Two consenting adults could be found anywhere on the planet misbehaving, why not a barn?

"This reminds me of explorers coming to the new world." He whispered while fondling her.

"Tell me this isn't part of a history assignment."

Digging deeper under the horse blankets Nicolas replied, "Back in Saratoga my students are old enough to discover new adventures in the back seats of their cars."

India rolled her eyes, "With each new discovery they're making history."

"You got it."

Nearby they could hear the horses pawing against the stall walls.

"We don't know what time it is. My friends will be here soon!"

"No they won't."

"What makes you so sure?" She asked.

"Because you're a single young woman and I'm a very handsome young man," Nicolas said as India groaned, "and we are old enough to have a good reason to be laying here naked."

Rolling out of the blanket she grabbed her pants, "Just the same, I don't need a new reputation. I was very comfortable with the old one."

Nicolas propped his head with this hand and relaxed as India dressed. Sun peeked through the barn door warming the dry areas of the dirt floor attracting a congregation of sparrows who chirped their opinion of the two lovers.

"I talked to my Aunt Ginny yesterday about your visit. She seemed very firm about you staying here in Kentucky. That seems odd to me, comments like that without having met you first. I wonder, if she walked into the barn right now if she would still feel the same way?"

Nic peeked under the covers, appreciating the fact that he was wearing nothing but goose bumps. "Naw, she'd like me right away."

Bending down India grabbed a handful of hay and threw it at him, hoping to get him off the bales and dressed.

Buttoning her blouse she asked, "Did you dream last night?"

Nicolas seemed not to be interested in the question, ignoring her as he pulled on his sweater.

She babbled on, "I did, so I assumed perhaps after that experience last night you would have some sort of fantasy as you slept."

Immediately his mood seemed to change into a gruffer tone, "I don't care to remember my dreams."

The sparrows lifted off together away from the barn just then, their tiny wings creating the only sound.

"I'm sorry, I didn't want to…"

"No, it's a place I don't enjoy going. My dreams I mean."

Now both dressed they stood together looking out towards the lake in the distance and the lodge they had left the night before. The new dawn brought a cold breeze moving the last of the gray clouds east welcoming a bright blue sky overhead.

"I lost a brother a few years back. Or, no that's not entirely true. I didn't really lose him at all. He appears in my dreams whether I want him to or not."

"That's awful."

"Some of the time I see him in a place, how can I explain it, where it's pleasant to see him but that's rare. Usually, I find our reunions in my sleep very upsetting." Nicolas lifted his arm to lean against the doorframe, stuffing his other hand into the back pocket of his jeans.

India softly spoke, "I'm thinking you were very close?"

"You might say that. He was my twin."

"Oh God, I'm so sorry."

He turned away from her to rub the forehead of a palomino near by, "Taken me a while to deal with being alone. Teaching helps, I'm never alone at the school but the rest of the time I just shut down. When I got your phone call I wasn't ready to change anything right away, or not until I saw the Fax. That was the kicker."

"What do you mean?"

"You won't believe this but my brother had a connection to those coins you sent pictures of, the one's you said had been in your family since the 1800s. My brother had some crazy idea to dive off the California coast and retrieve coins exactly like those."

"How do you know? Our gold coins are over 140 years old, sort of hard to come by. Perhaps he could have found a coin dealer to buy them from?"

"You don't know my brother."

"Was he as sweet as you?"

"We looked alike, but that's where it ended. Our interests were very separate."

"But you were still close."

"I used to call it 'The Nathan and Nic Show.' He was the entertainment and I was the commercials."

Far off a truck made its way toward them. Kids in the pickup bed meant that they would be saddling up again to ride their mounts back down to the lodge, pick up a few supplies and take to the trails once more.

"May I ask how he died?"

"Matter of fact going after those exact coins near Crescent City, California. Sort of shook me up to see your Fax when my original plan was to totally ignore you."

She stepped up to him, kissed his cheek and smacked his butt, "I have my ways."

Knowing that they still had work to do they walked back to their bunk. The blankets from last night needed to be refolded and packed. Sharing the task India said, "As soon as we return to Millwheel I will make it my first priority to show them to you. In all this excitement I forgot to do that."

"Slipped my mind, too. I thought of it a couple of times since I've been here but between our research, viewing the graves and wild sex I sort of put it on the back burner." He teased her with a bump of his hip, smiling broadly.

∞⦂∞

"I'm sick to death of this relationship! Time to light things up enough so lover boy will leave town." From his perch Lew Mills dropped his binoculars and hearing a noise behind him, turned to find a young boy with tight clothes and black hair in the process of cutting the head off a small gardener snake.

"Thank you for coming, Ukobach," Mills said, "Telepathy told me that you had time in your busy schedule and for that I am eternally grateful. Heard you had some high scoring events over the last hundred years. The Texas City Fire back in 1947, that was nice. 581 dead."

The boy picked up the remains of the carcass throwing it into the weeds. Only a moment later a large falcon swooped down to feed on it. "I was on my way to Columbia. Heard tell there's an earthquake happening on the 25th of January so I can't stay long. It will look good on my resume. Many will die."

The boy watched the bird enjoy the entrée as Mills spoke, "I am a bit squeezed as well. Impossible to leave now, but here's something right up your alley. A fire to start, nice and hot. Fry a few high school students perhaps, a teacher or two? In New York State. Will only take a day to cover then you can dash off for the quake. What do you say?"

"Just a school? I have an event guaranteed for over 1000 fatalities. Why would I go up to New York? That's out of my way."

"You will be well compensated for your time. Trust me."

"There's a steep price for your request."

Lew Mills rolled his eyes, "Yes, yes, I'm sure there is."

༄

"You own Millwheel? India shrieked, "Where the hell did that come from?"

"Wouldn't it sort of make sense?" Nicolas said quietly, "Sort of figures if Thomas Curran really did live here and he's my great-great-grandfather then we should be cousins or kin of some sort."

India grumbled as she walked outside into the backyard of the farmhouse. Slamming the screen door caused a cat nearby to run under the wooden steps. Nicolas followed, bringing his strategy along, "Isn't it true that Kentucky is comfortable with us dating or relatives marrying?"

"Oh boy, don't dig that hole so deep that you can't crawl out," India said gritting her teeth.

"It seems I can't say anything pleasant today but hear me out. Last week after we toured the cemetery I began to think, your, mine, our grandfather arrived here in 1868. He planted crops, built homes, made babies. Your half is here but my half was in Saratoga before he left. I'm just saying...."

"Don't say one more word. Everyday of my life has been spent here. Even as a little girl I was consumed by my obligations to this farm. I watched every blade of bluegrass grow, I repaired every damaged fence, delivered foals in snowstorms and I buried my family here.

You'd best choose your words carefully if you don't want me to...."

With that said India marched off, disappearing into the farm.

Nicolas saw that the calico cat had returned and was cleaning its paw on the stoop. Sitting down Nicolas was glad to have someone to talk to, "Geez, that didn't go very well. Maybe I should have waited a few days after she found out how irresistible I am. And that I'm a little nuts about her too." The cat stopped licking, "The idea of a co-ownership isn't that far fetched though...."

Looking around for his audience, he found the cat had left.

The fire in Saratoga Springs demolished the high school injuring three firefighters. The school mascot, a Falcon, was later discovered in the parking lot, melted.

ॐ

The next morning India found Nicolas busy in his room and inquired, "What are you doing up?"

"I got a flight out this morning." He replied, shoving his shirts into a duffle, "Seems not to many people going to New York from Kentucky today. That's good. My principal and I talked a few minutes ago. Seems the school has burned to the ground."

"That's unreal! Is everyone okay?"

"Yeh, pretty much. But the staff would like all of us together as soon as possible."

"I hate to lose you know with the farm's deed trouble still unsolved." India made a solemn face, "And things were getting pretty messy for us too."

"Our time here on your farm was nice. You're nice."

India looked at him with surprise.

"No, you're more than that and you know it. We have something that we should build on. The school is the least of my concerns right now except it has to be handled before I lose my job." He paused, "Will I lose you?"

India walked into the room closing her arms around him, "Our differences yesterday about the deed didn't help. I'm sorry. Your presence here makes me feel whole, complete. This is your home now, Millwheel. A place for you to come, stay, be a part of."

"Thank you. Although, I knew the first time I saw camels in the yard that you'd let anyone stay on Millwheel Farm."

She fell onto the bed, throwing her hands over her face. "Your awful."

Pulling the zipper on the duffle closed, he sat beside her, "Seriously, I can't feel comfortable anywhere, here or in New York. Three years ago after losing Nathan my life was over anyway. Some people can rise above catastrophe, guess I'm not one of them. Now back in Saratoga my classroom has been reduced to a pile of ash. I'm a mess."

Kissing him softly she whispered, "Your brother loved you. I would do anything to bring him back for you but you must carry on. What you leave behind in your life, Nicolas, is his legacy as well as yours."

Nicolas needed a minute to think. The last weeks had introduced feelings and relationships that he had not anticipated. "I need to find out what I want. Stay teaching? Join you here? Move to Crescent City and wait on the beach for Nathan to return? I thought by now I'd be over his death. You don't want some guy in a blue funk dragging himself around this place. You'd go nuts."

"I'll wait a while for you to return but not *too* long." Smiling, she needed to be close to him now. "How long until your plane leaves?"

"Just before noon"

"Good. There's plenty of time. Would you let me give you something before you go?"

"Yes."

❧

The ridge remained windy all afternoon.

Lew Mills stood on the peak of the Parker property looking down on the Millwheel Farm. "Such a beautiful place. Long white fences and sturdy buildings with all the trimmings. Trails to walk, ponds to rest by and watch nothing all day. People already in place to fill every need. Convenient."

He thought of how it might be different had he never left. "There's plenty of time to find out. Although the world seems in pretty pitiful shape, which is a good thing, this could become my headquarters, sort of a Shangri-La of stopovers for Grim Reapers. I might change the name. Something catchy, like "Death's Rest," or "The Motel Macabre.""

Lew Mills laughed out loud.

A woman approached from the hawthorn trees behind him. Her visit was expected but at first they did not speak. Side by side they looked like lords of the manor assessing their lands.

"I want it all" Mills whispered.

The woman did not speak but instead giggled a bit, pulling her shawl close around her small shoulders. Catching the breeze her long red hair whipped around her face and neck even slapping Mills. Under her shawl she wore a dark coat that almost reached the ground keeping most of her small frame hidden. A blood red scarf was twisted around her neck.

"You heard me. I'm dead serious. This is a great location. No hurricanes!"

Lew Mills was now looking directly at the new visitor known as Apollyon, the Destroyer. Her journeys throughout the world had been well documented and at times she had even outshined Mills in fatalities. He envied her but would never let on, impressed with the fact that she worked alone and handled chaos with little effort. He fantasized, 'Lovely to look at, might she be a guest on my Kentucky horse farm someday?'

Speaking out loud he inquired, "So your busy I hear? Spending time in the Dominican Republic, Haiti. Then off you went to the Gulf. Then it really rained on Biloxi. I salute you."

"Yes, four hundred dead total. But storms, you know how they are. Here today gone tomorrow. "

Mills thought back to one hundred and thirty years earlier, to the storm off the Pacific and his profitable success from the Brother Jonathan. "So true. But thank you for coming. How long can you stay?"

Apollyon was not used to this questioning. Other players did not welcome companionship at any level. She was hesitant to reply not knowing Mill's reasoning. And careful. Traps in the past had been laid for others like herself, eliminating players. Losers helplessly walk the earth alone until Hell froze over and that was not an option.

"I'm on my way to Bangkok, Thailand for a plane crash. Why?" She lied knowing that it wouldn't happen until late December but still needed to be cautious.

"I have my hands full here, what with my granddaughter's reluctance to sell. A shame, don't you think? I'd give her the world." He turned once more toward the estate, "This old farm was mine once. Sort of have a warm spot in my heart for it."

Apollyon laughed so loud that it caused the birds to scatter from the impending doom. "A heart, that's a hoot! This conversation in itself was worth the trip!" She turned and moved toward a stump of wood that had been resting in the forest for eons. Sitting down she rearranged her hair, taming it behind her back. "By the way, Reapers are talking. Where have you been? About a hundred years flew past and your fatality numbers over that time are way down. Any reason?"

"You could say I was tied up."

She smiled at him but had no allegiance. Because of the game he needed a large disaster soon. She would be pleased to take his position, for his failure to attend to the dead would damn him forever and he'd be out of the game for good.

The sun to the east was now behind clouds and the day was half over. Mills felt a sudden urgency to settle his request or loose the chance forever. "An issue related to all of this has again reared its ugly head. Seems there are powers as we speak that may alter my plans here at Millwheel. I need to gain total obedience with my relative to reach my goals."

"That's not my problem." She replied with a tone so dry it made Mills lick his lips.

"This is an easy mark. Take but a few minutes of your time. Put a feather in your cap!"

"Feathers I got. What do you want?"

Chapter 25
DEATH and DIARIES

"A few months ago I had never even heard of India Curran." Nicolas thought to himself as he dragged his bag down another ramp. He had a three-hour layover between Kentucky and New York, stopping in Minneapolis.

"I'll return to Millwheel, we'll fix the deed in her favor, I'll get over this mourning over Nathan and marry India Curran. There. I need to be the hero in this story."

Nicolas worked his way across the airport to a large food court.

Thinking about India he remembered what she had said about waiting. "I'll call her tomorrow, give her the run down on the school and promise that we'll celebrate New Years Eve in the bluegrass together."

Standing in the concourse mayhem surrounded him. An intercom overhead called for passengers, other noises, and people running late for flights. Suitcases so big, travelers reminded him of furniture movers. Slumped in their chairs some were sleeping, others scolding their children.

"Humm....Pizza, Chinese, Pickled Herring? Prune Kolaches? Yes, this is definitely Minneapolis food."

The guy in front of him pulled out a twenty and waited for the young attendant to make change. After the man left, Nic stepped up to place his own order at the counter. In a hall on the far side of the concourse he heard a loud noise and yelling. *"Probably teenagers going to Florida,"* he thought.

The girl employee asked him for $6.50 for the bagel.

"Too much," answered Nic.

Out of the corner of his eye he noticed two men wearing the same colored uniforms, yelling, and reaching for their sides as they ran. A man with long red hair appeared to be dragging a little boy, moving too fast for the boy to stay upright. Nicolas turned back to the counter girl now finding her down by the floor below the carousel that held the rolls. She looked up at him with a frightened expression. Nic turned, transfixed. Investigating the situation in the room he saw that the little boy had fallen onto the carpet. Uniforms yelled "GET DOWN!" Shots were fired, but Nic didn't see where they went. With the red haired man running past him there was yelling again. The running man pulled his gun out and aimed while falling down in front of Nicolas. Uniforms yelled once more and two bullets flew past. One bullet missed the red haired man, shattering the glass carousel on the counter. The other bullet found a home inside Nicolas Curran.

The burning of the high school never left India's mind as she took the two minute ride over to visit neighbors to the north, the Craft's. She had wanted to ask them about the deeds weeks ago but her guest from New York had interrupted her research.

"Nicolas must have landed in New York by now anxious to get in contact with school officials and offer help. Yet the more digging I do the better chance of side tracking that no good son of a bitch who wants our land."

A small rambler built in 1956, the Craft family's original home was destroyed during a cloudburst that flooded the entire hollow in the spring of 1955.

Seated in the living room India and Richard Craft got right to business, "Thankfully my sister Tina saved everything from the storm of '55," he said, "We had been lucky she was visiting us that day. Grabbed all the papers, notes, albums and lit out of here to higher ground before we knew how bad the storm would get!"

"It may be lucky for all of us." India replied.

"She had a couple of old books that you might find interesting. One's pretty big, over 125 pages. Mostly in longhand it tells about settling here, our family, some legal notes. My dad was good about that." Mr. Craft smiled as he flipped through the ledger. Then he pulled out a smaller leather covered book and handed it to India, "This diary is in the years that you're interested in, 1870—1895. It's a sort of a record of events. Good thing, too, had this inside," and Richard Craft produced a map measuring about 15 inches by 20 inches, a layout of the Craft farm.

India wanted to cry as she read the names on the document, "Craft Property, Curran Farm, known as Millwheel and here's the Parker property! Look, Virgil, Salem, and Isaac. They're all listed as we know them from the cemetery stones on the land east of us! How did you come to have this document?"

"My family sold some of our land back in 1880. See," Richard pointed to the name, " We had to pull a new survey and, as a seller, the county must have demanded that a new map be drawn of everyone's boundaries so there would be no arguments later about who owned what."

They studied the lines specifying roads on either side of the Parker's land. Persimmon Grove was just east of Millwheel bordering the ponds and crick. The map indicated that the same property swept east to Flagg Springs.

Richard broke her concentration, "You'll like this better. Its from 1877." He reopened the smaller book, "Here is my Grand Dad's writing about a housewarming long ago. Seems our family was there, too."

The script was illegible to India, "Please, you read it to me."

"Seems the Parkers were having a party or picnic." He said as he ran his fingers along the withered page, "The Curran's came, your folk, brought some wine. Says here we brought squash, some bread. Someone named Jefferson brought smoked fish, another person named Riddle brought venison. Let's see, here is a mention of cornbread. Then here," He pointed to a name, "Reverend John McGill had attended that affair, blessing the land and the new home which had simply been an older cabin with the land, it says, donated by your family. One of our Craft family members as well as a person named Benjamin Yobel were listed in the book as notaries on the deed transferring the acres east of the ponds and creek from Persimmon Grove to Flagg Springs. Gee, its pretty clear here how the Parker's came to have all that land."

India was overwhelmed. This was the information she had been looking to find. In her wildest dreams she would never had thought that the secret to the Parker land would be recorded here in these old diaries belonging to an entirely different family from hers. This moment would have been perfect if Nicolas had been there to share it with her.

Mr. Craft read more, uncovering others in the area that had attended, Baptists, Mormons, a German family.

"What's this here? Printing by itself on the side of the page?"

Richard leaned closer, turning the book a little sideways, "It appeared that the Parkers were considered at the time to be mulattos. This note may seem strange now, to mention such a thing, but after the Civil War any black owning the land, especially a free black slave would need some documentation. Perhaps my grandfather thought that later in history this note of his would be of importance."

Richard turned the page and read, "The night of the party there was a fire." The small ink lettering scribbled in longhand across the ancient pages made it difficult for India and Richard to precisely understand the notes.

"A fire started after everyone had left and gone back to their homes. It engulfed the house and all of the Parkers were burned to death save for two men that had been spending the night with cattle. Doesn't say their names. The entire Parker family was laid to rest at the bottom of the ridge near the creek that divided the two lakes."

India knew a wagon road split the lakes following the creek north and the cemetery today could still be seen from a dirt trail.

Richard read a bit longer to find that directly after the burials the only two men related to the Parker family had left Kentucky. There was no record of their destination or final location. Richard read more on the last pages about some Curran family illness and the return of a cousin Jennifer, no last name, who everyone had been glad to see.

As Richard finished reading India was thinking about the Parker family and their happiness, followed by such a devastating loss. She felt tired and it was still early morning.

"May I please borrow this book only for an hour. I need to move directly to a print shop, scan these pages and make copies of the map, too. This may have saved our farm. I'm eternally grateful that your father and grandfather thought it important to write about such a small event as a housewarming in Campbell County. Isn't that something? This will surly prove to that attorney, Damien Alva and his client that the Parker family had possession of the land separate from Millwheel."

Chapter 26
ROAMING GHOSTS

Hello Nicolas.

Hearing a familiar voice far off, "Excuse me?"

"Welcome to the afterlife."

"Nathan, is that you?"

"Yup, or just my spiritual realm. I'll be closer to you, with you actually very soon."

Nicolas wanted to cry. Confused but truly happy. Happier than he'd been in years. But where in the hell was he? "Nathan, don't leave me, don't ever go away again."

"No brother, I won't. In fact I'm coming closer."

"Where are we, me?"

"I'm wandering or that's the term some use. You've just arrived so we won't be together for a while yet."

Nicolas had tears in his eyes. "It's been so long. Your voice sounds so..so good."

"Missed you too, Bro. It has been too long since we've been together."

"Where's Jeremy? He was wonderful. What a great guy. Is he with you?"

"No, he drowned."

A silence stayed between them for a time. Nathan went on, "He just drowned."

Nicolas noticed a crack in his brother's voice.

"And yes, as you said, he was wonderful."

"Your best friend."

"A great guy to dive with, and be with."

"Yeah."

"Yeah."

The silence of the vacuum lasted a moment too long for Nicolas."Nathan!"

"Yes, I'm still here."

"Where am I?'

"You're near me and we'll be wandering together soon but first things first. Good news. There's been information within our group and you should know there are others wandering like me. Seems a Grim Reaper we've been seeking has been found. Now we know his location and need to get him, destroy him before he disappears again."

"Why?"

"If he stays on earth, alive among the living, well…. we'll always be lost. It's a curse to have no place, no home. You and I together again makes all the difference but its not enough."

Nicolas was ecstatic, "It doesn't matter what condition we're in, I love you. If we can just stay together we'll get by."

Nathan needed to make a point, "Wandering will wear you out. It's a never ending hole that you fall into and stay falling indefinitely. If we don't fix this situation we'll be falling forever."

Silence.

"Nathan, when you and I meet, are we both going after this Grim Reaper?"

"Yes."

"And then when he dies will we be in a better place?"

"Yes."

"So you're saying, flat out, that we're not dead?"

"Not yet."

The memory of a person walking through the grave-yard after Abigail Culver's death had caused India to be awake until long after midnight. "A dark figure in the cemetery creeping around the headstones. Did he stop to read each one?"

She wrapped the pillow once more around her head, "All the heartache of missing Abigail and Nicolas leaving me for New York, I still have visions of that man in black." She crawled further under the covers, "Almost two blocks away from where I stood, he must have been very tall, definitely over six feet. The hat he wore, a fedora of some kind made it impossible for me to see his face."

She had watched him fade away into the woods beyond the alfalfa field where she knew he would, to his surprise, cross a deep creek, slogging through water and push through dagger-like thorns on Hawthorn trees.

From under the blankets she asked, "Where the hell did he park? Either the guy was lost or he's nuts."

That following morning she called Nicolas once more, only to leave another message. Dragging coma-tosely around the farm she helped with chores until Jeff had suffered enough of her depression, "Go Ride!"

Admitting defeat, India headed for Willy's stall, not surprised to find him already saddled. "Figures. What a bunch of mother hens."

Waiting impatiently the short liverbay had been pawing the ground, a bad habit of his and the bluntness across the front of his hooves showed the results. Approaching, his head flew up and he turned his ears toward her in a type of salute. She acknowledged his greeting by giving him a hug around his neck. With that he dropped his head as she unhooked him from the crossties and lead him down the long aisle to the exit.

Together they would tour the Parker place aware that in the future the new owner may not approve of riders on his property. Especially now. India had made the copies of the diary and map, delivering them in person to Damian Alva's office. His reaction to her proof of ownership was cold at best, but he admitted, "You certainly surprised me and I applaud you. But there's still the matter of my client. He will not be easily vanquished."

Proudly leaving his office she paused when he asked, "Ms. Curran, aren't you curious to know why your family had given, at no cost, 800 acres of land to the Parker family?"

Crossing Persimmon Grove Pike that morning turkeys called from deep inside the forest as she wandered in that direction. Dew still glittered in dark recessed places remaining on ferns and moss all day without the sun to bake it off. Frosty fog rose from the hills making the air hazy blue on the horizon. Willy walked on wearing only a rope halter. Nearly thirty years old anything more was unnecessary as they both knew that a strong gallop was never going to happen.

Moving up the trail she remembered the last two months spent going over old family notes. "In years past there had been few opportunities to learn my farm's history. The first Curran's energy must have been infinite, taking incredible devotion to see it bloom into the estate it is today." Booting Willy to step reluctantly over a small ditch she had other thoughts as well. "I wonder what had caused the change of heart in the deed settlement? Alva and his client didn't seem interested in any further litigation. That makes no sense."

And then there was Nicolas. Like a knight in shining armor he had come to her aid. She giggled a bit picturing Nicolas dressed in such a romantic fashion. Under her Willy could feel everything she thought and at this point probably was rolling his big dark eyes. She went on to think about their tryst. *"Could this lead to something more permanent? At my age it's welcome, needed and I'd like to tryst more often."* She laughed out loud at the thought. Feeling the added vigor Willy picked up the pace.

They were now coming to the highest part of the ridge at the top of the Parker property. India was startled to come upon a large man kneeling on a pile of dirt. She watched as he raked his long fingers through the soil. Hearing India and her mount approaching he did not stand but instead raised his face to them.

"Do you have the time?" The stranger asked.

Not wearing a watch India stumbled over her answer. "I would suppose it would be 9, 9:30."

He smiled at her, "Time…A storm in which we are all lost."

"Excuse me?"

"Plato."

Under his hat the man's eyes were exceptionally dark except for a dull twinkle and large black brows hooding his lashes making it hard for her to see his expression. Broad shoulders, long arms, big hands, it was all supported by the frame that rose up to address her. Even with twenty feet between them India felt small looking down from the saddle.

He clarified, "Of course it all depends on each man's definition of time."

India was quickly becoming uncomfortable with this conversation and turned Willy away, back toward the trail that would remove her from this man's presence.

"Do you ride often? I would be pleased to see more of you on my estate."

India turned her head back around towards him, "Are you the new owner?"

An unexpected wind blew up the rise past them causing India's skin to grow cold as she thought. *'This would be the man that in the last few months, because of his own greed to own Millwheel, had caused us such anxiety. Now this place, this property where I've spent my life riding seems filled with evil.'*

He smiled at her.

Remembering the stranger visiting along the graves just below the swing of the old Sycamore, she asked, "I've seen you on our farm, walking through the cemetery. That was you, wasn't it? Why were you visiting our graves?"

"Just remembering old times, but I'll admit that I did not feel welcome there. It appears that you and I are now guilty of trespassing on each others land."

Slapping his hands against his pants the dirt seemed difficult to remove. "I lived there once, for a while. Seems to have become a proper place. A little paradise or bit of heaven perhaps?"

Willy was getting antsy, wanting to move off this ridge and down back into the hollow where he could collect himself and relax. India had to flick her fingers on the reins connecting into his mouth the message to be still for just a moment more.

"So are you a relation of ours?"

He studied his soiled palms, "Not considered a favorite I'm afraid. But then, even with my notoriety it would still be hard to find which family tree I'm hanging from." He kicked at the soil beneath his feet, perhaps to exhume some lost item from long ago, "My time here was very short-lived. Some might remember me as a black sheep. That would be one reason not to dig up the past, don't you agree?"

India tightened her grip on the reins before asking, "Then you must have lived here before I was born. Growing up my parents never mentioned you. If I am correct, you're the new owner of the Parker Farm?"

"Lew Mills at you service." And he made a small bow.

Chapter 27
INDIA'S EPIPHANY and the STEAMBOAT CREW

Taking a shower and changing clothes hadn't relaxed India. The ride earlier across the Parker's ridge with the surprise introduction of Lew Mills had her unglued. Rubbing her head with a towel she sighed, "Camels in the round pen, thank God they've disappeared. Strange children playing along fence rows, unclaimed jewelry, too many bizarre events to explain." Now dressed, she stepped over Maggie asleep on the floor, "And my new neighbor, Lew Mills, would he know any of the people living on Millwheel Farm now?"

India made her way down the main stairs of the original 1890 farmhouse. Stories over the years told of the original shelter, a small cabin made from gathered rocks and branches. Rotted and unsafe, it had been burned instead of renovated, or so she had heard. "This farmhouse must have seemed like a castle for ex-slaves who had chosen to stay here."

Stepping down into the living room she found herself alone, the house quiet. Standing in the vestibule to think India looked into the large entryway leading to the dining room and the old framed grouping of coins on the wall. Her family had once told her that it had been on the property since the farm was established in 1868. Moving closer she felt a bit awkward knowing this may be the first time in her life that she had ever really studied them. "Nicolas unfortunately, never had the chance to examine them before he left. A shame."

Three gold coins, each one mounted against a green velvet background under glass in a neutral maple frame. No reason to actually be drawn to the coins other than the fact that rare gold in any home might be considered a novelty. Two of the coins had been stamped with a woman's head, her coronet embossed with the word "Liberty." Thirteen stars surrounded her and the year 1865 sat comfortably below. A middle coin in the arrangement was a back view of the other two. It was a more elaborate design showing an eagle set behind a shield. The lettering read "United States of America" and the term "Twenty D."

"This was either the term for the number of coins struck or perhaps the value."

Her presence in front of these heirlooms found her thoughts and body unintentionally submitting into a different world, another place outside the vestibule. The quiet of the house that moments earlier seemed peaceful now crumbled away as she physically moved through emptiness. Exploding into an unknown vortex, she found herself in an environment of strong winds and crashing waves. Loud gales of wind asked to pull her body from a foreign structure. Under her feet water soaked wooden planks made it difficult for her to stand on her own. Gripping at a rail that had appeared from nowhere she dragged herself along an ancient steamship's gangway, grasping for handles with the fear that at any moment she would be swept overboard with the other passengers. There were hundreds. Appearing from cabins onto the decks some were swept off to drift silently away from the boat with the current. Many were screaming, calling names into the distance for others unfamiliar to her. Mothers, children, sailors and camels treaded the high waves only to be sucked under as India watched. Looking to the decks above, untied ropes swung carelessly, slapping at the hull. Out in the turbulent sea horses escaping the mayhem whinnied from far away on the horizon as a man alone on a platform below yelled for help, yet in an instant was swallowed by the surf, leaving no trace of him or his plea's.

As the phantom boat tipped and rolled a large man two levels above slammed a door and stepped out onto the deck of the boat. With the sudden noise she couldn't help but look up at the imposingly figure. He stood stock-still. Dressed in a high collared coat and white shirt his eyes watched the high sea approach, then crash against the side of the ship. He seemed oblivious to the fact that people and loose cargo were being washed into the sea. Her eyes moved then to notice on the same gangway toward the bow two men pointing forward. They were conversing to each other about something of interest ahead. The large man stepped over to join them but with no obvious motive proceeded to throw both men overboard. Dodging any reflection, he turned and stepped back around to enter a different cabin door.

Soaked and struggling to stay fastened to the railing India had no time to consider the murder of the two men that had just taken place. Waves reached up and over her, grabbing at her green velvet dress that she had never owned, a coat that hung down to the floor, which she had never bought. The fabric was so heavy with ocean water that with the next wave she felt herself helplessly cocooned, strangled within the surf. Spinning down the gangway in a paralyzing suction India Curran lost her grip, slipping into the sea.

Dark eyes stared directly at her as India regained her senses. Shaking her head, familiar sounds of Millwheel returned. Black as night, the eyes on her blinked once more, than a huge sweaty nose pushed against her shoulder causing her to stumble backwards.

"Are you going to ride that horse or just annoy him?" Jeannie asked while she used her fingers to comb through Tempter's mane. "He's been standing here waiting for you to get on for God knows how long. Something must be wrong. Come on over here and sit down."

Jeannie took India's arm and led her from the hitching post outside of the farmhouse to the first porch step. They both sat down. "You're not pregnant, are you?"

India was still dazed, somehow transformed to her home again from the hallucinating visions of a steamship and suddenly she recalled witnessing the murder of two men! Two murders! Had she then drowned? Thinking of the ocean storm she began to wobble.......

"Hey lady, just stay still. I'll go put up your horse, get his saddle off. You stay here and don't move 'til I get back." With that Jeannie walked off leading Tempter back to his stall inside the barn.

"A nightmare in the middle of the day? At least I'm back on solid ground." Thinking that something to drink might clear her head India rose up from the stoop and made her way back across the veranda of the house into the vestibule where the gold coins quietly remained hanging upon the wall. A clock ticked softly on the fireplace mantle. "Things seem normal in here."

Going through the kitchen India noticed a plate on a sunny windowsill covered with a cloth. Lifting the towel she discovered dough that had been formed into balls to rise. Then and there India decided, "The employee's have lost their minds. Since when did we stop buying freezer rolls that just pop into the oven? And who on this farm knows anything about yeast? Crazy." In the refrigerator were the remaining fresh cream from a few days ago and the apples. A bloody "something" in a bowl was soaking in milk. "Yuck. Why doesn't anyone tell me about this?" She moved back from the self, "I'm not a wild game connoisseur but if this is someone's venison I wish they would ask me first if it's okay to leave it here."

Closing the refrigerator door she caught the sound of conversation. Strange noises from around the corner made it seem like a town hall meeting was taking place in her dining room. Loud talking, some gruff, some whispers, than booming laughter.

Peaking around the oak frame to get a look India is shocked to find a dozen men of different ages, in clothes from a different era, draped around her large mahogany table upon which they had tossed their coats. Feet resting on elegantly upholstered antique chairs, they were comfortably smoking cigars and eating apples similar to the ones India had just seen in the fridge. One man appeared to be sleeping. All seemed very busy discussing a mutual subject, but India spoke up to introduce herself just the same. "I hate to intrude, but I'm India Curran and I live here."

Her opening statement fell on deaf ears. The men situated around the room carried on the discussion with no notice of her. Their topic grew into fervor.

"We followed him this far! Can't lose him now unless he finds a different destination. He might skedaddle if he comes across something of equal importance, a tornado or fire that would lead him off, then we'd lose him again. Came to roost here now, he has, maybe forever. Lazy son of o'bitch. Everyone else does the work. Man lives off the drudgery of others."

"And death." An older bearded man wearing a round cap and neckerchief reminded the speaker, "He gains when others perish. That seems to be the way of it. He can walk through time with no consequences. Lets wait n' see. We may be on to something now. A new twist. Young men, arrived dead of course. I passed them just the other day. One of them at home with the sea. Preferred to swim it rather than sail it and for that we lacked in a shared interest. But they filled my head full of tricks on how we get rid of the demon for good."

Fists on her hips India stepped into the fray, "If you don't mind, those cushions are very old and *expensive*. Could you remove your feet from them please?" India was becoming infuriated, "And cigars! Ashes falling onto my ancestor's wool rug. It's nearly a century old. The nerve."

Further down the table a black sailor barked above the throng. His head was wrapped in cotton rags tied and braided into hair that fell to his shoulders. The sleeves of a linen shirt that had once been white were smudged with earth and dust, the tattered garments hanging loosely about him hiding his skeleton. "And what if we can't stop him here? He'll move on to other accidents, faults of man or nature that will lure him out again. He goes where he pleases, sure 'nough. Lazy or no he'll always find amusement in destruction and death. First in line for calamity of any kind, we all agree. And the bigger the better!"

The bearded man spoke once more, "We'll have supplies! The dead boys told me a recipe to remove this Reaper that plagues us. Convenient for us, we have the answer right here in this house!"

Another sailor added, "And others here to help. Not hard to find having the same quest. People lost, wandering about, victims of other catastrophes where the Reaper walked. Gratefully too many to count! They come to do the same as us, lead him to hell."

Looking at the bearded spokesman India felt that he must be a commander or captain of some kind. He wore a lapelled long-coat, perhaps of wool with a high crowned hat. Introductions would be in order, yet with all the men ignoring her presence at their meeting it seemed futile. 'How long do they plan to stay here in my dining room?' She wondered. 'Would they be staying for dinner, or over night? How many beds would I need?'

Deep in thought India blinked, and the room was empty.

Chapter 28
OBOL'S for the JOURNEY

The cold and darkness of the evening did not stop India from walking outside to consider Nicolas and the unanswered phone messages. "Perhaps he had another girl in New York. Wouldn't surprise me. My luck with men never changes."

Crossing the yard a cold crispness enveloped her. Approaching the main barn she lifted her coat collar and folded her arms. From the corner of the building the tall dark man she had met on Parker's ridge, Lew Mills, moved to join her. Fear slid into her but she stood her ground, "I'm sorry Mr. Mills but the farm is closed for the night. Please return with any business in the morning."

"I have a proposition."

India thought about the bizarre men dealt with earlier in the dining room and wanted no more frustration today so she demanded, "I am in no mood for any propositions from you or anyone else. It's late. Time for you to go."

Mills was speechless but tried to relax remembering that this was his only living relation. "You will listen to my offer or shorten your chances of survival."

India tipped her head trying to make sense of what Mills was saying.

"This is your only stop, here on Millwheel. I, on the other hand, can come here as often as I like even after you're dead. Consider this. A castle, the largest estate in Campbell County, or Kentucky for that matter. You could raise the finest thoroughbreds in the world. And please, considering my history with horses any accommodation to equines is huge. I simply wish to retire here having family close."

She retaliated, "Millwheel was built from the men and women that struggled after the war, starved through decades of sever winters and all on a foundation of devotion and love. You are not family and you don't seem to know much about our history."

"I beg to differ, having been there, but lets not squabble. This is your last chance. Either side with me or meet your fate. And take my word for it, I've had larger targets than you."

As Mills thought of large targets he remembered the other Reapers. Their game was based on moving ahead, scoring, crushing the competition at any cost. There was a high price to pay if he were to fail now, especially with such small prey. But looking at India he considered, 'There might be something gained in killing my only living relative. A fine trophy she would make for the wall.'

Flip, Jeff, Jeannie and several of the other farm crew had now gathered behind India. Mills looked into their faces, "Like the faces of the people onboard the Brother Jonathan, children going into battle, many to die never understanding the war."

He then smiled looking past them.

Feeling the heat, workers all turned to look as well. Screams from the farm erupted, "The house, Fire! Look, the barns, too!"

The ground next to the foundations seemed to glow with flames that reached up to consume anything that stood, barns, hay sheds and the farmhouse. Panic consumed the Millwheel employees but the young farm owner noticed strangers somehow organizing the situation. Like a fire drill, they were coming out of the burning buildings carrying Millwheel valuables. Women walked off the porch with arms full of precious keepsakes, setting them carefully in rows on the ground. The young black children India had seen running in her pasture weeks earlier had the dogs following as they carried baskets of bridles from the tack shed. Sailors led mares with foals. A well-dressed woman in a long gown and feathered hat held a vase. Waking past, India noticed she wore the lacey silver bracelet that had been secured in the farm office drawer. "That's the piece with the engraved leaves initialed CVS!"

Turning, India saw dark-skinned strangers carrying saddles, furniture and pictures that had hung on the walls, placing them safety under the trees near by with no thought to the danger surrounding them.

But the fire was only a deterrent from the main threat. Lew Mills was now moving closer to India. With the entire farm ablaze there was no safe place to run, no doors to lock him out.

"So now you have nothing to live for. This is the choice you made. A poor roll of the dice if you ask me. First I'll take your wealth and then your life. I'll rebuild here to suit my own tastes. Sorry to lose you, such a short acquaintance."

"You're crazy!" India screamed, "My wealth? If you think a bunch of buildings make up a persons riches, your confused. My friends, this land, that's the value in my life. You might kill me, but can you kill us all?"

"I can certainly try."

Lunging toward India his attack came too late. The seamen that she had seen in her dining room earlier had pushed past her friends and advanced from behind Lew Mills. Their arms reached around his, trapping him with their embrace. As the captive struggled a tall black man wearing a wide brimmed leather hat and green vest stood close to Mills and although the demon squirmed the man's arms firmly held the Reaper's neck tight.

Through the smoke and flames the sound of familiar voices caught India breathless. She turned to find the twins, Nathan and Nicolas, walking into the crowd of seamen surrounding Mills. Nicolas held the framed gold coins that had hung in her dining room. India felt a need to run to him, yet he seemed to be unaware of her presence moving only to join the strangers holding the demon.

"Nicolas! Please, we need to leave here now before we all die!"

Nicolas and Nathan acknowledged her with a glance but at the same time got down to business. The ships captain and sailors stepped in front of the Reaper halting any hope of escape. Breaking the glass covering the coins, they passed the gold pieces to the tall black man clutching demon's neck. "These are for you, Jefferson." The Captain acknowledged.

Picking the coins from the officer's hand, Jefferson was joined by two small black women. "Emma, Rebecca, lets do this together." With the captain using his strong grip to pry open Mills mouth, the apparitions carefully placed all three coins inside. The twin brothers with the sailors firmly clamped it shut as the captive screamed from deep within, fighting, kicking to be released. Buildings still burned as dozens of spirits gripped at Mills, serving like pallbearers in his cremation. Jefferson, his two allies, the sailors and others made up the masses that clung to the fiery pyre as it levitated, collecting more bodies as it rose and with the smoke disappeared into the thick gray sky.

"I can't stay "

India turned to find Nicolas and his twin Nathan had not left.

"You're back! You're both here on the farm! Thank God, I'm so glad you've returned. Don't ever leave again!"

"I'm already gone, India." Nicolas said as he turned to walk away.

Nathan was already fading, moving further into the haze as he called for his twin brother to follow. India tried to grasp Nic's hand, to pull him back, but found nothing to hold onto as her fingers grasped at air. She cried out for them to return but both men had become difficult to distinguish from the fog. Unexpectedly a woman materialized out of the darkness and with little effort grasped Nathan's hand, leading him away. India would never forget the woman's long blood colored hair and a coat so dark that it melted into the ground. Closing his eyes, Nicolas silently slipped away with them, disappearing into the smoke.

Four Years Later

Carpenters worked all morning to steady the new sign at the entrance of the property. With tools and ladders scattered around India stepped back to see the results. Along the driveway in the distance a field of daffodils surrounded a new one-story cabin. Changes had included an outdoor patio facing the fields where, from a distance, an old sycamore tree could be seen. Wearing yet another new swing a spring breeze blew through the trees, just enough to make it come alive.

Young saplings circled the charcoal trunks of old oak trees that still stood tall in front of pastures where young colts where learning to fly.

Jeff and Flip complained "Why not name the place 'India's Eden' or just the 'Curran Place?' Even if you change the name, everyone will still find us."

"No," India was firm. "Millwheel it will stay. The past is behind us now. My legacy is to remain resolute, regardless of our history. Our journey was rough, but starting now this new journey begins with me."

Made in the USA
Charleston, SC
17 April 2014